The Falafel King is Dead

From the reviews of *The Falafel King is Dead*:

'Shilo's achievement is to evoke an Israel which the outside world knows little about, with a level of poverty and ignorance which typifies the lives of many North African immigrants from the 1960s.' *Independent*

'Affectingly bittersweet' *Metro*

'The novel carries a striking political message about class and marginalised ethnicities in Israel.' *Jewish Renaissance*

'Israel continues to produce fresh and talented writers and Sara Shilo is the latest addition to that growing list... This short and sensitive novel encapsulates so much... A story that may well become a classic.' *Birmingham Jewish Recorder*

'I could write extensively about how much it moved me, because of strong voices, and the way it draws the reader right into the heart of a huge family.' Geraldine D'Amico, *Bagels & Books*, Jewish Book Week blog

'Between the individual narratives of the Dadon family emerges a powerful portrait of the past, but one that resonates all the more because so many things remain much the same.' *Jerusalem Post*

'In her impressive debut novel, Shilo weaves a story out of this emotion-laden subject with sensitivity and flair… [Her] triumph is the lightness and deftness of her touch… *The Falafel King is Dead* is a beautifully wrought tale of one family's hopes and dreams.' *Tribune*

'Shilo's narrative is eloquent with the rusty reality of lives infused with fear and remorseless mistrust; its originality lies in the way in which her characters' monologues are infused with a kind of magical thinking that elevates their existence beyond daily hardships and grim reality… Shilo's story has the dimensions of Euripidean tragedy, but her eye for detail and her sympathy for her characters render *The Falafel King is Dead* a wholly believable story of a working-class family caught up in a series of events over which they have no control. One does not have to read the novel as a parable to appreciate the power and authenticity of Shilo's voice.' *Times Literary Supplement*

THE
FALAFEL KING
IS DEAD

Sara Shilo

Portobello
BOOKS

First published by Portobello Books 2011
This paperback edition published 2012

Portobello Books
12 Addison Avenue
London
W11 4QR

First published in Hebrew in 2005 as *Shum Gamadim Lo Yavo'u*
by Am Oved, Tel Aviv, Israel.

A CIP catalogue record is available from the British Library

9 8 7 6 5 4 3 2 1

ISBN 978 1 84627 222 6

Text designed and typeset in Apollo MT by Lindsay Nash

Printed and bound by CPI Group (UK) Ltd,
Crodyon CR0 4YY

MIX
Paper from
responsible sources
FSC® C020852

SIMONA DADON

1 Who would have thought the Katyusha would find me outside? I haven't been out, really, for six years. I just switch off and go: to work, to the market, to the market, to work. And the one time Simona does something different, the Katyusha catches her out.

I'd already put food on the table for them, the usual Tuesday couscous with chicken, pumpkin, chickpeas – all mixed together. I stand there, the sky falling in, and what do I think about? Whether they ate the couscous before the first Katyusha landed, or whether they went down to the shelter on an empty stomach. I count them, one by one, in my head, as I think of them running to the shelter: Kobi, Chaim, Oshri, Etti, Dudi, Itzik. Go home, I tell my feet. But they don't obey me.

I'm on a swing in the playground, my feet pushing the ground away from me. I just sit there, swinging back and forth, forth and back. It's pitch black. The first Katyusha hit the electricity supply for the whole town. Only the lights in the *moshav* on the hill are still on,

3

blazing from the houses and the chicken coops. There are lights in the Arab village on the other side, too. I swing. *Hey Simona mona from Dimoaona, hey Simona mona from Dimoaona.* The swing stops, and I sing, '*Put your ha-and in my ha-and, I am yours and you are mi-ne.*' Then I start to cry.

When the second Katyusha falls, I scream and throw myself to the ground. My mouth is open as wide as it can go, but no sound comes out. My scream comes from the heart, not the throat. And after I scream from the heart, I scream from the belly. And when I finish screaming, I throw up. I lie down in the pitch-black night, and throw up. I retch and retch, but it's too dark to see what's coming out. In the end there is nothing left, just water. After a while the water is finished, too. When I get up, I feel as though the lead weight that has pressed down on me for six years has gone.

Akh ya rab, that feels good! The lead weight, which turned my heart into a block of ice, has disappeared. How did I survive for six years with a heart of ice? I sit back on the swing and take off my head-scarf. I wipe my mouth with it and throw it as far away as I can. I think the second Katyusha fell somewhere near our apartment. I want to run and see if they are all OK: Kobi, Chaim, Oshri, Etti, Dudi, Itzik. Simona's feet push the ground away again. *Hey Simona mona from Dimoaona.* My feet don't listen to me when I tell them to take me home. I sit with my back to the apartment buildings. People are on the road now, shouting, running. In a minute the car with the loud-speakers will drive round, telling people to go down to their shelters. Then the ambulances and fire engines will come. My feet stop the swing then walk in the opposite direction to our apartment. I don't

4

know where they are taking me. I'm walking towards Ricki's house, but my feet take me past her shelter and down the hill.

If only I could divide myself into twenty pieces. I'd scatter the pieces all over town, so that at least one would be hit by the Katyusha. Then, at last, it would be over.

I open my hands and my mouth, gaze up at the sky. I'm like the little Moroccan girl I used to be, trying to trap the rain in her mouth, sticking out her tongue like a saucer, hoping to catch a drop. That girl loved the rain, thought it Heaven-sent, just as I love the Katyusha that will surely come.

It's quiet. The Katyushas have stopped. Here, it's quiet, and there, they're working on my Katyusha. God in Heaven, who sees that Simona wants to come to Him, help them send a Katyusha, and to do it right. God forbid it should leave me half-alive, lying in a hospital. God forbid. My only wish is not to be stuck in a wheelchair. I'm already half-dead. Let them take the other half and be done with it. God, give them the brains to do a good job! *Ya rab*, what a world. You even need luck to have the death you want.

Why do I have to go to the shelter? Why do I have to get up tomorrow morning? For the chores? *Ay*, that's sad. How *could* Simona leave her chores? What will Simona's chores do if she flies up to the stars? Poor little chores. They'll have to sit shiva for her.

In the morning, when I leave for work at the nursery, the chores sit cross-legged in the apartment, waiting for me to come home. They jump on me the minute I open the door. They've waited all day, and now they want to play. I feel like a ragdoll. The ironing chore throws me to the sink. The sink, as soon as it's empty, tosses me to the broom.

The broom sends me to the bathroom to wash the little ones. The bathroom orders me to the stove to make something to eat, and then back to the sink, to the laundry, to the needle and thread. The chores don't stop for a minute, and they laugh at me, laugh and laugh, until the very last chore takes me in its arms and sees there's nothing left, nothing to laugh at. No more Simona. Only then does it allow me to drop into bed.

Thanks so much.

I get up at quarter to four. If I'm up then, I can manage. If I leave it until ten-past four, or even quarter-past, the day's shot.

I can't function at speed until after five o'clock. My arms feel as stiff as sticks, and keep threatening to drop off my shoulders. My knees tremble. My lower back kills me. It's like a competition in pain between them all. My feet feel encased in iron, like horses' hooves. The veins near my left knee are on fire.

When a husband dies, they should transform the wife back into a girl again, exactly the way she was before she knew him. Let her start again. You shouldn't leave a woman stumbling in the desert with her husband's children, when she's exhausted from giving birth to them all, when her body bears such bruises.

At four in the morning, I do the quiet chores. If the twins wake, my morning's gone. Even if their blanket falls to the floor, I don't pick it up. I hang the washing outside. In the winter it's hell; in the summer it's OK, my hands aren't too icy. In the middle of winter, when the mornings are dark, I hang out the washing later, so that it can dry on the line all day. The washing machine has worked its magic. Without it you would see a family's daily news bulletin: what

6

everyone wore, what they ate, what they did, where they went, how they slept. When I've hung out the washing, I tighten the line on the pulley, and the clothes move away from me. I hope for a hot, thirsty sun that will drink up all the water.

When Mas'ud died, my periods stopped. What a stupid girl I was to think that my blood went with him into the grave. I didn't believe he'd left me anything of himself. I cried and I didn't eat and I almost fainted every day, but I didn't think anything of it. It didn't enter my mind that I'd been caught out, but everyone else knew. I'd see myself in people's eyes wherever I went, and I didn't understand it. I'd look hard into all those eyes, one after another, and see the same thing: a pregnant woman. I thought they were mad. How could it be? Then one lunchbreak, Ricki, the cook at the nursery, grabbed me, closed the door behind us, and began to talk. My mind went blank. I heard what she was saying, and I wanted to kill myself from shame. All I could think of was how to get out of her kitchen, when everyone had been gossiping about me for a month, about how I'd fallen pregnant at the last minute. But Ricki, however rude she can be, is the person you want when you're in trouble. She said: 'Simona, listen to me. You're going to sit with me until your head is clear. You're not going to think about tomorrow, or yesterday. You're just going to think about one thing: how you walk out of here with your head high and your eyes wide open. Remember, you didn't do anything wrong by falling pregnant.

'You just listen to me: this is a blessing. A kid that bears his father's name is a blessing. It might seem like trouble right now, but in half a year you'll see what's growing inside you at this moment, and it will have a new face. You have to let the gossip just slide right off you. Don't listen to them. I'll put oil on you, believe me I will, so that nothing sticks. Sit down, sit down. What did you get up for? Don't stand next to my pot; the soup will get all salty if you cry into it. *Aiwa,* that's better. Half a sour smile from Simona is still something. Where are you going? No, baby, you're not cleaning today.'

She gave me tea with *shiba,* then went out to the others, collected their finished cups of instant coffee onto a tray, and said: '*Yalla,* girls, to work. No cleaning elves are coming to help you today.'

Back then, I didn't know I was carrying two sons. I said goodbye to one person, and hello to two.

Seven months after Mas'ud died, they were born. Two of them with exactly the same face, their father's face.

They didn't take after me.

I put three pots on the stove. I always leave three pots for lunch. Yesterday I made rice, beans and fishballs in sauce. Today it's the couscous. I'd already put white beans in water to make their favourite soup for tomorrow. I'd also thought of making potatoes and fried fish.

People think Mas'ud is dead and I'm alive. That's wrong! Totally wrong! Mas'ud is alive and I'm dead. As soon as he died, I was finished. It was all over for me. Everyone knew him as the falafel king; I was his queen. And now? They're still talking about him. He will always be a king. No one can replace him. And me? Where am I? My days as a queen are long gone.

When your husband dies, everyone comes to check on you, to see how much you love him. When he's alive, who cares? Then, you can drive him crazy, talk about him to whoever you like, badmouth him.

No one sniffs about that. But as soon as your man dies, someone turns up every five minutes to check you're being respectful. The moment you get up the morning after shiva, a thousand people come to sit in his chair. What's their job? To see if you're treating him right. And they work hard at it. They don't leave you alone for a second, and they count your tears. Their ears, eyes and noses seem to grow, as if on the lookout for an out-of-place laugh, for perfume or makeup. They want you to die with him. He's dead, six feet under, so you should be dead, too, spinning on top of the ground, just for them.

If a man looks at you, if his eyes rest on you for two seconds, they'd kill him in an instant, to preserve your honour.

But when they see you're washed up, their hearts turn heavy and black. So they pour mercy, like a bucket of filthy mopping water, on to your head. Then their hearts are clean again, shiny with goodness. And you? You stand there, soaked to the skin, and dirty, too, from their black mercy.

But if you run away from the mercy, God forbid that you should fall into the widows' sugary trap.

Right from the start, I said to myself: Simona, don't go near the widows, because once you're stuck there, there's no way out. They'll pull you away from other people. They throw a party when they hook a new widow. Your luck and their luck have the same colour and shape. They only want one thing: for you to be with them, to sit with them, so they can teach you the widows' rules.

So I've been looking at my feet for six years, paying attention to my steps, just so I don't wake up one day and find out I've stepped in something nasty.

I don't have the strength to keep my hands high, stretched out for my Katyusha. I only ever had one thing in life that I kept my arms open for. When that was gone, I closed my arms.

Where is Simona going? Where are her feet taking her? To the football pitch at the end of town. No Katyushas have fallen there yet. *Inshalla*, let one come today. Simona throws her bag off her shoulder, stands on the pitch. The grass is dry. This country doesn't have enough water. It's a constant refrain. But they find water for the football pitch. It's only her good fortune that they haven't used the sprinklers today. Simona stands on the grass, her head spinning crazily, her mouth opening to sing: '*Why is this night different from all other nights, from all other nights? Because on all other nights Simona does chores and more chores. Tonight, tonight, a Katyusha will take Simona, who's waiting for it.*' She calls out to the angel of death, but it is the angel of madness that comes for her instead.

The poor kids. At least if I go, they'll get a little honour and some money because I died in a Katyusha attack. In this country, whoever manages to be killed by Arabs is honoured like a king. If you go mad, on the other hand, your whole family is ruined. Who would want to marry Etti if her mother is said to be *mahbula*?

2   Where can I lie down? This is a nice bed. A long green sheet. I lie down in the middle, where the game starts, in the circle made with lime. But after two minutes, my body starts to itch madly, just as it did when I had German measles.

Simona heads for the goal. Why there? Because there's no grass. She's the ball at the end of the game, the goal scored by God in the eighty-ninth minute.

I take off my shoes, put them near the goalpost, and lie down again. The netting of the goal makes a tray of *baklava* in the sky, and the stars are the almonds on top. I curl up on my side. My bare feet are crying out for mercy. I don't listen to them. I never do.

How did I turn from 'Our Simona' to 'Simona of the Chores'? How? Everyone used to call me 'Our Simona'. I was invited everywhere, adopted by everyone. What could I do? Our Simona used to laugh all day, until she brought the evil eye upon herself. The eye wouldn't go away. It stayed for six years.

When I wanted something, I only had to say the word, and five minutes later, my wish was granted. Not even five minutes. Anybody with a brain wanted to stand next to me, so that some of my luck would rub off on them and give them a rose-tinted life, too. That's why they used to hug me, to buy me little presents.

Every morning Our Simona would stroll around town. She'd go to the falafel shop, take some money from the drawer, just so she wasn't short. Not a lot of money, perhaps fifty or a hundred shekels. I knew everyone's break-times: at the bank, at the post office, at the school. I'd drink something with them – tea, instant coffee, Turkish coffee – and make the girls a little jealous with nylon stockings from the city, a new perfume or haircut, a bracelet Mas'ud had bought me . . . It was even better if men were there, too. I'd turn their heads a little, laugh, then be on my way. I'd go to the nursery, take a child in my arms for the fun of it, have a drink with them, too. I didn't have to work. Why should Our Simona work? Mas'ud would get up to mop the house with her; she'd put a few pots on the stove. We used to lock the door so no one would come in and see him mopping; being caught with a mop in his hands is the greatest shame for a man. We'd finish at ten. His mother would come and take care of the baby for a few hours. In those days, Our Simona would hang around town, and he'd grind the chickpeas for the falafels. It cost him pennies to make, but he made a fortune.

Wherever I went, people would look up from their work, laugh, forget their troubles, and dream that, one day, they'd be in my shoes. What was wrong with that? Even when I made the girls' eyes green, it was good for them. It stopped them falling asleep in the middle of their lives. Whenever I brought something new from the city, they'd ask God to give it to them, too. Why not? A month later, half a year, a year at most, they'd have it, too, and they'd be happy. And the men, when they heard what Mas'ud had bought me, would start to put money aside to buy something nice for their wives.

When Mas'ud died, his fortune went with him. He never saved a penny. He gave it all to me. And what did I do with it? The truth? It just ran through my fingers. So the nursery did me a favour and gave me temporary work. I was there for six or seven months. Then I had the twins.

Just after the twins' birth, Hani left the nursery, and I started a permanent job in the toddlers' room, with Aliza Fadida. We have eighteen children. Avi is the youngest – just a year and two months – and Miri the oldest at two years and seven months.

At six-thirty in the morning I rush to the nursery. At four-thirty

I crawl home. Every day someone brings up the days of Our Simona, the queen. All the envy kept on account, all the jealousy in their hearts, is given back to me with interest. And in instalments rather than one lump sum. I don't know when that account will be empty.

Last week I thought: One more word, and I will throw down my apron and run home.

When was it? Monday afternoon? Tuesday? Not Tuesday. Maybe it was Thursday. Why should I remember the days? What's so special about each one? A mountain of days lies upon me, smothering me, all mixed up like the laundry. Here's a sleeve, there a trouser leg, and a towel that is in fact a sheet. I can't remember a single day from morning to evening. There are no shining days, not one I can tell apart from the others. A day that I washed by hand so it wouldn't turn the same colour as the rest.

Why should I care what day it was? What I do know is that it was midday. We finished changing the nappies, put the children in their cots, ate, then sat for a while with a drink. Ricki came out of the kitchen, her hands covered with soapy water, and shouted:

'Sylvie, come here. Yehuda is on his way. Yehuda from the Council, from the maintenance department. Any minute now he'll come through the gate. I told Devora to call him about the drain, but really I want him to put a roof over the sandpit. Come on, give me your apron – *aiwa*, just the right dress for him – grab Shlomi, darling, and go out to him. Don't forget what we said. Get us a roof for the sandpit, just like the ones the Council put in the schools, and turn his back to my window. Girls, put some perfume on her, but quickly, he'll be here any minute. Come on! It's as if those children have put you to sleep! Put some rouge on her . . . a little more. Let your hair down, darling. Don't be stingy with it. When you've got it, flaunt it . . . I don't want another kid. It's got to be Shlomi, his nephew. How can he say no to his nephew? Bring him here. He isn't fast asleep yet. Here, darling, Ricki's giving you some sweet tea. Shlomi, do you know who's coming? Your uncle Yehuda! Want to say hello to Uncle Yehuda? No, Sylvie, don't go out yet – let him get a little closer. You remember what to do? Make the kid as if he wants to play in the sand. Now, go!'

Sylvie went out with Shlomi in her arms. Aliza and Lavana glued their faces to Ricki's kitchen window, peering out over the stove, hidden by a bush with yellow flowers. I sat at the kitchen door, turning my back to them, my hurt eating away at my heart. They used to send me out to do things like that. I would arrive at the nursery on my way around town, dressed just right, and I would get everything the nursery needed. Where have those days gone? Ricki would say: 'Our Simona, the man hasn't been born who can say no to you! If you want to learn about how to treat a husband, just look at Simona. You'll never hear her say, "My husband will kill me."'

I don't look out of the window with Aliza and Lavana. What is there to see? Just the remnants of my life, a reminder of the way it has been severed in two.

Lavana and Aliza are talking quietly, so Yehuda won't hear them, but Ricki won't shut up for a second. She's talking like a sports commentator: 'Look, look at Sylvie. I taught her that little laugh, but it's just for starters, like a shot of cognac. Just so he'll turn his head her way. I taught her everything, everything she needs. In a minute, she'll hand him the kid, and bend down to fix her sandal. What did

I tell you? She's even holding on to his hand so she won't fall. Watch his eyes . . .

'See how it's done, Aliza? It's a game. She'll hide something from him, and show him something else. She won't offer all the goodies on one tray. Look, lo-ok! See how she puts her head back, shows him her neck? Now a strand of hair behind the ear. Do you see how his eyes follow her movements? They're dangling on her earring now. She gives the kid's arm a stroke, and her nails brush him – half-tickle, half-scratch – so he gets a taste of what she might give him, the sweetness and the pain. Look, look how they've turned into a family: her, him and the kid.

'Of course he's standing close, Lavana. If he moves back even half a metre, he'll lose her smell. Without that, what will he have? Just his own sweat. Now she's showing him the outline of her breast. It's like a striptease. Ooh-ah! He'll think she's got watermelons there. Now she's closing her eyes. When she opens them, their colour will hit him harder. She puts her hand on her heart when he tells her his stories, laughs at every word. Boy, he loves telling stories! Believe me, girls, an ear is enough for that guy; he doesn't need the whole woman.

'Right, now she has to bring up the sandpit. She'd better not get caught up in the moment. O-K, she's taking the kid from him, she's looking sad, as if she's about to cry. *What can we do, Shlomi? Sylvie can't put you in the sand because of the sun. When the Council makes a roof for us, I'll let you play in the sand all day long* . . . That's what I told her to say. Now he's got no choice, girls. He's got to say something to make her smile again, yes? When a guy sees his girl is sad, it's like losing a war. Look, look how he's sweating. How he's moving the collar of his shirt – it's stuck to the back of his neck – how he's looking after her as she heads back inside . . .

'She didn't wait long enough! What's the hurry? She took his plate away while he was still eating. She left too soon. He wants to run after her. He still hasn't decided what to do. *Ay*, he can't say what he wants to say about the roof. He was already half cooked. Why did she take the pot off the fire so soon? He'd forgotten about the drain, the reason he came here in the first place. Now we can forget about the roof for the sandpit.

'Well, it's not like Our Simona's work. All Simona had to do was go out to him, and she would get ten roofs. What can we do? We don't have Simona any more. *Yalla*, girls, don't stand in Sylvie's face when she comes in, so she won't blame herself. And it's a quarter to two. At two-thirty the kids will start to wake up. No cleaning elves are coming to help us today.'

I didn't miss a word. I swallowed it all. I taught her all that stuff, and she stood there and talked about me as if I were dead. May-she-rest-in-peace. Have-mercy-on-her soul. You don't talk about the dearly departed the way she talked about me! Our Simona. She just didn't think. Her words scalded my heart like water on boiling oil. When I think of it, I burn inside. I hear the water screaming in the pan, *hisssssssss* . . .

But I just sat there, my lunch rising in my throat, and my blood to my head. I wanted to go home and never come back, but how could I leave? Who'd give me work if I stopped in the middle of the year? Who'd look at me? I was so happy when Ricki gave me a job that I kissed her fingers. It was like saying thank you for being sent to jail.

3   The moon looks down at Simona lying in
the goal. What does he see? A goalkeeper
that jumped to catch the ball in the right corner of the goal – only the
striker kicked the ball to the left.

A year after Mas'ud died, his whole family abandoned me. His
brothers don't set foot in our apartment. They're angry with me. They
think it's my fault the falafel shop didn't work out. I don't understand
what's the matter with them, what they have against me. Who am I to
decide if a shop will be successful? Who am I to tell people to buy
falafel there or somewhere else? And even if, for the sake of argument,
I am guilty of that, what did Mas'ud do to them? They don't even
visit his grave once a year. They have no shame. They threw away all
their money on the falafel shop, and failed, but they didn't have to
desert me and the children.

His mother's different. She doesn't have their nature, the way they
see money in everything. When Mas'ud was alive, she'd look at me
with suspicion if she thought he wasn't happy with me. Now, if she
sees me in the market, she grabs me and kisses me. My sisters-in-law,
Rachel and Yaffa and Shoshana, bring her in the car to visit me. She
checks they aren't looking, then stuffs money into my hands. I put the
notes back in her basket. She starts crying, quickly asks about all the
children. She doesn't forget any of them, says all their names in turn,
even the ones she only saw when they were babies, and blesses me in
Moroccan, wishing me strength and health.

I know she visits his grave. People tell me they've seen her there.
But what did I do to make the rest of them abandon me? Mas'ud's
family were all I had in the town. Now I have no one. I came north

17

from Ashdod for him. Maman died in Morocco, and Papa, God have mercy on him, was killed in an accident sixteen years ago. In one minute he was gone. My four brothers in Ashdod work like mules. They keep their heads down.

Who's Simona's best friend? That'll be the evil eye. Yes, just the eye. It won't leave me alone. It arrived two days after Kobi's bar mitzvah, and it took Mas'ud from me, as well as the crown from my head. And when it took the crown, my head fell with it.

Why did they have to bring the eye to the bar mitzvah? They wanted for nothing. I treated everyone like royalty that day, everyone. They couldn't have dreamed of such luxury. It would have been impossible. If you've never seen it in your real life, how can you dream of it? I hired four buses: one to take Mas'ud's family and their friends from the *moshav*; three to bring people from the town. There were a thousand stops along the way; the buses had to halt every two metres, so people wouldn't have to walk far. And they were tourist buses, not ordinary ones. Inside, the clean smell alone made you think you'd walked into a palace. No one wanted the bus ride to end, because it was like being on a plane. They had drinks and mixed nuts and fruit and the most expensive chocolates. What didn't they have? Nothing! The music system played songs all the way, and, one by one, they went to sit next to the driver, telling jokes over the megaphone, drinking, and eating sunflower seeds. When they arrived at the city, they climbed out next to the most beautiful place they'd ever seen in their lives.

At the entrance of the hall, on either side of marble steps, were two water fountains. Just inside, two girls pinned a red flower to every guest. There were mirrors everywhere; it was as if the guests had been multiplied a thousand times, to remind them of how attractive they were that day. People looked at themselves in the mirrors and rearranged their hair. They smiled, talked politely to each other, picked up a glass for the *lechaim*, checking the mirror to see how they'd picked up the glass. Every guest's eyes were fixed on the mirrors all the time, and they all put on a show, because they wanted to look their best for the mirrors. If a woman made a face, she'd see it reflected back. And if she moved away from one mirror, her sour expression would reappear in another. She couldn't run away, so she had to look happy instead.

And the food? We ordered the best dishes. Not chicken but meat with four side dishes and ten kinds of salad. We paid 300 shekels per head. That was a lot of money back then. Who could pay 300 shekels per head six years ago? All their gift cheques put together didn't cover a quarter of the party. At home they must have thought they were putting the same amount in their envelopes as we paid for them. Forget it! It wasn't like any party they'd ever seen. Even so, they couldn't have known how much it cost.

I see the bar mitzvah in my mind, everyone laughing, dancing. Why'd they have to bring the evil eye with them? We made every man feel like a king, and every woman a queen. We hired the very best band. We didn't begrudge them a penny. From Yom Kippur until Lag b'Omer, all I did was organise that bar mitzvah: hiring the hall, sending out the invitations, buying clothes, booking the photographer and the band. I rushed here, there and everywhere. Whenever I visited a venue or a shop or a supplier, I would think: yes, that's it.

But rather than booking or buying it there and then, I'd say I had to talk to my husband first. Then, at home that night, I'd imagine the bar mitzvah. I'd see Kobi, the family, the guests, the candle-light, the dancing. Finally, I'd picture Simona. If she wasn't shining like a diamond, I'd get up the next morning and look for an even better hall, an even shinier dress, even prettier flowers. That's how it was. I'd examine, look, ask questions. In the end I always went for the best option.

_When Mas'ud said he didn't want something expensive, I'd appeal to his heart, kneading it like dough, softening it with my tears. I'd feel my way slowly, with patience. 'All your money comes from their pockets, Mas'ud,' I'd say, 'from the falafel they eat in your shop, so what's the problem? They'll see you giving some of it back.' I used to talk to him in the morning, when no one could interrupt me. Also, when your man opens his eyes in the morning, he looks at you like he's seeing you for the first time. You and him, Adam and Eve in the Garden of Eden. And, if you don't get lost in the moment, that's the time to get what you want. 'Then they'll come to your place and talk about the bar mitzvah,' I'd say. 'They'll take out their wallets, buy another falafel and a drink. Everything you spend will come back to you in no time. In three months you'll get it all back.' Three months? He didn't see three days after the bar mitzvah. Not even three days.

How did they bring the evil eye with them? Poor Kobi. He didn't even have a proper Sabbath in the synagogue. Instead of his bar mitzvah service, he had to sit shiva for his father, poor kid.

Two days later they came to the house. They came on foot. Kobi's invitation had a gold border. Mas'ud's announcement was written on the walls of the building, and the border was black. We lay on the floor with torn clothes and broken hearts.

When they came to tell me, I wanted to run and see him. I didn't believe them. I started running there, but they stopped me. Three or four of them grabbed me, and took me back. In the apartment the enormous bouquet from the bar mitzvah sat on the table in the living room, and my hair was still in place, held by hairspray and twenty invisible pins. I went into the bathroom, and pulled out all the pins. I washed my hair in the sink. I changed clothes. What did I forget? To take off the nail varnish. Mas'ud's sisters noticed, and quickly took me into another room. From the look on their faces you'd think the world was about to end because of my red fingernails. Rachel and Yaffa each took a hand, and Shoshana poured nail varnish remover on cotton wool. They used a ton of remover, and practically removed my nails. When I think about that time, my strongest memory is the smell of nail varnish remover. The funeral itself has disappeared from my mind, but that smell lingers.

After the first month, I cut Our Simona's hair, which used to hang down to her waist. I took a pair of scissors, went into the bathroom, and cut it myself. Afterwards I put on a headscarf, like an old woman, and then I was finished with Our Simona.

Early tomorrow morning we all have to go to the cemetery. If a Katyusha comes, they'll throw their mother into the ground, too. The world won't stop. Why should it stop? Etti's a good student. She could go to a boarding school like Ricki's daughter. Itzik and Dudi are already grown up. Itzik, even with his hands, will get by. He doesn't have a choice. I'm not worried about Chaim and Oshri. I'm just afraid of what people say. When gossip starts, it's impossible to know where it'll end. But I don't have to worry about what would happen to them if I died, because they think Kobi is their papa. If only people kept their mouths shut. The two of them could stay with Papa Kobi, and he could marry, with God's help. I can't keep him for myself any more. If he married, the twins would have a young mother.

I'm thinking about them again. Are they hungry? I shouldn't have been sitting down quietly. I should have run home, taken the pot of couscous down to the shelter, and filled their bellies. They haven't eaten properly all day. They ran around in the street most of the morning, just coming home to eat some bread with *matbukha*, then running out again. Even if I'd said, 'Come and sit down; let's finish lunch', no one would have listened.

There was a time when they used to stay at the table. Mas'ud would sit in his chair, and no one would move until Mas'ud got up. It's not like that any more. They come into the kitchen, grab what they see, taking it straight from the pots, and leave their plates on the table.

Kobi thought he could make them all sit down at the table, but he couldn't control them. Only Oshri and Chaim listen to him, because they think he's their papa. They're little, so they believe anything. I hope they still call him 'Papa' when they're older.

Their food is all I can think about. My belly is wild with their hunger.

When you have a baby, its belly is connected to yours. At the hospital they cut off the cord that used to feed him, they cut it in front of your face, so you know, from this moment on, that there isn't anybody to feed him other than you. If you don't give him food, he'll die. You're his angel, or his angel of death. When he was in your belly, he ate with you. No one asked you if you wanted him to take food from you. The air that he needs, thank God, he takes from the world by himself, and he cries about that, too; he's not used to it. But the food, no. Every child that comes out of you leaves his worm in your belly.

A woman with six children has six fat worms in her belly that go wild when they get hungry. Even if you're bursting, and you don't feel like putting anything in your mouth, or you can't stand the sight of food from the nausea of pregnancy, the worms will cry in your belly, because you're their feeding tube. You have to cook for them. And you never get a break from it. A man's work always has some freedom, he can slip away, but there's no break in a mother's job of putting food on the table.

And after the first baby, if you think your body will return to what it was, forget it. Even if you get rid of your baby weight, and squeeze back into your trousers, your bra, you'll never go back to how you were.

When a man gets into you for the first time, it's supposed to be an amazing moment; when you open up down there, you become a woman. But no, that's nothing. All you did was let him into a little room at the entrance, with a red ribbon for him to tear, as if he's the mayor or the head of the Council at the opening of a new building. It's all about honouring him and his ego, so he'll be nice to the child that comes from you, rather than kill it in jealousy. So he knows he was first. But when do you really open up your whole body? Only when you give birth. The baby comes out, and a lot of blood and water; it all comes from inside you. A man will never understand that. The feeling of seeing the face of a person who was inside your body, and not just for a day or two but almost a whole year. For nine months you feel him, but you aren't allowed to see him. You suffer because of him, throw up, drag him around, see your veins pop out and brown marks appear on your face. At night you wake up three or four times to pee. But you can't say anything. You can't say, '*Ayuni*, sweetheart, you can stay inside, but you're not allowed to press on the pee-pee place.' You can't have a heart-to-heart and tell him that you don't like the spicy sardines in vegetables that he makes you buy. There are ten cans of spicy sardines in the cupboard, untouched. There's no one to talk to. And you definitely can't ask him to stop making you sick, which happens like clockwork every day at four. No one will listen. What are you supposed to make of it all? There's only one explanation: you came into this world to bear the people who will live in the world after you leave it. Your job is to suffer and shut up. That's how you become a mother. You learn to close your mouth tight, to keep all your pain inside you, and not to scream.

As soon as the baby comes out, your breasts start working. You're now his personal fridge and milk store. You can't begin to understand it. You don't have time to stand still and understand it. It happens so quickly, just like when we came to Israel. One moment I'm in Morocco, certain my life will end here where it began, just as it will for Maman and Grandma and Grandpa. Then, suddenly, they tell me I'm going to 'the Land of Israel'. A day later I'm in the car that's taking me to Casablanca. Now I'm in Casablanca, then in a camp in Marseilles, a week later on the ship, *Jerusalem*, learning how to dance 'Hava Nagila'. A thousand times I think about the day Papa explained we were leaving Morocco. A thousand times, over and over again.

If something happens to you so quickly, it doesn't matter how many times you go over it in your mind: in the morning I did this, and then we travelled there, then they said that. To your last day you won't understand it. You ate without chewing, and so it comes out the other end whole, just as it went in.

After Kobi was born, what did I wish for? For God to make me a girl again. I felt like my semolina sieve. Full of holes from top to bottom. Water gushing out. The hands of doctors and nurses pushing inside me. The baby appeared, followed by the blood and the placenta. They stitch you. Then you start to leak at the top, too. You didn't know how many holes you had in your breast. Suddenly you see: three on the right side; four on the left. If the baby sleeps for too long, your milk starts flowing all by itself. Nothing stays inside you.

For the first twenty years, your mother, grandmother and aunts shut you down and close you up. When you pee in the bathroom, do it quietly. Don't let anyone hear you pee. No one should see your menstrual blood. Put your hand over your open mouth. Your whole life is about closing up. And don't forget your legs. You should practically sew them together when you sit down, so you feel like a tree. Then your wedding day arrives. The talk changes. It's like the difference between black and white. Now they want you to open the way for your husband at night. And on the day of the birth, they want you to open everything – and not only for your husband, but also for your baby and for anybody else who might walk into your hospital room.

Three days after you give birth, your eyes also start to leak, without asking permission. You don't just cry, you drip from the eyes, whether you want to or not. After Kobi's birth I also thought I was going bald. My pillow was full of hair in the morning. Mas'ud's mother said to me, 'Don't you know what they say? That the baby takes away his mother's beauty! Don't cry, *binti*, everything will come back.' Was she right? She was. It did come back. Then it disappeared again. Came back and disappeared. After the twins, it didn't return. But Simona doesn't care about that. Who looks at her now? Mas'ud from his grave? Etti doesn't look at me. But then, she doesn't look at herself in the mirror. Not even Kobi looks in my direction. These days his eyes flick away from me. In our bedroom he turns his back, quickly closes his eyes to me.

And what about men? How do men feel about all this? Only that they got in there, and a baby came out. How puffed up they are! Their chests become so full of air that they can't let it out. They look as though they're about to burst. And what happens to *their* bodies? Nothing. Not a hair out of place. How does that make them feel? That life is a game. They scored a goal, and so they cheer. They hold the baby in their arms at the *brit*, and wear their *tallits*. They pick up a glass, drink a *lechaim*, and they laugh.

4   The ground feels like ice but the air doesn't seem as cold. I put my bag under my head. Now I'm the ball in the goal: half the crowd is ecstatic I'm here; the other half frantic. And no one else gives a damn whether the ball went into the goal or not. The rest of the world couldn't care less.

I bring my knees up to my chest underneath my dress, and tuck my face inside, too. I listen to my heart and breathe in deeply. *Akh ya rab*! The scream even affected my nose. I've already forgotten how to smell. I could put my face into a box of turmeric and not smell a thing. The stench of the nail varnish remover won't go away. It has blocked my nose to new aromas. For six years I haven't been able to smell or taste anything I've cooked.

Ah, how I used to love curling into a ball when I was a girl, tucking myself away from the outside world. Simona became her own world. God gave her ears to listen to her heart, a nose to smell her own body, and closed her eyes, as there was no need to see anything. Her hands brush over her skin, bringing to her nose the scent of places it can't reach.

Dogs. I can hear dogs. I pull my head out of my dress to listen. No, no dogs. Just the loudspeaker car, sending people down to the shelters. It's too far away to hear properly but, even so, I know it's not telling everyone to come out. Now the car is closer, on the road next to the football pitch: 'All residents are asked to remain in the shelters.' It's trying to get through to the old people, the ones sitting at home saying, 'Everything comes from Allah, and whatever is written in Heaven will be.' The loudspeaker is trying to scare them into moving. Only Simona and the old people are careless of their lives. What's the point of protecting them? If you've lost everything you leave the door open. All thieves are welcome as there's nothing to take.

I imagine them all in the shelter. Dudi and Itzik are sitting together. I'm sure Itzik has brought his bird with him. He takes as much care of her as if she were his wife. I hope he's not annoying the neighbours. I don't know why Dudi sticks with him. He'd be better off spending time with Kobi, who was a man even before his bar mitzvah. I expect he and Etti are trying to get the little ones to sleep. They might be crying because of the Katyushas, although it isn't the first time they've heard them. But today's Katyusha, the second one, was the most powerful we've ever had.

In my mind's eye, I see Kobi taking a child in each arm, throwing them in the air and spinning them like a merry-go-round, making them laugh. Kobi loves them. Etti does, too; she's given them her whole heart. She'll be OK. She realised their mother had no time for them, so she took over, gave them what they needed.

Etti's their big sister and Kobi is their papa. But they don't know he's not their real father.

Why not? Let them enjoy it. It was their choice. They picked a young, handsome and healthy dad. Who am I to say otherwise, when they've already decided. They even call him Papa. He was about fifteen when they started calling 'Pa-pa, Papa' as he came home from school. Like two little lambs, they toddled up to him: 'Pa-pa! Pa-pa!' Who am I to destroy their dream? I don't have the heart. What should I do? Take them to the cemetery, knowing their little heads are full of sweetness, full of honey, and say, 'You see that stone, kids? Well, under that stone, rotting in the ground, is your real father.' Is that what I should do? Or should I show them a picture and say, 'Oshri and Chaim, my precious ones, take great care of this picture, and give it a kiss, because it's your father – Mas'ud.' What kind of a father is a picture, or a gravestone that you visit once a year? Can a picture or a stone take the place of a real papa?

So that's how Mas'ud became their grandfather. I told them they were named after him. They know it all: that Mas'ud means 'happiness' in Moroccan, just as Oshri does in Hebrew; and that Chaim, which means 'life', was an exchange for his death. They know everything about their grandfather Mas'ud, how he was the falafel king of the town, and that one day he died at his falafel shop. They looked at Grandpa's picture, and heard stories about his life, but nothing about their father. They decided not to be orphans all by themselves.

5   What's going on? Why is it so quiet? From the day we arrived in this country, we have heard nothing but war. And now that Simona is asking, nicely, to leave the world, they've suddenly run out of Katyushas.

Wait, the lights are coming back on. All the mice are sleeping in their dark shelters, and their houses are full of light. The world's topsy-turvy. When the nursery heard there was an alert, we were sent home straight away. We didn't sit around in the shelters but wandered the streets. So the Katyushas caught everyone hanging out. When did people go down to the shelters? When the attack stopped. Now half the army is standing guard so no one comes out, and they're suffocating in those shelters, afraid a Katyusha will fall on them the minute they put a foot outside. Simona's the only one praying for one to fall. Let's have a few of them in the goal, at least five, to finish her off tonight. I don't want to see the morning. I don't want to!

I'm not crying. When I clung to my life, I couldn't stop crying. I could have filled a bowl with my tears every day. Now that I want to die, there's no reason to cry.

Why do we hold on to life? What is it, really? What is it made of? Ricki says, 'For every quarter-cup of sweetness, life gives you five cups of fear, and the fear takes away all the sweetness. So everyone's afraid of everyone else.'

We work eight hours a day at the nursery. We feed the children, sing to them, tell them stories, run after them to wipe their noses – I carry a toilet roll around all day – cuddle them if they cry, change their nappies, arrange their toys, wash their hands and faces. Eighteen of them, one after the other. We feed them at midday, and change the nappies again, like a factory assembly line. Then we pull out the metal cots, put the children down for their naps, clean the whole room, get them up, change their nappies again, give them an afternoon snack, and get them ready so that when the mothers arrive to pick them up, the children are dressed, with their bags packed, ready to go. The staff that work a split day rush off to do errands.

We work like mules at the nursery. You might think we float around on cloud nine all day, thank yous ringing in our ears. Forget it. We're all afraid, afraid of everyone: of the mothers, of the nursery inspectors, of Devora the director, who is paid a fortune for answering two phone calls a day and shuffling paper at her desk.

Ricki says that on the days Devora doesn't have meetings with the inspectors, we should make her lie on the marble worktop in the kitchen and spin her like an egg. If she spins fast, she's obviously hardboiled and you know the day isn't going to be good; if it's a slow spin then she's soft. On those days, the soft yolk days, we are afraid for no reason; but on the hardboiled days, she goes on the rampage, and God help you then. She grabs hold of the kids who have trouble chewing, squeezes their faces so their mouths open, and shoves the food in with a spoon, right down their throats. So they choke. She doesn't care. So they vomit. When she leaves, half the room is crying because they're afraid she'll come to their table or just because everyone else is crying. And what do we do? We look at each other and don't say a word. Who could we tell? Who would listen to us? Also, everyone knows she is the way she is because of the Germans, damn them. What can we do to her? You look at the number they put on her arm, and you shut up. You don't want to know what happened there. That number on her arm is a permit, allowing her to do whatever she likes. She came to Israel with a doctor's note that will be valid for the rest of her life.

Two women control the nursery.

One is Ricki, who puts her heart and soul into her cooking – as much as is possible with the ingredients she is sent by the cooperative. She often brings trays of eggs from her mother-in-law's chicken farm, and doesn't ask for payment. And she cooks as much as she can, in the biggest pots she can find, because the children must leave something on their plates. If we don't have any leftovers to throw away, how do we know they've eaten enough?

The other controller is Devora. When she's on the rampage, she can't bear to see a crumb left on a plate. What can we do? She suffered over there, and we're suffering in the nursery. Poor Miri is not even three, but Devora grabs her mouth and forces the food in, just because she eats slowly. In the end, she does eat well, but Devora doesn't know who eats quickly and who eats slowly, who likes pudding and who won't touch it. (And pudding, in any case, is just some thin cream cheese with raspberry juice poured in to make it pink. Not everyone wants to eat cheese in the morning.)

Even when Devora is having a soft egg day, she doesn't know what to do with the children. She's got no instinct. She'll buy a new doll, for instance, telling us to put all the kids on the rug, which is a metre and a half by two. Then we settle eighteen kids on the rug. She wants them to sit like soldiers, absolutely still. Then she sits on a high chair, talks to them in a little girl's voice, as if they're retarded, and sings some song with the doll. Then she puts it on a high shelf so it won't get ruined. How could you give one doll to so many kids? They'll only fight over it then cry. And all the time, her smile is stuck to her face, as if it's held in place with clothes pegs.

Until she goes to the bank or on an errand at the Council – invented by Ricki so she'll leave us to work in peace – we don't stop trembling. And the worst thing about our fear is: who is she, anyway? We say it all the time: 'But who is she, anyway?' She hardly steps foot out of the gate, and we start up, like stuck records: 'But who is she, anyway?' Until Ricki sees her from the kitchen window and shouts, 'Girls, you have a guest!' Then we start to shake, and immediately begin singing to the kids, really loudly. If one of the girls is sitting down, even for a minute's rest, she jumps up to show she's working. Devora hears four songs at once when she comes in, as everyone's singing something different. Wherever you are, you grab a couple of kids and sing to them.

So when is she happy? When she's eating our food. She loves the homemade cookies we bring into the nursery after Sabbath. Then, we're the best staff in the world. Her mouth is full of Sylvie's peanut cookies as she corrects her Hebrew: 'It's "apron" not "aprin", and I don't want to hear you saying "I could of" instead of "I could have". The little children are *tabula rasa*, blank slates, and they remember everything they hear. Don't forget it's our responsibility to teach them correct Hebrew. You say "I could have" not "I could of", Sylvie. And I don't want to hear a word of Moroccan in my nursery, either. Tell Lavana to keep her Moroccan for her husband.' She laughs at her own joke and closes the door of her office. The whole nursery entrance made way for that office, just so she'd have a desk, a telephone with a lock on it, and a noticeboard, where she writes down everything we do. She sits and looks at her diary and the menus for the week, and spies on us through the two windows that overlook the baby and toddler rooms. All so she can see with her own eyes that everything is working as it should, exactly as it is written on the noticeboard.

As soon as she takes a bite of a peanut cookie, she doesn't listen to a word of what Sylvie's telling her. She forgets to write down that she needs to order seven 'aprins'. But so what? At least she speaks good Hebrew. You have to give her that. Ricki says, 'They mix up all the new immigrants, pour us into a baking tin and into the oven. We don't even have time to cool before we're divided in two: one half to correct Hebrew, and the other half to be corrected.'

If you're the half that is corrected then listen to Simona: you're better off sitting in the goal of the football pitch on a Katyusha night.

To fear Devora is to fear the temper of one woman. You get to know her rampaging moods. They're nothing new anyway. At six-thirty in the morning, we have eighteen rampaging mothers, dumping their bags (containing clothes, nappies and plastic bags) and their half-asleep kids, who don't want to leave Mama. Sometimes the children are crying. Other times they have a bewildered look, as if they don't want to know where they are: neither asleep nor awake; neither sad nor happy. Just blind, deaf and mute. Your eye is drawn to the quiet one, but you can't look at him. You've got to have eight ears to catch what the mothers are throwing at you: this one can't eat beetroots; that one didn't sleep all night; another has nappy rash (there's cream in the bag); this one has medicine that you have to keep in the fridge and give him twice a day; and this dummy was dropped on the way and has to be rinsed. On Devora's noticeboard this time is called 'Reception of the Children' and it is allotted ten minutes. You don't know who to listen to first. You have no idea which kid you're holding. They all have to be picked up. Every one has to go from his mama's arms to yours at six-thirty in the morning. And you have to be a really good, quick listener. At quarter to seven, the factory bus arrives. The mothers don't have time, either. They have to run.

When the factory mothers go, it's as if they are still watching us, thinking we're having a great time. At the factory, they're not allowed to move. When they're sewing they have to raise their hand to ask to use the toilet. They sit in the factory, bitterness eating away at their hearts, and imagine us drinking coffee all day long, ignoring the kids and gossiping.

In between Devora's rampages, we have the mothers' black days. Without any warning, at perhaps nine or ten in the morning, one of the mothers suddenly appears to take her child to the clinic for a vaccination. She didn't tell us about it. Why should she? As soon as she opens the door of the nursery, her eyes turn into a camera, taking a picture of everything: who's crying, whose nose is dripping, whose wet nappy has come undone, what we're all doing. What she saw the minute she opened the door is the truth, a blueprint in her head. She'll tell all the factory girls about it later. She won't leave out a thing. More than that, she'll exaggerate it, blow things out of all proportion. It'll be the highlight of her day. The factory girls wait for her to return, just to hear what she's got to say. She'd better have something good for them. At four o'clock they arrive at the nursery. Devora's already left for the day. So has Ricki. It's just us. Us and the kids. We wait, and we know what's coming. As soon as they walk in, they're on the attack, like screaming banshees. Someone highly strung like Shoshi can really lash out. And the ones who don't have a reason to complain help the others to shout.

My hands are so cold they're hurting. The wind has started up. Why now? Well, as long as it doesn't change the Katyusha's course. My legs are cold, too. The wind even managed to get through my black widow's nylons, which only come up to the knee. Everyone says to me: enough is enough. It's been six years. It's time to stop mourning. You can wear any colour you like. But I don't want to. Who are they to tell me when to wear colourful clothes? Who are they to tell me when I should stop mourning? Listen to me, just for once, as I sit here at night in the football pitch in the middle of a Katyusha attack: Simona is not mourning her husband. She is mourning for her old life, the one that was severed in two. Can't you get that into your heads? Simona's mourning isn't at an end. But in another minute, her life will be over, and so will her mourning.

6   My head is spinning. I'd better lie down again. What was I thinking about? When my fate was written on the same piece of paper as Mas'ud's. When we came to the camp in Marseilles and they told every family how long they would stay. They'd count the time according to the *sehina* of Sabbath. They'd say, 'You're sitting four *sehinas*.' Then you'd know you'd have to wait four Sabbaths in the camp before the ship would take you. Papa greased the palms that needed to be greased, shaping the path of my life, and Mas'ud's family got on the same ship: the *Jerusalem*. I didn't see or hear him in the camp, but on the ship I heard him for the first time. His voice was like fire, shooting into my ear, playing with me. It was the first time I'd felt such fire.

I was fifteen, a quiet girl, but in one day I changed. Mas'ud's fire found the seeds of laughter in my belly, and it heated them, making them jump, the way corn seeds jump, hop-hop, opening and exploding, brown skins breaking to show the white inside. My laughter on that ship was like the white of corn seeds, their lightness, their swelling. My laughter and his became travelling companions. Every time I heard his voice, the hard seeds began to heat and pop. My laughter followed Mas'ud's voice all around the ship.

He didn't talk to me, though. What would he have to say to me? He walked around with his brothers and his friends. I didn't listen to everything he said, just the sound of his voice. We were just two kids who didn't know a thing. But then, we started looking for each other. As soon as I heard his voice on the deck, I would go out and pretend to be looking at the sea or the white birds. When his voice went into the dining room, my laughter followed it. Then my laughter went into

Mas'ud's ear, tickling it, and he started to laugh as well. He'd wander around, then come outside, too. All the way from Marseilles to Haifa, my laughter was like the popping of corn, the sea salt sticking to it, and his like the moment the juice is squeezed from purple grapes and turns to wine. Our laughter became companions on the ship. We didn't say a word to each other, but our laughs became married for life.

Our eyes met just once. Like a zip, we were caught in each other right to the top. We couldn't breathe. Then the zip opened, all the way to the bottom, and we turned away. We stepped from the sea to the land, and the fire in me went out.

My family went south, to Ashdod, and his went north. For two days the hot seeds in me kept popping. Then they cooled and hardened. My belly hurt all the time. The officials threw one family here, another there. But we had our luck, and it didn't abandon us. After a year and a half in Ashdod, my brothers bumped into him at the port and brought him home, just some guy that was with us on the ship. They had no idea what we meant to each other.

Akh ya rab, what wouldn't I give for Mas'ud's hand now? He'd reach out and I'd put my hand on his. His hand was the car and mine was the driver. Like on our wedding night, at the beginning, I took him on a journey of my skin. I didn't let him wander around by himself. I treated him like a child, teaching him how to touch my body. His left hand had a callous on the little finger, and I loved to put it on my body. His whole hand was like butter, the callous tracing patterns on me.

Simona's gone mad. She's sitting in the goal of the football pitch, and what is she doing? Trying to prise a little stone out of the dirt. But all the stones have been hammered into the dirt by the energetic running men. If she had found a stone, she'd have taken off a nylon stocking and put the stone inside, so it would feel like Mas'ud's left hand, the one with the callous.

My hand on yours, Mas'ud, my eyes and my mouth closed, just our hands on a journey. Where shall we go tonight? Where didn't we go, Mas'ud? We went on hundreds of trips, ones that were short, funny, dangerous, scenic, direct, backwards and wet. Then there were the ones when I'd hold your hand, and you'd lower your voice and whisper in my ear, 'Simi? Simi? Put your hand in mine. I'll be yours and you'll be mine.' Instantly my body would be filled with soda, with little balls of air.

At first I was afraid of the nights. I didn't want to be in bed with him all by myself. My throat would start to hurt. I'd start to shake and feel sick. What to do? My fingers were more useful than my brain. Ever since I was little, since the day Maman died, I understood that my head was just for school. What does my head know about improving life? It's little better than a lump of rock. But my fingers, which are light and move where I want them to, have power, the sort that can help me to live. So I'd think with my fingers. I'd put them on the table, quickly, like a touch-typist, and, one by one, creep each finger onto the knuckles of its opposite, until they were interlacing. Then I'd put them on my chest and let them talk to my heart: Stop asking to be sick, Simona. Why do you want to be sick? What good will it do? At night, with Mas'ud, you can forget about being human. In bed your head will shrink, until there's no room for thinking. Close your eyes, free your mind, as if it's a bird, and your body will do what it wants. Anyway, what's in bed? Just two bodies behaving like animals, not people. When you wake, everything will come back. Don't be afraid. In the morning, nothing stays the same.

That's how it was. In the morning I'd be afraid that I'd get out of bed and find out I'd turned into a cat or some other furry creature, and, to tell the truth, I did smell like an animal in the morning, my hair all knotted and bushy. My eyes in the bathroom mirror didn't seem human, and my tongue would move in my mouth as if trying to remember how to make words. I'd walk out of the house in the morning, looking from side to side like a child crossing the road for the first time. I was always afraid I'd bump into someone who'd see through me. I'd shake until I realised that there was nothing to be afraid of, that no one could see what I'd turned into.

I used to walk from our apartment to the grocer's, and my face was like an open book, like a shaken soda bottle that spills half its contents on the floor when opened. In the first month after our wedding, I had to put a lid on it. I'd look at people and wonder how they walked around with such sour faces if that's what they were doing all night. I'd look at Yaffa, who lived next door to us, searching for evidence of the night on her. I'd visit you in the building where you were plastering, seemingly to bring you food, but really because I was going crazy not seeing you all day, and also to look at Zion, Yaffa's husband, who was working with you. I'd look for traces of animal in him, but never saw anything. I could never work out how people had the strength to work all day when they hadn't slept all night. I was always dead tired. I'd have a shower, comb my hair, which came down to my waist, plait it, buy some groceries, cook, bring you lunch, wash the few metres of floor we had, look for whatever else I had to do, then fall asleep until you came home.

It took me a long time, until I was already three months pregnant with Kobi, to work out that not everyone did it all night. What a stupid girl I was. A sweet girl, with a stupid head.

Akh ya rab. Maybe before the Katyusha gets me, I'll get that stupid head back for a minute. Listen, I'm only asking to have it back for just a moment, the head of that girl who didn't have a care in the world. Eighteen-year-old Simona who had no troubles, and no fear of future troubles, which sit, like twin towers, on everyone else's shoulders, stopping their heads from turning. Just for a minute, put the spinning top of that girl back on my body, the head of a girl who thought people were all the same, except everyone else could control themselves, hiding evidence of the journeys they took every night.

What did I love about you? When you lay beside me and slowly untied my plait. If you did it too fast, I'd jump so you'd think you had pulled my hair. Then you'd light a match in my ear and whisper, '*Kshhh, pshhh.*' Your fingers were like the feet of four dwarves, climbing barefoot up the ladder of my body, and your voice filled me with laughter, just as it did on the ship. Then I'd turn to you and put my hands in your armpits, which were like the part of the corn-tassel underneath the outer layer. It was the most delicate part of you, a secret part that didn't fill me with shame. I'd bring my hands up to my nose to discover your smell. It was different every day. When you came home, I'd tell you not to have a shower for that reason. I'd smell your work day on my hands, knew if you'd been afraid or angry, if you'd had a good day. You wouldn't tell me anything. When I asked, you'd just throw out, 'Thank God', as if you were gritting the husk of a sunflower seed between your teeth. I never managed to get any more out of you.

Ay, Mas'ud, your smell is still here, I swear. Not the smell of falafel oil, but the smell of Mas'ud the plasterer. You're here! I'm not going to open my eyes, but my nose is searching for you in the air. *Ay*, Mas'ud, how am I going to talk to you now? I haven't spoken to you for six years. I haven't looked at your picture. I just wanted to forget about you. Tonight it's over. This is my last night, Mas'ud. How can I tell you about the day they took your body away from me and put you into the ground? How can I bring you Simona, when they left her body outside?

All our hidden, secret things were there, the things people don't talk about. But I knew they were there. I clung to them, made them stay next to me, but you were stronger, and they all fell into the grave with you. Nothing stayed in my world. I haven't thought of them once in six years. They were buried. But tonight, I'm going to exhume them, pull them out one by one.

Do you remember, Mas'ud, how I used to get you out of bed to come and help me? 'Can you put Etti in her cot for me? Look, she's fast asleep. She had a tiny feed, then she closed her eyes.'

'Bless her, look at her hands,' you'd say to me, but quietly so she wouldn't wake up. 'Her fingers are always open. That girl is not the type to be frightened, Simi, believe me.'

'Come here, Mas'ud, look at Kobi. He always sleeps as straight as a board, as if he went to sleep like that and won't move until the morning.'

'That's why he wakes up so strong,' you'd say.

'Look, Mas'ud, Itzik and Dudi are sleeping back to back. Come on, close the door and let them sleep.'

Give me your hand, Mas'ud, just as you used to do. Not your right hand. The other one. Here, here's your hand. Let's go on a great adventure. Come back to life, just for a while. In a few minutes, a Katyusha will come and then I'll go with you to your place. We'll go tonight, together. My hand on yours. That's how we'll go. We won't let anyone separate us.

I won't open my eyes until you come to our apartment with me. I need you to come now, so I'll believe you came back from the dead. That you time-travelled through six years and fell into my world. Won't you come with me? Here are the stairs. You go first. Open the door; walk in. Six years is a long time, yet it flies by. Now you're with me, I can't remember anything of those years. They've become just a moment in time.

Open whichever door you like. Both apartments are ours. Two and a half years ago, the Elmakeises went to Tiberias, and we got their apartment. We knocked down a wall and made two homes into one. Back then everyone was moving because of the elections. Amsalem moved to the terraces; Dahan and Biton also knocked two apartments together. The Romanos from downstairs went to the new development near Magen David. Everyone with half a brain moved or extended their apartment back then. What's the matter? What's the matter? Why are you leaving? Why aren't you coming in? Are you angry?

I'll tell you what happened. Look, I'm telling you. They asked me, and I said 'Fine.' What's the matter? I just said, 'Fine'. At the polling station, no one looks at your ballot paper. They don't know how you've voted. *Ay*, Mas'ud, what are you trying to tell me by rolling your eyes like that? What should we have done? Stay in a two-room apartment, just so some guy gets a piece of paper with his name on it? Look at me and I'll tell you the truth: I voted for the right person. I did. But they can all go to hell. I couldn't care less who won.

At first I didn't think I would vote. Then, suddenly, they were at my door. They took me in their car, as if I were a queen, gave me a ballot paper. I left the house just as I was, no bag, no pockets, just my identity card. I went into the polling station. I thought I'd change my vote for what you would have wanted. I stood there, shaking. I had no idea what to do. Would they find my paper in the box and know that I'd switched votes? The paper was creased with the sweat from my palms. I was convinced they would have recognised it. Then I thought they might be timing me, to see how long I stayed inside. So I quickly put the paper into the ballot box. Then I went back to the car, and they brought me home. Four months after the elections I got this big apartment for the kids.

What do you want to do now? Make the apartment small again? They told us we didn't get the new apartment because of the elections, that it was just gossip. They said that it was because they were constructing new buildings anyway, new places for people to move to, that they wanted the Home Office to think the town was well populated so they'd invest in it. Listen, even Edri got a house, and everyone knows how he votes. Enough of this. Stop rolling your eyes and open the door, but quietly, so they don't wake. How would I explain that you came back just for the night?

Itzik made the old kitchen into his bedroom. I have no idea how he got his bed in there. Kobi and I shouted at him, but he didn't listen. He pushed with all his might, and in it went. Now I don't have anywhere to keep the mop. What can I do? His bird nests in the sink. It's a good thing it's asleep. I'm afraid of it – and I'm afraid of him, too. He just looks at it all day long. You'd think they were married. He only talks to the bird and Dudi. He dropped out of school and wanders the street. That's his life. At least he doesn't steal. Why are you standing over him, Mas'ud? Don't you want to see the rest of the apartment? Why are you worried about him? That's just the way he is. I don't know why he's lying like that. I've never noticed it. I don't know what's going on in that head of his. His face is like a stone, unreadable. Quite honestly, I've only ever been in here once, and I had to run out again because of the smell. That's the truth. Once was enough. He's a teenager now. I don't know how I didn't notice him growing up. I didn't notice he was shaving, either. How can he shave with those hands? How could I not have noticed my boy was growing up? He's already bar mitzvah age but how I can organise a bar mitzvah for him? He doesn't have a father to take him to the rabbi, and I don't have the money to pay for it.

You go on, Mas'ud. Leave me here with Itzik for a minute.

Wait, wait. You can't go on your own. Wait. Look, here's Dudi's room. He never sleeps in his own bed until the morning. He gets up every night, and walks into the new apartment to sleep in his brothers' room. Look, here it is. However big the house is, they sleep like sardines. Etti's grown up already. Look at her, there in the other bed. And Dudi's in the bed next to hers, see? And here are the new children. I'm picking up the blanket so you can see them, the two of them. Chaim and Oshri. Your twins. You left them inside me when you went. I named both of them after you. What should I say now? Congratulations? Should I congratulate you, Mr Dadon, on the twins you had five and a half years ago? I'm playing the part of the nurse who comes out to tell you the good news.

No, you can't pick them up. No, Mas'ud. I will not allow a dead hand upon them. The living and the dead don't go together.

Now they've woken up. I'll tell you why they're saying 'Grandpa'. It's because that's who they think you are. Don't scare them, Mas'ud. Where are you going now? To our room?

That's better. Rest. No, wait there. Don't go by yourself.

Ay, why are you turning to leave? Look. That's not a new man. Come back, look properly. It's Kobi. Our Kobi. What's the matter? Didn't you recognise your eldest son? Kobi sleeps with me. I didn't bring a new man into our home. It's just your boy lying there. From the day the twins were born, he's been with me every step of the way. Bless him. He wasn't even fourteen and he stayed awake all night long, helping me with the little ones. Where would I be today without Kobi? Etti slept like a log. In the morning she used to say, 'Why didn't you wake me so I could help?' But Kobi was there every night: giving bottles, changing nappies, bathing them, never leaving me alone for a minute. Look at him now: he's nineteen, working, bringing home a salary. He's a good boy.

Why does he sleep with me? It's because Oshri and Chaim think he's their papa. So that they have a papa and a mama like all the other children, a papa and mama who share a bedroom.

It's not the end of the world. Not really.

Look, Mas'ud, the world didn't stop turning. That's the way it is. When something new happened, you'd stand there, your two strong legs apart, and your face white. You'd say, 'That's it, Simona, you've gone too far. It's the end of the world.' But life went on. While you were lying in your grave, you had two more children. What other proof do you need? Look at me. It's night-time and I'm lying outside waiting for the Katyushas, but it's OK. The world won't stop turning because of Simona. It just won't.

Look at Kobi, and see what a fine man you made. He's changed a lot since his bar mitzvah. Ask yourself why I would need a new man when I've got Kobi at home? Why would Chaim and Oshri need a new papa? Look at his nose, his delicate, little girl's nose. Like you, his strength begins just beneath it, on that little hill between his nose and his mouth. And his mouth is like yours, too, as it was when I saw you for the first time on the ship. A plump red mouth, which makes him look as though he's wearing lipstick, and a little laugh upon it, as if the mouth is laughing by itself. He's a good boy. Even when his heart is heavy, you'd never know it. His chin is strong, and his ears are as little and pretty as a girl's. When you glance over his face, looking from one detail to another, it's as if he's a mix of man and woman. You start to feel confused. But when you look at the whole thing, it all makes sense.

You're running away already, Mas'ud? That's it? You saw Kobi in your bed and now it's the end of the world? Come here. Lie down with me in the goal of the football pitch. That's right. Don't go back to the apartment. It's too hard for you to return to a home you left six years ago. I still need to talk to you. When Itzik came out, you thought it was the end of the world, and it wasn't. For an hour and a half I lay there alone, my legs on iron stirrups. Why was I alone? I'll tell you. Because after the baby came out the way it did, everyone ran away from me, and they took him, too. They didn't tell me a thing. The nurse screamed when she saw his fingers and toes, and everyone came running. They grabbed hold of the baby and left me lying on my back, my legs in the air. They didn't sew me up or anything. They just got the placenta out, then disappeared. They took my baby. They didn't let me see him. If I'd given birth to a monster with three heads, they shouldn't have run away like that. I lay there like a dog. In fact, if I was a dog, I'd have quietly licked his head clean. No one would have screamed in my face. And what did you do while I was lying there? You went crying to your mama. That's it! Mas'ud says it's the end of the world! You didn't think to ask me how I was. Now you can listen to me. The blood gathered behind my knees. I was cold. I was thirsty. I screamed. I cried. No one heard me. Just the bare walls as my baby was taken from me.

I thought it was the end of the world, too. I thought I was going to die right there, with my legs wide open. Who came to my rescue? A cleaner. She came and gave me a drink, then went to find someone to sew me up.

For a year you wouldn't say *kiddush* at home. You wouldn't look at the baby and say *kiddush* on Sabbath. I dressed him in big shirts, the sleeves covering his hands so you didn't have to look at them.

47

Nothing helped. You'd look at him then turn away. I had to take you by the hand again and show you that the world hadn't come to an end. Quickly, very quickly, I got pregnant with Dudi. That was just for you, another child to bring the colour back to your face. In less than a year, I gave you a healthy child. It was lucky I had a boy. A gift from God.

Every time you ran to your mother's, I'd die of shame.

You'd say, 'Simi, I'm just popping over to Mama's to see if she needs help with the chicken coop.' As if she really needed help from her strong boy. But I knew what you really meant was: Simona didn't make your life good enough, so off you run to Mama's. Fifteen minutes on the bus to her house. You'd sit there half the day: eating, reading the paper, drinking, sleeping. You wouldn't come home. I used to go to the *moshav* to see you sitting in her kitchen; two little turtle doves with full bellies, and me the cat in the middle.

When I got there, you wouldn't look at me. You'd take Kobi or Etti or Itzik, whoever I'd brought with me, and your mother would get up to make me tea. She'd turn her back to me, her mouth closed, her eyes like ice; I knew what she was thinking. The words she wanted to say seemed to stand behind her teeth, like the children stand behind the nursery fence to watch a bulldozer working outside. 'You've taken my boy away from me, Simona. I put honey on his tongue, but you should be spreading it. You didn't see what he looked like when he came home today. He was as white as a corpse. Look at his colour now!' After five minutes she'd come back with a cup of tea, her manner changed, looking me in the eye: 'What can you do? All men are like children. That's the world, *binti*. Always be patient, and life will be good.'

My sisters-in-law, Shoshana, Yaffa and Rachel, are all made from the same mould. They'd come in, kiss me, talk to me about all kinds of things: 'What a pretty dress, Simona, where'd you buy it?'; 'Kobi's such a cute kid'; 'How Etti's grown. What a pretty girl – and no evil eye, either.' Their words were like sugar. But as they opened their mouths, their twisted laughs escaped, showing in their eyes: 'Is that how you keep him? Like that? What's the use of your beauty and your dresses if you have to follow him all the way here?' I'd suffer it so I could buy you back from your mother.

They didn't think that in town. I know what they used to say about me: 'Look how she keeps him twisted around her little finger.' When I went to the cinema, Shushan talked about me behind my back: 'Mas'ud Dadon? He has to ask his wife's permission to pass wind.'

Mas'ud's gone. He just came and went, without leaving me a memory of his face. He turned it away, didn't look at me, so he didn't see what has happened to me in six years. And he didn't even try to find out how I was coping. He escaped to his grave all alone. And if a Katyusha won't come for me, I can't go with him. I don't have his back, his hand or his smell to lead me.

7 If I could, I'd take the netting of the goal and wrap it around myself. But how can I get it off the goalpost? I haven't got anything to cut it. Just Our Simona's handbag, which I haven't opened in six years. Maybe she left nail scissors in it? What is inside Our Simona's bag?

I can't open it. I still can't do it.

I put my head back inside my dress, hoping for sleep.

I'm at the cemetery, looking for Mas'ud's grave. I can't find it. It has disappeared. In its place is a patch of dirt with six tall thorns growing there. I don't understand it. I touch the solid dirt. They haven't yet dug the grave. My fingernails are blood-red among the thorns. On the other side of the cemetery our rabbi is saying psalms. How didn't I notice there was another memorial happening? I quickly check I'm wearing my headscarf, and my finger brushes a hairpin. I don't understand. My hair is the way it was for Kobi's bar mitzvah. I look up to see whose memorial it is. But instead of the rabbi I see it's a bee whose humming sounds like a prayer.

Now I'm in the middle of town, with my bar mitzvah hairdo and my yellow cloche skirt and the black blouse with the yellow collar. I go to Mas'ud's falafel shop. Again, he turns his back, and I say, 'Quick, Mas'ud, leave everything and come with me now!' He doesn't reply. Someone behind me is laughing. It's his father, and he's saying, 'Shim'ona, Shim'ona, what'll we hear from Shim'ona today?' It's just how he used to laugh at me when he was alive. I turn. He's sitting on a crate, which Etti used to sit on when she helped Mas'ud, and playing with the till like a kid. 'Look at me, Shim'ona, look at me!' He pushes a button, and the till rings and opens up. He laughs and closes it with a bang, then presses the button again. I turn back to Mas'ud and walk into the shop. He stands with his back to me, cutting vegetables. I tell him to come home, to leave everything, but he just points at a big bowl with his knife. '*Behayat,* Simona, look how much houmous I've ground today. There's six thousand shekels in houmous here. It'd be a terrible waste. And what about all the people who are coming into town today because of Rabbi Kahane? They're checking the loudspeakers right now. He will be here soon. It'd be a crying shame to lose all that money. I'll make at least half of what I make on Independence Day.' I cry, 'Mas'ud, I'm hungry, make me some falafels.' He turns to his father, saying he doesn't know what's wrong with her, that she's never touched one of his falafels in her whole life, that she's never even visited the shop. He sounds like someone who's won millions in the lottery but doesn't quite believe it yet. In a little girl voice, I ask him for falafels. He says, 'Just a minute, I'll get some for you. How many do you want, Simi? Four?' He's so happy that he starts to dance, his hands spinning the falafel balls. I tell him I want lots and lots, but he still doesn't look me in the eye, so I tell him I want everything he's got, that he should make all the falafels just for me. I don't know how I'll get through them, but I say, 'Tell everyone the shop's closed. I'll finish every last mouthful you make, but we have to go home now, quickly. We don't have any time.' And then his father calls out, 'Shim'ona, come and look at this big heap of money. I've made piles. I did it all by myself. Look, the notes are nice and neat; the hundreds and fifties and tens all separated out for you.'

I don't want to look at him because he died of a heart attack before we opened the falafel shop, and Mas'ud is still alive. Mas'ud turns to me, and on each of his fingers is a falafel ball. I fall on his fingers. The falafel burn my mouth, but I finish them all and ask for more. But he doesn't make any more, just looks at me steadily, his eyes not moving, as if they are stuck. 'Eat for your health, Simi. Eat as much as you

51

want. Eat and eat.' Then he lowers his eyes to the floor. Now he sounds like someone who has realised the lottery money is counterfeit, spoiled like sour milk: 'I'm not coming home today, Simona. As soon as I finish the houmous I'm leaving with my father. I'm leaving, Simi, I'm leaving.'

I start to hit him, punching him in the face. I hit him a thousand times. In a minute I'll knock him onto the burning pot of oil. He shouts, but doesn't hit back, just tries to stop himself from falling, then he starts to shrink under the weight of my punches, becoming smaller and smaller, until he's the size of a child, the height of my waist. I grab him, pick him up like a baby, with one hand behind his knees, the other on his back. How heavy he is. He's smaller but he weighs just the same. I put my back into it, pulling him off the floor. I straighten up and turn to go, holding him in my arms. I've got to get him home, so he doesn't leave with his father. His smell is killing me – the oil, the coriander on his clothes – but what do I do? I bury my face further into his shirt. Now I can't see. I move forward in the direction of the door, and just as I think I've managed to get him out his father grabs me, taking him from me, laughing all the time. *Shim'ona, Shim'ona, what do we hear from Shim'ona today*? Then he stops laughing and grips my hand. 'Come on, take the money. We won't need it where we're going. Take it, take it. Why not? Don't be ashamed, Simona. Come on, we'll open the till together.' Then he pushes my finger onto the button that opens the till, but it doesn't open, just rings and rings and rings.

I open my eyes. It's a dream. Dawn is beginning. My mouth is dry. The grass of the football pitch is covered with dew, as if it was listening to me all night, as if it was crying for me. I turn onto my stomach, pressing my mouth against the grass. Dew is the cleanest water there is. I sit up and open my handbag. The smell inside is the smell of Our Simona, of perfume and powder. It's as if everything is looking up at me: the round brush, the makeup kit – dried up over six years – the compact mirror and the tweezers. The bottles of nail varnish and perfume, and the white headscarf for the bar mitzvah Sabbath. Spare nylon stockings in case I had a ladder in the middle of the party. My hand delves in. What's at the bottom? I have no idea what it is. I take it out. It's a knife wrapped in a napkin; a souvenir from the bar mitzvah.

I unzip the side pocket, take out the box I put there, open it. Inside is the ring Mas'ud gave me at our wedding, lying on a bed of cotton as though suffering from a terminal illness. I don't put it on my finger. Instead I put it in my mouth, holding it with my teeth. I close the handbag. I want to stand but I can't move my legs. Holding on to the goalpost with two hands, I pull myself up. I've got pins and needles in my feet.

The sun is rising from behind the little hill of the cemetery. The trees shade half of the sun's rays, the other half creeps to my legs like an unrolling carpet. From here it's no more than fifteen minutes to his grave. I won't pray for him today, as I have done every year. I'll come alone, dig a small hole in the ground next to his grave. Then I'll put his ring into it, next to him, fill in the hole with the earth and divorce him.

I want to step away from the goalpost but I can't. A picture comes to mind. A day of first steps at the nursery. It's a day none of us have forgotten, when the crawlers gave us the best present: seeing them walk for the first time. What a day! Almost all the crawlers walked. Shlomi started it. He took two steps, grabbed a table, then took a piece of banana from a plate as if it was nothing, as if he'd been walking for a hundred years. Then it was Ziva's turn. She'd been crawling with her knees off the floor. Suddenly she picked herself up, slowly, slowly, and stood in the middle of the room, her legs spread, wobbling until she fell. Twice more and she learned how to stand with her feet closed up a little. Then she took her first step and fell on her bottom. She was quite old to start walking, a year and five months. After Ziva, others started to walk, too. We laughed and laughed. We forgot to put them to bed, forgot to clean, forgot everything. Instead we picked them up and kissed them all over their faces, on their legs, and put them in the middle of the room so they'd walk. And then Avi got up. Avi! He was just ten months old. He stood on the side, watching the others, holding on to a table, rocking and making happy noises. I wasn't looking at him, was looking at myself in the mirror for a minute, then suddenly I saw him in the mirror, taking a step, then getting scared and falling onto the other table and bursting into tears. After half an hour he was walking just like the older ones. We thought it was a miracle, to be walking when he was so little. When the mothers arrived at pick-up time, they didn't believe us. All we heard was: 'Come to me! Come to me!' Then they saw we were telling the truth, and they started to laugh, too.

I leave the goalpost and start to walk, holding the wedding ring in my mouth and breathing through my nose. In the air is the smell of a new morning, and it gives me the strength to walk.

54

When I get close to the cemetery, I have to stop myself from running. I don't want to put my ring there, after all. I don't want to make a grave for it, sit shiva for it, and say prayers for it for the rest of my life.

I sit down where I have stopped, take out the bar mitzvah knife and dig a little hole. Then I open my mouth, watch the ring fall into its grave, and cover it up.

I get up and walk towards the cemetery. After five or six steps, I turn back. I can still see the place. I walk forward again, then turn back once more. The sun is behind me. I look. Maybe it's here, or maybe it's there. I think I know. Yes, I'm almost sure.

I walk further, look back again. The sun is in my eyes now. I can't see a thing. The ring is gone. Even if I want to go back, I don't know where it is any more.

When I turn to go, I hear voices in the cemetery. It's my children. Who's there? Is that Etti? And Itzik or Dudi? Maybe it's Kobi. Now I'm sure I can hear Chaim and Oshri. How can it be? It's only five o'clock in the morning, five-thirty at the earliest. The loudspeaker hasn't announced the all-clear. Who would have thought they'd get up so early to say prayers for their father?

DUDI AND ITZIK DADON

Dudi and Itzik

'Bring her over here. Come on. Watch how you're holding her. You're strangling her! Give her to me. Look what you've done. Another minute and she'd have lost a wing. She's delicate, you know. Get it?'

'But Itzik, you said she was strong, really strong. You're changing your story again. You're always changing things.'

'Of course she's strong, but she's delicate, too. You have to be careful with her! Think before you act. When we got her, we had to work out how to get her down, remember? So we still have to do that – to look at her from all sides and angles. Get it?'

'Watch out! She's shitting on your hand!'

'Let her shit. It doesn't bother me. Even her shits are beautiful. Everything about her is beautiful. Nothing's disgusting. She's like a queen, this one, queen of all the birds. Have you ever seen her piss?'

'She can't piss.'

'How do you know?'

''Cause I'm always looking at her. She only does white shits. Let me have her back. I'm not giving in to you again. You promised we'd have her fifty-fifty.'

'Go on, then, take her. But be careful, OK? Look how I'm holding her. I'm not afraid to let her use the whole of my hand.'

'I can't do it. I can't have her on my hand. You keep her, Itzik. Your hands were made for her. You don't have any feeling in them, so you can keep them open for her. When she pecks your hand, you don't feel the pain. You just laugh, like she was kissing you.'

'OK, OK, give her back, then. You need to wear gloves, like the ones the disabled JNF guys wear when they're weeding thorns. Then we can sort out the other thing. Now take out some meat for her, just a little so she doesn't get used to too much. We'll need it for her training. Cut it up for her. Don't forget she eats like a queen – little bits at a time. I have to think what to do next. I need some leather cord to tie around her foot.'

'Wouldn't shoelaces be good enough? I thought we could tie some laces together. I've already bought some.'

'Shoelaces? She's a queen, Dudi. You don't use shoelaces for a queen. Anyway, they'd just rip her leg. As I said, she's strong but delicate. I'm going to guard her with my life. There's nothing in the world I wouldn't do for her. I'll get her everything we saw in that film *Kes*, everything. She'll never want to leave the palace I'm going to make for her. Get it? Why are you making faces?'

'What do you mean? I'm in pain. I bet I broke a finger when I fell.'

'Where'd you fall? You can't have fallen that badly.'

'Not when I was holding her; when I came down with the bird book. I thought I heard you whistle, and jumped down into the bushes. I didn't look where I was going. I was afraid I might drop the book so I took it out of my mouth. I forgot all about that bastard piece of iron stuck in the ground.'

'OK, OK, come and sit down. Have a rest. Just don't start crying on me. And have a good rest, because you need to go back up for one more thing.'

'Go where? You said we'd finished! You're changing things yet again. First you said we'd just go and get her. Then you said we needed the book, so we'd know for sure if she was a girl. Now it's something else. And you said the book was a little thing but look at this finger. It's like a hotdog. My fingernail is killing me.'

'I swear this is the last thing. We just need something to hold her. Dudi, how can we train her otherwise? All we need is a leather cord.'

'Why did we cross the street? Ten metres later and we're crossing back again. Is it because of Mordi? So you don't have to say hello to him? Where's the harm in saying hello? Now he'll think we've got something against him, and he'll tell Kobi.'

'So what? Kobi's not our dad.'

'He'll get angry, and Chaim and Oshri—'

'Leave them out of it. They're just babies. One day they'll find out the truth about Kobi.'

'Itzik, don't be like that. He'll get angry and then he won't give us money for the cinema. I can't live without films.'

'OK, OK. She looks like she's listening to everything we're saying. Her eyes seem to understand everything, don't you think? She understands the past and the future, and she doesn't care about any of it. I love the way she grabs my finger with her foot. Do you think

61

she knows she's ours? Wait, where are you going? We're heading this way.'

'No, no, Itzik. Not that girl-soldier-teacher place. I said I was never going back there. I swore on Dad's memory!'

'What's the matter with you, Dudi? I swear I'll never understand you. Either you want her or you don't. How can we train her without a leather cord? All right, calm down. Why are you jumping up and down? I've already thought it through. On Monday all the girl-soldiers have classes in the adult education centre, where Grandma goes'

'How do you know where Grandma goes? We haven't seen her in ages.'

'I saw her going in there last week with all the old ladies. It starts at four. There's nothing to be afraid of. And I don't want to hear you swearing on Dad's memory again. We don't have a dad. You can't swear by someone you don't have. Get it?'

'And what if one of them doesn't feel well and decides to stay at home, eh? Did you think of that? Or if she just didn't fancy teaching and pretended to be sick? Come up with me yourself. We'll knock on the door and see if anybody's there. Then I'll go. But how do you know they've got a leather cord?'

'Believe me, they have.'

'A leather cord?'

'Have you forgotten about that tall girl's sandals? She probably gets up at six in the morning to criss-cross them up to her knees.'

'Course I know her. She's a friend of Liat's. Her name's Shulamit.'

'So if we tie the leather from both her sandals, we'll have a great

62

cord. She doesn't like to wear them anyway, because people made so much fun of her.'

'Her legs look like meat tied up for the Sabbath stew.'

'So let's go and get it. We'll be done in less than a minute.'

'At least let me give back the book, Itzik. I'll just rip out the two pages we need, then put it back on the shelf.'

'What's the matter with you, Dudi? I swear I'll never understand you.'

'But you said we'd give it back! You're changing your mind again. You said we'd just look up the bit about hawks and then give it back. You promised we wouldn't steal!'

'What's the matter with your brain? If we put it back now, they'll be onto us right away. Forget about the book. One day, when they're hot under the collar about something else, then we'll give it back. We'll bring it to the school, make it look like they did it, that they forgot about it. And bring me some more meat, too. She's still hungry. Listen to that screeching! But I've just remembered they fixed the shutter after their radio-cassette went missing. You can't go in that way again. Get it?'

'If Liat's there, I'm dead, Itzik! I'm a goner the minute I look into her eyes. I can't cope. If she catches me, she'll cry. She won't tell anyone, but the way she looks at me, the look in her eyes, it's a kind of death.'

'You're off again! When will you get it into your head that that's how she's holding on to you? Liat in the morning, Liat in the afternoon, Liat at folk dancing, Liat at the cinema, Liat at school, Liat in the centre, and Liat in bed – in your dreams. It's like a Bollywood film. You spend your life doing things to raise half a smile from that girl, and you haven't even seen her bedroom. She'd slam the door in your face. I swear, Dudi, you'll never ever see me tied to someone like that. Get it? She'll soon be finished with the army, and then she'll go back to wherever she was before. She won't bother to piss in your direction.'

'Why do you have to ruin everything for me? Just because you don't like people doesn't mean I have to run away from them all the time. And why should it bother you if I dream about her at night? Is it any of your business? And her smile – maybe she has a smile Itzik's never seen, eh? Maybe she gives you half a smile but I get the whole thing, and laughing, too. She comes up close and looks into my eyes, and she laughs. You know something – I won't sneak into her house. I swear that's the truth. I'll just go to the front door, if she lets me.'

'You won't go in?'

'I won't!'

'You know what your problem is, Dudi? You always go after the birds that flit from place to place. What do you think you're doing? Those volunteers will go back to America in six months, and you'll never see them again. Just don't tell me that you're dreaming of the day some volunteer girl says, 'I love you, David', and takes you back to America with her. Dudi, you will never see America. Listen to me. The best you'll be is background in the photos they take back to America. A photo, that's it! What do you get from the girl-soldier-teachers who are just dying to get out of here? Shoot me if I'm wrong. Every Friday morning their eyes are glued to the clock, counting down the time minute by minute. If you saw them in the city tomorrow, Dudi, they'd cut you dead.'

'That's enough, Itzik. Enough!'

'I haven't finished yet. Listen to me. Even the ones that are here for two years tops, what do you get from them? They're only living here because they ran out of money in the city, and can live here cheap. They look at you as though they were nice and clean after a *mikve*, and God just got mixed up and threw them in the rubbish by mistake. Every day they count how much money they've got, and how long they have to wait before they can fly back to the city. Those people will fly away, and those and those, and they'll have a good laugh about what a moron Dudi was. He thought he'd fly away from here, too. He didn't see he was just a chicken in a coop that couldn't fly for more than two metres. Dudi, remember this: I've got no faith in people who come and go. I don't wear my heart on my sleeve, so they can do whatever they like with it. They came, they stayed, they went. It's not my problem. I forgot about them before they even arrived here. The only people in this world you can really lean on are your family. Get it?'

'What family? I talk about Dad; you tell me we've got no dad. I mention Kobi; it's like you've been bitten by a dog.'

'Forget Kobi. He only thinks about himself. I've told you that a thousand times.'

'I've had enough. You're making mince-meat of my heart. I'll go in one last time, but not now. I'm dying of hunger. I can't go in if I'm hungry.'

'Why don't you have something to eat while you're in there? Go into their kitchen. You've got loads of time. I'll cover you from behind Cohen's grocery. Eat something quickly, but just bring the sandals.

You shouldn't be more than seven or eight minutes, even after eating.'

'Where will I find food? In the girl-soldier-teachers' house? You make me laugh. You've never been in there, have you? They've got nothing. The kitchen is empty. There isn't even the smell of food there, just the smell of the black mould that grows in winter. They can't get rid of the smell, even though they whitewash it before Pesach. I don't know what they eat all day, I really don't.'

'Our problem is that Cohen won't give us any more credit. If only Kobi would pay him. You can smell the bread from here. OK, we'll go home and get something to eat there. I got hungry thinking about those hungry girls. Afterwards, we'll come back for the sandals. We've got until seven, when the class finishes. We'll put her in her kitchen cabinet while we eat. You did make holes in the cabinet for her, didn't you? I hope you did, Dudi.'

'I made five holes. Five!'

'So we don't need to worry. We'll put her in the cabinet and nail it shut. Then we'll come back here at six, before it gets dark. That'd be all I need, for you to turn a light on while you're inside.'

Dudi If it wasn't for Itzik I would never have thought of breaking into houses in a million years. If Itzik didn't have those hands and feet, maybe he'd go instead. Itzik's my big brother and he's just like me. We're practically twins. When he takes off his hat you can't tell us apart, except for his hands and feet, poor guy. What can you do? That's how he was born.

It's Itzik who tells me how to climb. Without him I'm nothing.

I've climbed houses, rocks and fences hundreds of times. Itzik tells me how to do it. I wouldn't know how to climb something new. He knows how to read walls, and I don't.

He looks at a building from the top to the bottom. He starts to read it. I don't know what he's seeing. I don't understand why you can't just go up to the wall and start climbing. He doesn't talk. I walk around, kick stones, mess with my hair, take a piss, come back, and find him lying on the ground like a bug that's turned over. He lifts his screwed-up hands and feet, moves them as if he's climbing, but without getting up. How could he? He just shadow-climbs, his eyes moving up slowly, and he puts his hands and feet in exactly the right places. He marks out in the air what I'll do on the wall in two minutes.

After that he'll say, 'See the bars on Hazan's window? You put your right foot there. Then you climb the bars to the end of the window; just be careful not to wedge your foot in too hard or your shoe won't come off again when you pull it out. You lift your hands, grab the pipe and pull yourself up till you can put your left foot on the new awning of Edri's laundry balcony. Just be careful there. That plastic is slippery. Now, you don't put another foot on the awning, Dudi. You still hold onto the pipe, just hold it a bit higher, then lift your right foot up to the concrete strip. From there it's easy. You see the little windows where the birds make their nests? You put your left foot in the lower window, and grab the other window with your hand. After that you put your other foot there too and hold on with both hands. Go up like it's a ladder till you can climb the bars of the girl-soldier-teachers' laundry lines, then you bring up your feet one after the other, and you're on their balcony.'

67

When he finishes talking, I go up exactly as he said. Luckily I find Shulamit's sandals right there, thrown onto the laundry balcony. I make a victory sign to Itzik. He mouths, 'God is great!' Then I go to Liat's room, but it's locked. I have no business being there. Itzik signs that the coast is clear. I throw him the sandals, grab the pipe, and slide down.

I've been getting things for him since I was nine. At first I used to fly up, fall down, and the whole world would spin and go dark. I'd fall down, almost break an arm, but Itzik's face never moved. I would cry and scream with pain, and he never budged.

It wasn't that he didn't want to help me. He wanted to help me as much as he could, except his hands drop everything. After I'd finished screaming, he'd say, 'You know what your problem is, Dudi? Just when things are going well – maybe you climbed the right way for a metre – you get excited and forget where you are. Think about John Wayne, how he shoots three Indians, *tak-tak-tak*, and they fall down before they even saw him. What if he got excited, went to sit with Itzik and Dudi in the cinema, just to see how great he looked? Another Indian would show up straight away, and whack him with one arrow. Get it?'

He'd say the same thing every time, till I learned to climb. Now he just puts his hand on my shoulder. He doesn't pat me on the back, just places his hand. That's the best thing in the world, his hand on my shoulder. Except it reminds me of Dad and then I want to cry. As soon as Itzik senses that, he removes his hand. Then we go quiet. We never talk about Dad.

What is there to talk about? Dead is dead.

I only borrow things for him, and I always think I'll stop tomorrow. Itzik doesn't have the same sense of not being allowed to steal. He always says something to change my mind. You think something is good and the other bad; Itzik will get you to swap sides.

He has his Commandments, too. You're allowed to steal something if:

1. You return it exactly as it was.
2. The person you're stealing from doesn't need it.
3. The person you're stealing from has stolen from others. It's even a good deed then. (Assouline from the grocery puts up his prices because he knows people can't drive to the city where the same thing is half the price. A month ago we stole batteries from him. Itzik wanted them; I don't know why. He was in the back of the shop and knocked over a box of tin-openers with his screwed-up hands. Assouline came to help him pick them up, and that's when I put the batteries in my pocket. Then I went to help them as though nothing had happened, and we left. The minute we're outside the shop I start to shake, and Itzik says, 'I'm taking you to see the villa he's just built in the flashy new development. How did he have the money for that if he didn't steal from everyone?')
4. It's for someone else. Then we're transferring, not stealing. (Itzik says you can take something from someone if it doesn't mean a lot to them but the world to someone else.)
5. You're stealing it back. That's allowed, too. (Itzik says, 'That

book isn't theirs, and the girl-soldier-teachers didn't buy it, either. The stamp says it belongs to their high school.)

6. You're getting back at someone.
7. It's for an important project. ('Think of the people who have died in terrorist attacks, Dudi. If we went to Shulamit and said, "Give us your sandals, and your best friend won't be killed by terrorists", don't you think she'd give them up for Liat?')

When I start talking about something we stole, he brings up God: 'What's right? Who's right? Did God make everyone equal? There's no such thing as justice. He doesn't deal the same cards to everyone in life but he gives everyone the same Ten Commandments. Why is one person born in a castle and another in a tent? You tell me. Do you know why? Because God steals and replaces, just like us. Just so the world doesn't become boring to look at. When we lift something, God's happy, really. He sees we understand His game.'

That's the way Itzik messes with my mind. When I'm with him, I believe every word he says, but the minute I'm alone I can't think that way. I go home, look at Dad's photo, and I want to cry. Dad looks at me and says, 'Is that what you've become, Dudi, a criminal?' What can I tell him? What Itzik told me? 'You can't be toeing the line all the time, Dudi. You've got to decide when to be inside and outside of the law. What is a good person, anyway? Is it somebody who sticks by all the laws to make God happy? Don't make me laugh. Someone who pretends to think about God is only thinking about himself, so he can go to Heaven when he dies. Listen to Itzik.'

Itzik Since I was small, I've thought about what God was thinking when he stopped my hands and feet growing inside Mum. There's nothing God doesn't see, nowhere he can't go. He doesn't have eyes like ours, which can only look forward and see a tiny bit of the world. He sorted out something better for himself. I don't know exactly what, but there's nothing he can't see. He sees everything, God, everything from miles and miles away.

No one could help Mum see what he was doing to the babies inside her. She had no choice. She just had to put herself in God's hands. Like Suleika the blind woman who crosses the street by herself, she could only pray that God would watch over her. That's all Mum could do until the baby came out, ready-made and too late to fix. She couldn't say, 'He's not mine.' How could she when everyone saw him come out, the cord still attached to her? That's how God teaches people that they're small and blind, and he's big and all-seeing.

When I was little I used to lie on the floor a lot, as if I was a carpet. The floor and I were stuck together for most of the day. I'd try to do things the other children at nursery would do, but nothing worked. When this happened, I'd lie on the floor quietly, shut my eyes, and imagine I was back inside Mum's belly, listening to God decide about each of my fingers, when to stop it growing. I'd see God walking by silently, each week pointing at a different finger, and the angel flying with him writing down on my notes what God had ordered. I'd see the picture of my feet and hands on the note in the angel's hand, and that he'd written to stop the fingers that had begun to sprout.

Then I'd feel my heart exploding with pain, and I'd go beserk. I'd head-butt the floor – *buf-buf-buf* – bang with my hands and my feet and my knees as hard as I could, and scream just so I couldn't hear my thoughts. I'd do that for a while, until my body hurt more than my head, and I'd only stop when my body couldn't take any more. I'd stay on the floor, listen to my beating heart until it slowed, listen to footsteps. I'd become a part of the floor, just listening to footsteps. That was good. Lying down, listening to all the banging around, feeling the heat of my cheeks wanting to heat the floor tiles but the tiles cooling them instead. I'd smell my own sweat and breathe loudly. When my sweat cooled, I'd get up and start trying to be like all the other kids again.

At first, they tried to pick me up. They tried to talk to me, shout at me, drag me up. In the end they left me alone. They'd circle me, blocking their ears and screaming, 'Itzik! Itzik!' I felt like a football player, urged on by the crowd. They'd all shout, even the girls, until the teacher came to take them away, to make them sit somewhere else.

One day they decided to give me my own special space. The teacher's assistant took me by the hand and said, 'Itzik, when you need to lie down on the floor, come over here.' She put me in a little cupboard near the kitchen, where the broom, the bucket and the mop were kept, and said, 'You've just got to hold it in until you get here. Then you won't disturb anyone else and no one will see you.' She explained it in exactly the same way she'd explain to a kid who peed or pooed his pants, that there was a place for such things, that you shouldn't do things like that near other people. So I'd go and lie there instead. Instead of smelling my own sweat, I'd smell dusters and cleaning liquids. I think it was then that I got addicted to the smell.

Even now, if I want to calm down, I go to the bathroom, pour some washing powder into the sink and breathe it in. Then I can calm down, clear my mind.

At first I used to hate God for making me this way for his own fun. Just to see what a person looks like who can't hold anything in his hands, who bleeds whenever he tries something for the first time, who falls over when he tries to walk, because his feet aren't like other people's feet, who sweats with the effort of trying to be like everyone else.

Then I used to curse him, deep in my heart. God's name and a curse, as one. I'd curse him in Hebrew, in Arabic, in Moroccan. I'd invent curses. And I stopped going to synagogue on Sabbath, so he could see I wasn't playing his game. What's he after anyway? Is it just to have everyone go the synagogue and sing songs about how wonderful he is?

Show me the person who wouldn't sign up to that. To have everyone read a book that's all about him, which if it fell on the floor is picked up instantly as if it were a baby, checked to see it's OK, its dirty cover given a kiss. Show me the person who wouldn't dream of everyone reading this book together, a book that commands them to sing about him, about his goodness and strength, and to obey him. You can look all you like, you won't find anyone who'd say no to that.

When did I get my new idea? Four months ago, when I turned thirteen without a bar mitzvah or anything. I don't know how it started. Maybe God saw I wasn't his pet, and gave me this new thought. I used to think God wanted to see how someone managed with hands and feet that were different, but maybe he just wanted to invent a new type of person altogether.

Maybe God wanted to create a person who had no use for normal machines, cutlery, tools, weapons, clothes, shoelaces, pencils, erasers or razors. None of that was any use to him.

Why not? I bet he wanted to see how inventive that person would be.

Even a *tefeillin* is no good. He'd even have to invent a new way to tie himself to God. And a *tefeillin* isn't something someone else can do for you.

But truthfully, I don't know what to believe. If God had made me mute, I might think he just wanted to make fun of me. But he gave me brains to think about all the things that happen in the world, so maybe he did want to try something new. Why would he watch all the people in the world, doing the same thing, for a million years? I think he must always be looking at me, God, why else would he make me this way? He chose me when I was in Mum's belly: Me, Itzik Dadon, the first boy of a new kind of people.

Dudi

Today we're going down into the wadi, taking the path lined with boulders, far away from the houses. We're neither too cold nor too hot. Itzik's big hat sits above his ears like a helmet. He never takes it off. He even sleeps in it. He only ever washes it at the outdoor tap in the wadi, then puts it back on straight away, soaking wet. I wish I could take it off him – the hat and the fingers together make him ugly – but Itzik doesn't think about his looks. He never looks at himself in a mirror. He walks around like he's invisible.

Itzik and people don't go well together. But I'd like to live in a world filled with people and nothing else. I'd take that.

He thinks everyone and everything is a traitor. Once he said to me, 'Look how our clothes betray us. On Pesach Kobi gave you the blue shirt, remember? When you first put it on, it was like you were wearing Kobi's shirt, that you'd dressed up as Kobi. The next day it was the same: Dudi's wearing Kobi's shirt. The shirt didn't forget its owner. But after a month, it's over. The shirt has passed itself from Kobi to Dudi. Now when you walk around in it, it's yours, completely. You can't tell that it transferred from one person to another! And it's exactly the same thing with cars. When Reuven first sold his pickup to Makhlouf, you'd see the pickup turn into the street, and you'd think: Here's Reuven's Amar. Even when you saw Makhlouf in it, you'd still think he was driving Reuven's pickup. But after two or three months, you look at it in the street, and you say: Makhlouf. That's it. Finished. The truck forgot the person who sat in it for three years. The things we think are ours betray us without a care in the world. Now, if cars and shirts are like that, it can't be any different with people, can it?'

We go further into the wadi. I lead, choosing a path he can walk on without falling. The way I'm walking, you'd think we both have a problem with our feet. As soon as I hear the sound of his breathing behind me, I pretend I have to pee, or that I'm tired, or that my foot hurts, and we find a stone to sit down on together.

All of a sudden he starts to talk, slowly. It's as if his words are rocks and he doesn't have the strength to pick up too many at a time. 'Say, Dudi . . .' he begins. I know what's coming. When he starts like that, I just don't know how it's going to end. Once it almost ended with the police. Heavy words start to fall. 'Say you were a terrorist. What would you target? Our building?'

'I don't know. You're making me into a terrorist now? What did I do to you?'

'Think, Dudi, think for a minute. Let's say we're terrorists. What would we target?'

'Why are you talking like this?'

'Listen, Dudi. Are you with me? Let's sit on this rock for a while. Close your eyes for a minute and think.'

Obediently, my eyes close. That's Itzik's power. I could beat him up even if I was sick. But he can finish me off with two words.

'We're terrorists now, Dudi. You and me. Imagine . . . We've carried out a thousand training missions. Our hearts are as strong as iron and beat slowly, never racing because of fear. Then our moment arrives. We break through the border fence at night. They don't catch us. That's how good we are. There are no more than two hundred metres between us and the Israeli army, and they can't see us, even with all their searchlights. Are you with me?'

'You've got to say it in Arabic. I can't think like a terrorist in Hebrew.'

'*Ahalan wasahalan, tefadalu, Allahuakbar! Allahuaakbar! Ru'h min hon! Itba'h elYahud*!'

'OK, so we're terrorists, with our *keffiyehs*.'

'Now it's midnight, Dudi. We walk at night. Ten or twenty miles, with the guns and bombs on our back. We crawl, too, crawl really quietly. They don't catch us. We move here, to the wadi, to the big boulder. We climb it, feel the cold when we lie on it. We go past the red tree. Can you see us?'

'Yes, I can.'

'It's starting to get light. Open your eyes a little – no, not all the way, more closed than open. Ex-act-ly. Now we can see houses, streets, a water tower, but we don't know the town. We don't recognise a thing. Get it?'

'What do you mean? What don't we recognise?'

'We've never been here before. How could we recognise it? We don't know who lives where or if they're Romanian, Sephardim, Tunisian, Moroccan. We don't know where anything is. We're not from here. We don't know a thing – whether people are young, old. Nothing.'

'We don't know nothing.'

'Now, listen, Dudi. If you see people's faces, everything we've done goes down the pan. If you look at people, you start to think: I like him so I won't target his house, but I don't like the look of that other one. You're a terrorist. You've got no family, no friends, nothing. Get it?'

'Totally!'

'Now you have to pick a house, to make a choice. You, alone. So, which one are you going to choose?'

'I'll tell you something. If I was a terrorist here in the wadi, I'd go up to the closest house, the first one I could see. I'd go straight up the path, and in without a second thought. The railroad apartments, say. Right, Itzik?'

'No, Dudi, that's not right.'

'Why not? I don't understand. Why wouldn't we just go to the railroad apartments and get it over with?'

'OK, I'll explain. Now imagine that I'm the terrorist. I choose my building carefully. I know I'm going to die there, and I don't want just any old place. You only die once, don't you? I also know the newspapers will come and take my photo afterwards.'

'What, your photo will be in the newspaper?'

'After something like that, definitely. Why wouldn't I be? Who doesn't want to be in the newspaper? So I look at the buildings to see which is best. Not all buildings look good in photos. And I want to make a statement, too. I think you've forgotten we're terrorists. What good would it do to blow up the railroad apartments? We'd get one family, and then we'd be caught and that would be the end of it. Before we could do any more, the people in the other apartments would hear and come out for us. Get it?'

'What do you mean? So we shouldn't go into the railroad apartments? People who live there are always afraid because they're at ground level. The minute Rafi's family hear about a break in the border fence they get out the axes his dad's hidden under the bed. They sleep with them at night. His dad probably got them from the JNF. What's up, Itzik? You've gone deaf all of a sudden? So where would you choose? You still haven't said. What about the terraces? Why not? Where, then? I bet you're thinking of our building.'

'What are you on about, Dudi? I'd never choose our building in a million years. No way. Even if it was an option, I wouldn't choose it because of the rubbish. Maybe if it was cleaned up, so there was no stinking rubbish or graffiti. Maybe then. But not definitely.

Let's walk to the carob tree so we can see it.'

We walk as far as the carob tree, past the tall oaks, then up the path slowly until we can see our building.

'I'd never pick it, Dudi,' he says. 'Look at it. All that rubbish from the big families on the ground floor. If they cleaned it up, I'd think about it, but not as it is. I'd never target it. They should clean it up first. Clean it, then paint it. Why are you making that face? They're just sitting there waiting for City Cleanup to come and do it for them. They should do it themselves. They can dilute the paint with water, but the materials wouldn't cost much anyway. Two pots would be enough for the whole entrance, although they shouldn't put too much water in. Why? Because it wouldn't get rid of the graffiti.'

'You want terrorists to bomb our building? Is that what you really want, Itzik? You've lost your marbles. Wait till Kobi hears about this. I'm not going to keep quiet about it. As soon as he comes home from work, I'm going to tell him.'

'Leave Kobi out of this. What did he ever do for you? He's paid you off with a few pennies for the cinema. When the terrorists turns up, what good will that do you, eh? The minute he hears them coming, he'll run into the cupboard. He practises. You won't see him for dust. What sort of a man is that? You tell me! Someone who trains how to hide. He's not your dad, someone to say, "Come on, sweetheart, you go into the cupboard. It's better that you should live and I should die!"'

'As if you've got any better ideas.'

'But I'm not afraid of the terrorists! I don't shiver and shake like the rest of the town. Let 'em come, let 'em come. Itzik's got a little

79

plan. Believe me, Dudi, if you just do what I say, they'll curse the day they ever came here. And they'll curse the day they were born, too.'

Then he began to explain his plan: the kestrel might not be able to kill them, but she could take out their eyes. She wouldn't need to attack them all, just the leader. If you kill the leader, the other terrorists are finished – everyone knows that.

When he was satisfied I understood, he said, 'We'd get a medal of honour for that. At the very least. All I want you to do is to talk to that volunteer, what's-his-name, the one who paints the shelters and the rubbish bins. Let's get him to come and do some painting for us. That'd be better than a normal paint job. He could cover up all the holes and also the shit that Motti spread around after Beitar lost the game.'

'Mike?'

'What Mike? Who's Mike? Motti Abarjil did it.'

'No, I'm talking about the volunteer that paints. His name is Mike. I've been to his house loads of times. He even made me a coffee once. You leave Mike to me, Itzik. I'll tell him what to draw. If you tell him to put in mountains and snow, then he'll do that, as well as trees and waterfalls, just like in films. That's what he did in Shimmi's building. You tell him to do an ocean with boats, that's what he'll do. I'd let him draw the Wailing Wall if he wanted to.'

'The Wailing Wall? What are you talking about that for?'

'Since he went to Jerusalem at Pesach, he's been dying to paint the Wailing Wall. He's painted a little one in his room. You give him a big wall, Itzik, and he'll give you the Wailing Wall. You'd swear the stones were real. Only when you touch them can you tell they're painted.

80

And he'll do the religious guys, too, the ones in black with the round hats, as well as the notes and the grass. Whatever you tell him to do, he'll do.'

'How long would it take him to paint the Wall?'

'Three or four days. A week at the most. And he does it for free. You could have a sunset, too, or a blue sky, with birds even. He'll do whatever you want.'

He listened, waited until I had finished, then said I should stop getting so excited.

'What's so great about the Wall? It's just a pile of rocks. What does it have to do with God? And what's it got to do with us?

Then he said he had a problem.

'I didn't sleep all night because of it, Dudi. All I could think about was a name for her. There's no way, no way on earth, she can't have a name. She sleeps with me, but I don't know her name. My brain was on fire trying to think of a name, but nothing came to me, nothing. My mind was a blank. She's not a dog, she's a raptor. If you say "Blackie" or "Spot" to a dog, he'll come. He'll come running up, tail wagging, to any name you give him. But she's got more pride. Her place is in the sky. She even shits in the sky.'

'You're after a name? I can think of hundreds of names. I'm great on girls' names.'

'Just don't call her Liat. Or after any of your volunteers from the Absorption Centre. Not the name of someone you've got a crush on. Get it? I need an honourable name. Not the name of just anyone.'

'Liat's not just anyone! Even Kobi and Mordi, who saw her on Memorial Day—'

'Forget Mordi and Kobi! I need you to think of a name as if you were looking at her, how she flies then homes in on something, how she grabs food, tears your hand with her claws, how she gets hostile when she's hungry. Even though she's strong and fearless, she's still a girl, as you can see by the colour of her feathers. And don't talk to me about Kobi again. You and Kobi. Don't you say one word about Itzik's plan. He's not our brother any more. It's over. Mum made him into Oshri and Chaim's dad instead. He can't be two things at once. That would make him God.'

'Delilah.'

'What about Delilah?'

'Delilah. We'll call her Delilah.'

'Isn't she someone from the Bible?'

'Of course she is. Samson's wife, Delilah. You haven't been to school for two months and already you've forgotten about Samson and Delilah?'

'I don't remember. It just disappeared from my head. De-li-lah. I really like that. It's got honour, but it's not too heavy. It's delicate, too. Delilah. Well done, Dudi, you got it just right. I wouldn't have thought of that in a million years. Delilah. *Yalla,* let's get her some food from the butchers. Did you talk to Moshe about giving us scraps? You're a great guy, you really are. And then we'll start training her with her name. You remember the boy in the film, how he shouted to the flying bird, "Kes! Kes!" And the bird to flew to him. That takes training, Dudi, a lot of training. Get it?'

We go back to the town. Again I can see Itzik's weighty thoughts. His head is like a cement mixer. After two or three days, every thought in his head has spilled out and turned into something real.

If I have a thought, on the other hand, it's invisible, like the wind, like a plastic bag tossed into the street and whisked up until it's like a little fly in the sky. Soon you can't even see it, and after five minutes, no one will care that one of Dudi's thoughts came into the world.

Itzik

When I wake in the morning, I just want one thing: a mountain.

I want a huge mountain right by my bed, brown with white rocks. So that as soon as I open my eyes, as soon as I put my feet on the floor, a mountain is standing there ready to be smashed, by me, Itzik Dadon. I'd make no allowances. I'd rip it up with my hands, the ones God decided would come into the world, hands of a new kind.

I think about the mountain next to my bed. I've got nothing against that mountain. It hasn't hurt me or bothered me. It doesn't know me. Don't think it's Mount Anything Special. It's not Mount Sinai, a mountain with a name everyone knows. I'd get out of bed just as I am, break that mountain into two pieces with one punch. Then I'd go back to sleep. I'd lie in bed for a while, rest a little, and then get up the way people expect me to.

Everyone in the house wants me to get up like newly-baked bread, which they can mould into any shape they want. When Etti gets up, she looks like a mouse peeking out of its hole. She can't decide whether to come out or go back to bed. She hasn't taken off her dreams. She stands still, not moving, her mouth open, as if she was in the middle of a word. Her fingers are wide open, too, as if each one has slept alone. I watch her as she takes two steps, then stops. Then she goes into the toilet, and stays in there so long, you think she might have fallen asleep. And just when you're about to break the door down, she comes out. She stands still again, next to the bath. Everyone files past her. She doesn't say anything. When she does open her mouth, even if it's just to say 'yes', a bird-like squeak comes out.

I could look at Etti all morning. I'd like to get up like her, just once. She looks as though she's sitting in the cinema, in the middle of a film, and Shushan isn't around to kick her out because she's only got half a ticket. I'd love to know what films they're showing in her dreams. If she'd been born a boy, I'd wander around the wadi with her. She could help me with Delilah, and I wouldn't need Dudi. I have to explain everything to him a thousand times, and even then I have to check that he has understood.

Since I stopped going to school this year, I only get up in the morning for Etti, just to look at her. The anger I feel when I wake starts to disappear. But then I see her turn into Oshri and Chaim's mum, remembering she's got to take them to nursery before she goes to school, and that makes me mad again. It's not enough for Kobi to have turned into a dad. Now she's their mum and she has to let go of her dreams. She's turned into an old woman and starts to run around all day, just like everyone else.

As soon as she leaves, I start to think about what I could do to make her happy. I have an idea: to get her more batteries for her radio. Whenever she doesn't have something to do, she goes under a blanket with the old radio from the falafel shop, and listens quietly. As soon as she falls asleep, I have a look in her bag and see how long she's got until the batteries are dead. Two days after they've run out, Dudi and I get more batteries. I take the old ones out, put new ones in, and watch her laughing when she sees them in the morning. She has no idea who does this for her. Maybe she thinks elves come when she's asleep.

Dudi

Every Thursday, in the middle of the night, Itzik and I wait until the last person has gone to sleep, then we quietly go into the bathroom so I can shave him.

First I put water on his face, spread the shaving foam over all the hair that has grown during the week. I know each hair. When you don't shave someone, you think all hairs lie the same way. It's only when you are close up that you see there are families of hairs, each with their own side. One family goes to the right, another goes down, another to the left. One hair stands alone, undecided.

You hold the razor and cut the hair in the opposite direction to how it grows, close to the root.

Itzik closes his eyes when I shave him, presents me with his whole face. I can move from side to side, and he doesn't budge.

I have to be careful, though. I'm not shaving Formica. The razor has to cut the hairs but not the skin underneath. Trouble is, the hairs and the skin are in the same place. The first time I shaved Itzik, he had five or six cuts. That doesn't happen now. The blade is straight on the skin, and my hand dances to where it's needed. Neither of us says a word during the shave, and the following week we pretend it didn't happen. Itzik closes his eyes and his hands, and I close my mouth. It's as if there is one person alone in the bathroom. The space between the bathroom wall and the sink is only big enough for one person.

If I ever do cut him, he doesn't move or say a word. I put bathroom tissue on the cut until the blood stops. When there's a cut, I'm the one to cry out. If anyone was listening, they'd think I'd been cut. When I shave him, the smell of the foam gets up my nose, hiding the other smells: the mildew on the bathroom ceiling, the bleach that Mum uses by the gallon, and the combined whiff of Itzik and Delilah.

The first time he tried to shave himself, he put a rubber band on the handle of the razor, came to my bed at night and woke me, asking me to tie it on to his hand so it wouldn't move. He thought he'd do it himself. After ten minutes he came back, his face covered with foam and his eyes black and strong, as they are when he's about to explode, when something hasn't worked. There was no need to say a thing. We went to the bathroom together and I did it for him. He stood there with his eyes open but unseeing, burning a hole in the mirror. My hand was shaking. I cut him, shouted softly, and wiped his blood with tissue paper. I don't know how long it took, but finally we finished and went to bed. I didn't sleep all night. My whole body was a stone and my hands were shaking. I put each one into the opposite armpit to warm them and kept them there until they had pins and needles. I thought: What next? Is this the way it's going to be? Do I have to shave him every night? Then I cried for myself, that I had a brother who was born that way. All night long, I kept wishing he had died when he was six years old, and then four years old, and then I got to the point where I thought: If only he had been born dead. I would have been born without a brother like that. Sometimes I see Kobi looking at him that way, too – disgusted. Maybe that's why he didn't have a bar mitzvah for him. Next year, when it's my time, I'll be sure to have one. I'm not Itzik. They'll have to do it for me.

The morning after the shave I went to school without seeing him, but I just walked the streets all day. I can't remember what I did. I came home in the evening and went straight to bed. I waited for him to come and wake me, but he didn't come. Nor the next, nor the next. I kept looking to see if the hairs were starting to grow back, until the next Thursday he came again, and again we went to the bathroom. As soon as we got in, he closed his eyes. He looked as though he was asleep. Suddenly I liked doing it for him. I don't know what happened or how. I just changed.

Itzik always breathes slowly. I know his breathing well. He takes three normal breaths, and I breathe with him, my belly touching his when we inhale, then I find I'm exhaling by myself. I'm afraid he'll stop breathing, that the air is stuck inside him. It makes me panic. So while he's not breathing, I breathe really fast – about three or four times – wondering if it's me that ran out of air, until I hear him let the air out in one whoosh, and then I can start to breathe normally with him again.

Itzik's skin and mine are the same; both of us have Mum's colouring. We have the same nose, too, Dad's nose. When I see a girl I like, I show her my profile, so she can see how my forehead goes straight down to the end of my nose. Itzik has the same mouth, too, except he keeps it closed, as if someone was coming to steal his teeth. I don't close my mouth for a minute, and I move my tongue around on my lips, like the way Dad used to clean the Formica worktop of the falafel shop. When I shave him, my tongue pokes out, moves around. You would think it was trying to help with the shaving. The best bits to shave are the bones that lead to the chin. Then I do the chin itself, which is the hardest place to shave, because no two chins are the same. I move the blade in a circle, but I don't look. My hand seems to trust the razor more when I don't look at it.

I watch Itzik's eyes. There's nothing more beautiful than the skin of a person's eyelids. It's like looking at a baby in the womb. The eye moving underneath is the baby in its water, and the eyelid is the mother's belly. Sometimes I have an urge to touch it, to feel the eye moving.

As soon as I finish the chin, I wash his face with lots of water, wipe it, look for any forgotten hairs, run my hand over it to check it's smooth. I always want to use some of Kobi's aftershave, but he'd kill me. Even if you just say 'Kobi', he gets annoyed. Anyway, Kobi hardly talks to us. As soon as he finishes eating, he goes to his room and sleeps with Mum so that Oshri and Chaim will think they have a mum and a dad. Those little ones will believe anything.

After Itzik goes back to bed, I take a good look at my face in the mirror. I have nothing to shave yet. I go to bed, place my fingers on my eyes to feel the mothers' bellies and the babies inside. Then I move my fingers lower, touch the eyelashes below. I can't do it for more than a minute. I imagine my hands are blankets, tuck in the mothers and babies, and sleep. I tell Itzik the dream I have after I've

88

covered my eyes. But he doesn't dream about girls. His dreams are twisted. When we slept in the same bed, his tossing and turning always woke me.

Itzik

I give Delilah a feed last thing at night.

I've caught two mice in the trap. I'll give her one mouse now and save the other for the morning. I put her into the kitchen cabinet with the live mouse in its trap. Then I hit the stick that opens the trap, pull my hand away and slam the cupboard door. Three mice escaped before I got the hang of this, one biting my hand on its way out. Now it's just Delilah and the mouse inside, and I'm outside, listening.

I hear her pounce.

People who live on the border have different ears from others. Cats' ears. We hear everything: our raids over there, Katyushas falling here, sonic booms. We can even tell where the Katyushas fall, and when they're still buzzing in mid-air. After a few days of Katyushas, my tired ears are confused. If a door slams in the wind two days after a ceasefire, you think it's a Katyusha. You jump at every little noise. Even the radio or a dog barking sounds like the loudspeaker car sending you down to the shelter. Not to mention Arab villages shooting in the air to celebrate a wedding. You want to send your ears to a mental hospital until they're back to normal.

Aliza, who works with Mum at the nursery, told us about one night when the cupboard in her living room fell off the wall. All the pretty dishes they were given for their wedding were inside. They didn't move all night, thinking there was a Katyusha or a terrorist in the house. In the morning they saw the cupboard on the floor and the dishes smashed into tiny pieces.

It's quiet in the kitchen cabinet. Delilah's swallowed the mouse in one gulp.

In a while, our building will start its night-time routine.

Until the day of the terrorist attack, we didn't have a night-time routine. Everyone went to bed whenever they liked. But after the attack, the whole block starts the night together. I sit on my bed and listen.

First the Dahans on the top floor shout from the balcony to Moshe that he should come in now. Then they unplug their fridge and start pushing it up to the front door. It's a heavy fridge without wheels. Kobi put wheels on ours. Their kitchen floor is the ceiling of my bedroom. Until they started dragging their fridge, I thought my ceiling was the sky, that there was nothing above my head, just God. The terrorists put a stop to that. Whenever I talk to God, it makes me cross that the Dahans are between us. What can you do? You can't imagine the sky is over your head with that noise going on. The fridge isn't an easy fit through the kitchen door: I hear breaking tiles or shouts that someone forgot to open the door in time. Each person swears that they're taking most of the fridge's weight. Everyone wants to be the project manager, to sit on the kitchen counter and instruct his brothers.

I can hear everything they say. Their voices jump from their kitchen balcony to mine. Then their dad shouts and they all shut up. After ten minutes the dragging of the fridge is over. Now they're locked in their prison. No one goes out or comes in until the morning. Sometimes I get so cross that I imagine the terrorists shooting down their door, the bullets spraying the fridge and everything inside: blowing up the milk, peppering the *matbouha*, coming to rest in a cabbage. I imagine lots of different things flying around the fridge, decorating the inside.

After the Dahans' fridge, which the whole building can hear, Iluz and Cohen put an iron bar across their door. For them the night begins with the pounding of iron. Now they're in their prison, too. The Bitons are watching television, Albert sitting with the Kalashnikov across his knees for security. There are no bullets, but his mum and sisters don't know that. Dudi's the only person he's told. His mum can't sleep at night until he takes out the Kalashnikov and sits down with it. As I think about Albert Biton, I know that Kobi's about to go to the cupboard.

I don't have to listen to know he's going. He walks to it as if he's just passing by, so no one will notice. Then he stands with his back to the door, leaning his weight against it, checking its strength, locking and unlocking it. He thinks he owns the cupboard. As far as he's concerned, everyone else can just die. At last, without looking at the cupboard, he moves away. Now Etti goes to the window that looks out over the wadi. She stands there like it's nothing, as if the terrorists hadn't come from that direction, as if she just feels like looking out into the darkness. As I watch her, I want to tell her to stay calm, that I have plans for the terrorists, but I never say anything. I don't want to see her fear, her fear of me and Delilah.

I used to stand at the window, too. But I soon realised that if you stand there at that time of night, you can't leave it. A minute standing there will keep you awake all night. You strain your eyes, trying to spot a terrorist in the dark. Then you start seeing things. A tree transforms itself into a man, and your heart beats faster, before you realise it really is just a tree. Satisfied the wadi's empty, you move away from the window. But the minute you do that, you convince yourself that terrorists emerged just as you moved. They materialised from nothing. Quickly you return to the window to catch them before they crawl underneath the building with their bombs. Now your stomach begins to churn, working as hard in five minutes as it would do all night. You run to the toilet, then back to the window again, and that's how it is for the rest of the night. You want to leave the window, but you can't, and then you have to, just to flush the fear down the toilet.

Since the day I brought Delilah home, I don't need to stand at the window. I've finished with fear. As soon as I hear she's stopped eating, I take her out of the kitchen cabinet and call Dudi to tie her and clean up what's left of the mouse. He ties her to the tap, puts the plug into the sink and creates a little river of water, so she'll have something to drink in the night. Dudi and I made the sink into her place, creating a little forest there so she'd feel at home and still a bird. Who needs another human? There are too many already. We poured cement into the sink, stuck a nice piece of wood into it, and some pretty round stones that I picked up from the stream in the wadi, added some big leaves and acorns. Delilah stands in her sink wadi, cleaning herself. She cleans her beak first, scraping it across the wood from side to side, like Edmond the barber sharpening his leather strap. Afterwards she tucks her wings behind her, looking like Shmuel Cohen, who walks with his hands behind his back after synagogue on Saturday.

After that, she scratches the feathers of her neck with one foot, ruffling them into different directions. When they fall back in place, they look puffy, like Mum's hairdo in the photo of Kobi's bar mitzvah. But Delilah's beauty lasts. It isn't created by the hairdresser and washed off in the shower. Her feathers are always combed the same way. Her plumage isn't dyed and she doesn't have white hairs like Mum. She doesn't change.

After she puffs her feathers, she starts to arrange them. It's the best show in the world. Her beak moves quickly over the feathers, missing nothing. Then she raises and lowers her neck – it's the thing I like to watch best – as if she has a mechanism inside it. Humans can't do the same thing. Maybe she's arranging her thoughts, as she's arranged her feathers, ordering them, making them clean and tidy.

After Delilah's training, I will put her next to the window that looks out over the wadi. She'll wait there for the terrorists, and I will sleep like God after he finished creating the world.

The last sound of the night-time routine is Biton going down to the entrance and closing the iron front door with a chain and a lock. My grandma's got the same lock on her chicken coop. The iron door was put in after the terrorist attack. Now we all know the night has begun. No one can enter or leave the building until quarter to six in the morning when the buses to the factories start to run. Fear doesn't leave, either. We're trapped inside with it, just like Delilah and her mouse in the kitchen cabinet.

Dudi   As soon as Dad died and the twins were
                                       born, which made seven people in the
house, the housing department gave us the apartment opposite ours.
The Elmakeises, who'd lived there, moved to Ashdod. Everyone in
town was moving then, trying to make their homes bigger. In the
street I'd see people carrying cardboard boxes and chairs. Kobi said
they were only giving people apartments because of the elections, and
that for six people, as we were before Dad died, we should have had
another 56sqm of space. Trouble was, Dad wouldn't vote for the right
people, so we didn't get it. After Dad died, Kobi had a quiet word
with those people, saying Mum was 'OK'. Then builders from the
housing department came and broke down the wall, making the two
apartments into one.

Our apartment is the shape of a butterfly now. We have two of
everything – two kitchens, two big rooms and two small – and a long
hallway. When you stand at one end of the hallway you think you're
looking into a mirror.

When they made our apartment bigger, we all grabbed a corner.
We moved as far away from each other as we could, and everyone had
their own space. After a month we started sleeping together again.
Who wants to look at a bare wall before going to sleep? I can't sleep
without the sound of two or three other people breathing next to
me.

Until Itzik brought Delilah home, he'd sleep with us, too. But now
he says it's better to put her in the old kitchen where there's water and
no one to disturb at night. He put his own bed there, too. Mum and
Kobi shouted at him, saying he should get her out of the house. When

94

that didn't work, they tried being nice to him. They tried everything. They said it was written in the Torah that you weren't allowed to sleep in a kitchen, that the kitchen didn't have a *mezuzah*. Itzik pretended not to hear them. Then, one day, when they were both at work, he started to drag his bed to the kitchen, as best he could with those hands. No one helped him. We just watched him fall and bleed, watched the bed getting stuck in the hallway. We wanted to help him, but we were afraid of Kobi.

After Itzik got the bed into the kitchen, it blocked the whole room. Now, if you open the sliding door, you can fall right onto his bed. The bird is tied to the tap and he sleeps next to her. There isn't a clear patch of floor.

Itzik   I lie on my back in bed for half the day. I'm completely still.

I dream about terrorists at night. They're always in my dreams. Every time I hear shouts or explosions, one of them is standing over me with a gun. Then I'm on the floor, and he's hitting me on the head with his shoe. The mud from the shoe gets into my eyes. I see them grab Etti by the throat, stuff a rag in her mouth, smash her radio. I see the rest of the family murdered in their beds, a bullet hole in each head, dripping blood on their pillows. I see Dad, too. He's in the house with us, a hole in his head where the bee stung him. He's time-travelled to die with us.

Last night the dream was different. For the first time I dreamed the terrorists were standing next to the building, waiting. I was so happy

I could hardly believe it. I brought them here! They walked right up to our building without a care in the world. Everything I arranged worked. Delilah and I looked out at them from our fourth-floor window.

Three fat terrorists standing under a streetlight. I don't know how such fatties made it here from the border. They look up at the flags I've hung from my window. The middle terrorist looks just like Shushan from the cinema, except he's wearing a *keffiyeh*. The other two I don't recognise, but they both have moustaches. They aren't afraid. They stand, their legs apart, and laugh. They're laughing so much they're crying. They'll wet themselves in a minute. The terrorist that looks like Shushan puts his arms around the shoulders of the other two, and they hold their dancing, laughing bellies. I wait for Delilah to go for them. Nothing. She's not interested. Suddenly the Shushan terrorist takes his hands from the shoulders of the others, and turns. The other two do the same, turning their backs to me. Now they look like a row of hand grenades, laughing then dissolving into the darkness.

I'm going mad. Why didn't she attack them as they stood and laughed? I'm holding her in my hand. She's as hard as iron and her sharp feathers pierce my hand. I look at her. Her eyes are glassy. She doesn't recognise me. Angrily, I throw her out of the window. As soon as I throw her into the air, she turns into a real bird. Then she flies away, disappearing into the night sky, lost to me.

I hear Mum in the kitchen. I open my eyes. It's the beginning of the end of the night. Delilah is still tied to the tap. No terrorists, no grenades. Nothing.

The dream's over, but I'm left me with a question: how can I get Delilah to peck out the eyes of terrorists? Until today, I didn't give it a thought.

I close my eyes again and think about all the animals in the world, not just birds. Big animals, little animals, birds and fish – they don't play the same game. They don't run into shelters when the Katyushas are falling. Then I wondered if it would be better to be an ant than a person, because an ant doesn't fear war. He doesn't know any different. If a Katyusha falls on him he dies, and if it doesn't then the possibility wouldn't even cross his mind.

I hear Mum leave for the nursery. I go back to sleep.

When I open my eyes, the room is light and quiet. Everyone has gone.

My mouth and throat are dry. I'm dying to pee and to eat. I look at the ceiling, questions spinning in the air. Do Israeli soldiers fight because of fear or pride or hate?

Delilah definitely has no fear. The way she flies, why would she be afraid of anything? And her pride comes from deep inside; it doesn't ask favours. Then I think about hate. After a while I have a thousand more questions. What is hate? How does it begin? Where in the body does it live? How do you get soldiers to hate? Is it like a one-off injection that lasts for life, or do you have to keep topping it up, like food?

Can Delilah feel hate or love? I raise my head from the bed and look at her. I can't tell whether she's happy or sad. Her face always has the shape of anger, that's just how her eyes are. The black feathers in the middle make me think of an angry person's wrinkled forehead. But that's just my imagination.

In any case, birds can't smile. Only people show their feelings that way. A person's face is like a blank cinema screen with the film rolling inside. But Delilah has pride. What's inside her stays there, even if a judge ordered otherwise. When people put on a face, it's a mask, a sign they're lying. If they're burning with anger, they'll look cool. If they're happy, maybe because they met someone they like or saw the girl of their dreams in the street, they pretend they don't care. God gave people faces so they could tell each other everything without speaking, but then we started messing around with the design, wearing masks and telling lies.

Delilah won't ask you how you are, meaning you have to reply, to put on your mask. She's not interested. She wouldn't lower herself to bother with human stuff. I've been with her for seven months and I don't know what's in her head. I don't even know if she likes me. I'll never know.

If she did understand our language, I'd take her to hear Rabbi Kahane when he comes to town, as that could be her injection of hate. If she understood him, she might then go for Hassan, assistant manager at the bank, because Kahane says all Arabs are terrorists. He doesn't make any distinctions. When I saw him the first time – what was I? Just seven, playing in the centre of town – everyone suddenly ran to the falafel shop. Dudi and I went, too. We had no idea what we'd see there. How could we? Dad was lying on the floor with the bee-sting under his eye, raised like a little mountain. I had no idea a bee could knock someone to the floor like that.

I get out of bed, holding onto the old kitchen counter so I won't fall. I have a Yom Kippur headache. It's probably midday. I go to the bathroom to pee. I push down my pants and underpants. All my clothes are elasticated with no buttons so I can take them off myself. I have one long finger, a good size but twisted at the end. I call it Elijah because it reminds me of Raphi's grandpa, who always stoops. With Elijah's help, I pull my clothes back up.

I wander into the kitchen. Mum has left us three pots for lunch. I move the cover of one aside, count the chicken pieces and take two: one for me and one for Delilah. When I see how she pounces on it in her sink wadi, I get the answer to my question: there's nothing Delilah won't do for meat.

Dudi

I brought home three rows of flags from the Absorption Centre so Itzik could hang one across our window and two on the trees in the wadi to bring the terrorists to our building. At first he wanted me to go up the wall of the Union to get the flags. 'No way,' I said. 'That wall was made for lizards to climb.' Luckily I remembered somewhere else I could get the flags. I went to Sally, head of volunteers at the Centre, and said, 'Yehuda from maintenance sent me to collect flags for the town hall. No need for you to call Gid'on; I'll get them down.' It wasn't a problem. She brought me a ladder and held it for me so it wouldn't wobble. She even said thank you.

Afterwards we went straight home to the old kitchen where Itzik sleeps with Delilah. He said we were going to make a terrorist mask, an Arab face, for her training and he wanted me to make it out of Dad's white plastic bowl, which he used to wash the falafel-making equipment. I said white was not a good colour, but he told me not to think too much, that we'd colour it with burning matches.

All Dad's things from the falafel shop are in a cupboard in the old kitchen. When Mum moved everything to the new kitchen she left them behind. Why should she have taken them? She didn't want to look at them.

I made two holes in the bowl for the terrorists' eyes. Itzik couldn't do that with his hands. Then I painted the whole thing black with burnt matches, and painted on a nose with Etti's marker pen. For a beard and eyebrows I used steel wool, which Mum uses to clean the stove, and glued them on with contact cement that we nicked from Assouline. The mouth turned out looking like a clown's, so I covered it with a moustache made out of more steel wool. What else could I do? When I cut the mouth out with a knife, that's how it ended up. He was laughing in our faces, unconcerned about the end of his life. With the moustache, he looked like he was thinking about his final hours, and that he knew what was in store. I made a *keffiyeh* out of a white vest, with a black shoelace to hold it on to the bowl and my head, so I wouldn't have to hold everything on with my hands, although in the end I did hold it at the edges.

Daoud only has a face. His body is mine. I stood in the bathroom, scratched his beard, practised Arabic words and tried to get inside his hate, although I couldn't see my own eyes. I said all the swear words I knew, then turned the tap on, so no one would hear me.

So Delilah will learn how to peck out their eyes. We put some meat through the mincer in Mum's kitchen, together with some bread soaked in water for an hour so it would harden when dry; that's how we managed to glue it to the eye holes. The only thing we didn't think about was how I would see once I was outside. It wasn't a problem in the apartment because I know where everything is. And we didn't think about the smell. After the meat had been outside for a few hours I'd have been better off sticking my head in a toilet full of shit.

Dudi and Itzik

'And I'm telling *you*, Itzik: why don't *you* put it on? I'll stand on the rock and let her go, and you put on the face.'

'Do I look scared? Come here, then. You hold her. Just don't forget to give her a lot of rope, so she can get straight to my face. Get it?'

'You don't have to, you don't have to. I'll put it on. It's better if you let her go. With you she knows what to do. She can read your mind. OK, I'll be the target. It's just the smell makes me feel like throwing up.'

'*Halas,* stop moaning. I'll count to seven and then let her go. Stand still and hold onto the face. One, two—'

'*Behayat,* Itzik, do we have to have so much meat?'

'Stop talking. Are you scared? She's going to fly at you any minute now. I'm going to let her have all the rope so she can attack without stopping. Just stand still. Still, Dudi, like an electricity pylon. You'd better not move! Three, four, five—'

'Wait a minute, I've got flies now. They don't care about the smell. OK, I'm standing still. I'm not moving.'

'Six, *dir balak* if you move!'

'I didn't move!'

'Seven! Delilah, Delilah, meat! Meat! Grab it . . . You're an idiot! It's all gone! Gone, in less than a minute. I should have brought Etti. She'd have been more help.'

'Etti can't stand Delilah. Didn't she tell you?'

'She must think it's Yom Kippur. She's been screaming with hunger all day, and now she's eating meat on the ground like a queen. She doesn't care about the smell or about anything else. She's probably laughing at us.'

'I told you to do it yourself!'

'You told me I didn't have to!'

'But Itzik, another minute of holding that bowl and I'd have been dead. I saw her swooping down on me, I know I did. Do you know what one of those claws could do to someone's eye? One scratch and I'd never see another film in my life! And anyway, do you think terrorists would stand as still as electricity pylons? You'd be dead first. I don't see terrorists putting down their bombs and saying to each other, in Arabic, "Itzik said not to move. Itzik said stand still. Itzik said please wait until Delilah comes." Anyway, the meat's finished now. I already told you but I'm telling you again: there's no more meat.'

He told me to get the meat from Moshe, and I've been telling him for three days that Moshe won't do it any more, but he doesn't listen. We haven't caught anything in the trap, either. I have to tell him again that Moshe wants a partnership in Delilah, but I know that'll make him angry. I don't care if there are five partners.

When I first told him, he fired back, 'No partnerships. No! No! No! I'm not telling you again. We already know what partnerships can do.

Once there was just one falafel king. There can only ever be one king, right? When he became a couple, what was left? Nothing. Do you think you can divide a king's crown into five?'

'But why, Itzik? Is it really better if she dies of hunger? Then all the training's wasted and we lose everything.'

'She's not going to die! She'll be fine. Listen to Itzik: this one is the queen of birds. Show me another bird that flies like she does. How can I explain it? Let's say you got married but you can't feed your wife, who you chose to marry because she was a queen, the best girl you knew. Now, say you start to work in a factory, only the factory suddenly runs into trouble. The consultants turn up with their fancy clothes and their nice cars, and they say, "Get rid of twenty workers and the factory will be fine." You were last in, Dudi, so you're first out. Two days' notice and you're out on your ear, so the factory can recover. You try to get welfare, but they say you're healthy and must work. So you look for work – it's not as if you're not looking, and every day you go to the employment office – but you can't find anything. Meanwhile, your wife's at home with a baby, and both of them are hungry. What would you do, Dudi?'

'I don't know.'

'I'll tell you what you'd do. You'd come to me, cry on my shoulder, say you don't have a thing to eat. As your brother, what would I tell you? I'd say, "Go to Moshe, Dudi. He'll give you some food. But he also wants to share your wife, like a business partner." How's that, Dudi? Is that what you want to hear from your brother when you're in trouble? Would you let him share your wife? You'd punch him. You'd beat him up.'

'OK, Itzik, how would you beat him up? Think you're Samson, do you? Come on, beat me up. I'll even stand still for you – like an electricity pylon. What are you going to do?'

'Did you tell him anything else about her? Just tell me the truth.'

'I told him . . . I didn't tell him . . . I don't remember what I told him. What would I say anyway? I didn't say a thing about her training, honest. You don't have to worry about that.'

'Now look – she's eating everything.'

'Why not let her eat? Enjoy your meal, Delilah.'

'If you see someone coming, Dudi, put the mask in the bushes until they're gone, and I'll take Delilah away from the meat.'

'What is there for them to see? They'll just think she's eating rotten meat. They'll think nothing of it.'

'Don't underestimate people, Dudi. Don't assume what they do and do not understand. They wouldn't want you to, either.'

'Everyone's the same to you. You'd throw them all in the rubbish bin if you could.'

'How can you try to understand someone who doesn't have a clue himself? He doesn't even know if he'll be alive in a minute's time. That's the honest truth. One minute you're standing, the next you're on the floor. And while he's standing there, what's he thinking about? God, is this my last minute? No, he's thinking about nothing much. I need a pee, maybe. Or, I'm hot and I'm thirsty. What's on everyone's mind? I'll tell you, Dudi, they're thinking about rubbish. It's only us – you and me, Dudi – that have grand plans. We're not like everyone else. Who is ever going to hear of them? Who's going to write about them in the newspapers?'

'I don't care about newspapers. What's a picture in the paper worth if my eye's been scratched out?'

'And if I tell you that God sent us here to prepare things for the terrorists? Do you ever think about God, Dudi? Maybe he's the one that put the plan in my head! So what should I do? Complain that he didn't give me a leather strap or meat or flags? I'm not a moaner, Dudi, understand? I don't moan to God. That's how he likes it. He laughs at you; you laugh at him, too. In the end, he'll respect you more than those who fear him.'

Itzik

When I want to understand God, I sit down by an ants' nest. First I decide which ant I'm going to watch. So what? you might think. But it's harder than it looks.

The ant you've chosen is running around, and there are a thousand ants just like it running around, too, and your eyes always want to look at the other ants. It's boring to watch one. While it's just running, suddenly you see another one dragging something, and you want to know what it's dragging. But as soon as you move your eyes, your ant escapes, and then you've lost it amongst the others. So you start again. You think you're getting to know this one. You watch it go into a hole and then you wait for it to come out again. But ants are coming out of the hole all the time. You think: Maybe that one's mine, or that one. But you have no way of knowing. Before it went into the hole it was dragging food and that's how you could recognise it. But now there's nothing.

I'm half a metre from them and I know they can't see me. That's how it is with God, too. We always think he's hiding or far away, but why should he? He's so big we can't see him. Even if the ants lifted their eyes, they wouldn't be able to see more than the sole of my shoe. I'd like them to know a god is sitting half a metre away from them. How do I do that? Well, I have two games: Good God and Bad God. The problem is, you have to know what an ant would think is good or bad.

Bad God is easier and more fun. I don't know why. It's like Chaim and Oshri having fun making a tower of blocks in nursery, but having more fun when they kick it down. When they're building, their mood is serious. As soon as they smash the tower, they shout and laugh. Then they're happy.

I might pour water from a bottle straight into the ant's hole. For the ants there are no choices. Some will die instantly; others will struggle out and then die in the mud. The survivors on the side might stop for a minute and ask why there's so much running about. Did something nearby cause it? They'll ask questions. Maybe, amongst all the questions, they might think about a god. If I did something nice for them – brought them a mountain of food, say – they wouldn't stop. Why would they? They'd just start taking everything into the hole. A lottery winner doesn't shout, 'Why, God, why?' It's only when bad things happen that you start to think.

You might think it cruel, that God is bad. No. He is no worse than me with the ants. He's just too big for us. If I wanted to talk to an ant, what could I do? I can't talk to it. I can't put my hand on its shoulder and say, 'Hot day, isn't it?' As God, I made the ant, but I can't talk to it. I don't know why God made us so different from him. Maybe he made us small because he wanted to look at us with one eye. Maybe he's alone now because of that. His people invention didn't do him any good. Why? Because there are more non-believers than believers.

Now if I want to pick an ant, I have to find one that isn't the same shape as the rest. I must be able to pick it out so I don't kill it. Whichever way I look at it, there's only one answer: God decided to put a sign on me before I was born, so that, no matter where he was, he would be able to pick me out and not get me mixed up with everyone else. And sometimes, at night, I see that he is suffering, too, because he can't be a part of the world he created, so I don't pick a fight with him. God's chosen one knows how to see God, too.

I thank him for choosing me, and don't ask why he puts ideas into my head. I just rack my brains to work out how I can do things the way he'd like.

Dudi

I'm in bed when suddenly I feel Itzik's hand nudging me. I turn over onto my front, but he won't leave me alone. I shout at him to go away.

'What's the matter with you, Dudi? Why are you shouting? You'll wake the whole house. Shut up. There's no need to go mad. It's not as if I wake you every day. If I'm waking you now it's because of something important, right, Dudi?'

'You ruined my dream, Itzik. What a dream . . .'

'What were you dreaming about?'

'I can't remember now. I don't remember anything about it.'

'So why are you moaning about it?'

'Because I can't remember. That's why. If I could remember, I wouldn't be moaning now. Wait, wait . . . it's coming back to me. The horse. I had a horse. And what a horse! It's completely black, with just a patch of white on its forehead, and as I climb onto it I hear a beautiful song that brings tears to my eyes. But that's all I remember. The rest is gone.'

'And was there a pretty girl? Wearing a long black skirt and a white apron, with hair longer than Etti's? Was she standing on a balcony, crying as you left?'

'How did you know that? How did you know what I was dreaming? Don't tell me we dream together, too.'

'What dream? I haven't slept all night. I just know because I went to the cinema with you. Your dream is the film we saw, Dudi. She was crying just before the interval. And then Shushan threw us out. Too bad he didn't throw you out before you lost your head.'

'*Walla,* you're right. My head's a mess. But why did you wake me? I was dead to the world, then you woke me. What's the matter? Tell me why you're going on about the cinema. What's happened?'

He wanted me to tell him the colour of Delilah's head feathers. I thought he was mad. He'd told me that when everything was ready, when we'd trained Delilah, we'd put her next to the wadi window and sleep like kings. Like kings, he said. Now, suddenly, he wants to know the colour of Delilah's head. He grabbed me like a raptor and wouldn't let go until I told him that the feathers on her head were exactly the same as the ones on her body. Exactly the same. After that he made me come into his room so I could see her with my own eyes.

'So her body was the same colour?' he said. 'And that's how we found out in the bird book that she was a girl? Well, look at her now. I didn't want to believe it. She's got male feathers! In a couple of days her whole head will be like a male kestrel! Look for yourself and tell me if I'm wrong.'

'I can see she's got some grey and light-blue feathers.'

'What's the matter with her, Dudi? When I first noticed her tail had changed colour, I thought it was to do with the summer heat, you know? Then her front started to turn red, but I thought nothing of it – thought perhaps, like girls do, she just felt like changing colour, like putting on a red dress with black polkadots, and that she'd take it off soon enough, go back to how she was. But she's not changing back. She's turning into a boy. Betraying me, just like that. Why? Why, Dudi?'

'Stop it, Itzik. Look at you – you're shaking. You know why she's changing!'

'Don't say it!'

'I will! You ruined my beautiful dream, so I'm going to tell you: she's changing because of the training you're making her do. Because you don't let her have fun outside, don't let her enjoy life. You just bother her all day long. Even army recruits don't train as hard. At first you said she was a queen of the sky, queen of all birds, God's neighbour. You even said her shits were beautiful. But what have you turned her into? A border guard. Show me a queen that screams with hunger all day. I'm telling you, Itzik, if it wasn't for the leather cord, she'd have escaped a long time ago rather than be tied to the sink. Now she's showing you she's not going to be your slave any more.

She's had enough of doing what you want her to do. As from now she's making her own decisions. That's why she's changed! When you get something in your head, you get so full of it and your great plan, that you don't budge one inch. She's got no voice. This is her way of saying no.'

It's seven o'clock at night. I'm with Itzik in the school. We're alone. There was an alert that lasted all day. We needed to have another look at the bird book I put back in the staffroom, but we couldn't get in. Everything was closed. Then at six-thirty Zion the caretaker went in, leaving the door open. We crept in after him, then hid and didn't move until he left. Itzik was afraid Delilah would make a noise. As soon as Zion left, we found the book in the staffroom, exactly where I had left it, and saw it was true that Delilah was becoming male.

I was afraid this was going to make Itzik mad, so I told him all sorts of stuff – that maybe because we didn't see the end of *Kes*, the female kestrel might have turned into a male; that if Shushan hadn't shouted from the stage of the cinema in the interval, 'Time to leave, Dadon brothers!', we might have seen the same thing happen to Kes.

I remembered how we stood at the cinema door with one ticket, looking at the film posters outside, and Itzik said, 'You know, Dudi, when you go into a cinema, you enter a different world. It's paradise, I swear. A sky that blue, snow that white, and such horses don't exist in this world. Only in films. Trouble is, guarding paradise is that son-of-a-bitch Shushan rather than some angel. Stay close to me when we go in.'

So he went in first with the ticket, and I followed quickly, looking the other way. Shushan tore the ticket and let him through, but caught me by the trousers. 'What's the hurry, Monsieur Dadon? Where do you think you're going? Tell me, Dadon, did you ever hear of anyone going to the cinema without making his pockets lighter?' Itzik stopped, too, waiting for me. Shushan saw this but went on. 'For your information, skinny Monsieur Dadon, I now count people by the number of legs. That's why I sit on a small chair. I used to count heads, and at least three or four people would sneak in underneath. You two had it easy. Now, for every two legs I count I tear one ticket. It's like Noah's ark: right leg, left leg, each with the same trousers and shoes. Why? Because, Dadon, you can put your head wherever you like, but the man who can fly hasn't been born. No way around that. Everyone has to stick to the ground, so they don't forget where they came from and where they're going.'

I made my face crumple as if I was about to cry. He remembered Dad then and looked uncomfortable. Quickly I suggested we had half a ticket each and left at the interval. 'Two halves equals one,' I said. He forgot about Dad, and laughed, along with everyone else going in. 'I'm quite good at arithmetic, skinny Dadon. There's no such thing as two half-tickets for one movie. When you were born, did you say to God, "Let us in on one ticket. We swear we're only coming into the world for half a lifetime"?' I could see Itzik didn't like the way he was talking about God, that he was about to have one of his quiet tantrums, so I said, 'But why? You'd be doing a good deed for the same money.' Then he started to say our dad, the poor guy, would be ashamed to see us this way, that he had never asked for something he didn't deserve, and gave nothing for free, either.

I was almost crying by then, but Itzik grabbed me to stop me leaving, making a stand. But Shushan didn't shut up. 'Do I owe anyone an explanation? That's the problem in Israel. You've got to explain everything. And why should a grown-up explain anything to a kid? Why should kids talk back to grown-ups? They should know their place. Right, Shula? No, the film hasn't started yet. Two minutes to go. How's Zion? Where was I, Dadon? So, that's how it is. If a kid is the height of his dad's legs, he spends a year looking at his knees. Everything he's got to say goes straight through his dad's legs. Yes, that's just how it is. It's all unripe, not worth hearing. And in return, his father's wise words fall down right into his head, rather than through his ears. Thirteen years old and he doesn't look his dad in the eye.'

I looked at Shushan's watch. The newsreel would start in another minute and we weren't in. Knowing Itzik, he'd have a fit in that minute, and then we'd both be kicked out. I said to Shushan, 'Just this once. You've already ripped the ticket, so what do you care?' He was as hard as iron. They'd already closed the cinema door and we could hear the newsreel starting. He looked me in the eye. 'Well, Monsieur Dadon, what have you decided? Maybe you'll make a grand gesture and let your brother go in. It'd be too bad if he missed the start.' Luckily for us, Rachel came in then.

'Isn't that right, Rachel?' he said in a completely different voice. I thought then he might let us in but keep us waiting for a while longer. 'See how I'm counting, Dadon? Two stockings, two new high-heels, one ticket. Come here, beautiful Rachel, and listen to this. The film won't start without you. It's just the newsreel on now. These two kids want to see the film on one ticket up to the interval. What do you think?' Rachel said, 'What's the matter with you, Shushan? You're penny-pinching with two orphans?' And she went in. But he still wanted us to promise. 'She said, she said . . . I want to see both of you here at the interval, asking to leave. So honest that you'd say to Noah, "We only have a single ticket, so let us out into the flood. We're not liars." *Yalla,* the film's starting already. Go in quietly and don't disturb anyone. It's not a great film anyway – just about some kid and his bird. I think they must have sent it to me by mistake.'

Who would have thought what that film did for us? Itzik was still angry at the beginning. 'I'll get him back,' he said. 'He'd better not talk about God like that. You'd think he was God's best friend. I bet God's never looked at him once.' Everyone told him to shut up. Another minute and someone would have punched him, so I quickly found seats for us and put him behind a small child so he could see. When I sensed he'd got over his tantrum I let myself sink into the paradise of the film. What a paradise, though! The kid in the film got it from everyone: his teacher, his brother, the football coach. There wasn't anyone he didn't get it from. And all because he didn't have a dad to protect him. But that's not how Itzik saw it. As soon as he calmed down, he only had eyes for the kestrel, how the kid trained her, how he stole without giving a damn, just taking whatever he felt like.

It's getting dark outside, and we're still in the school, just the two of us. I'm talking and Itzik isn't. He started to walk and I followed him, not knowing where he was going. He went to the craft room, took Simcha's big scissors, and then, that second – that second, I swear – while we were standing there with the scissors and Delilah –

two big Katyushas fell. In the town, no question. The first one even took out the electricity.

In the dark we made our way down to the gym, which was the school shelter, and sat there, with the new emergency lights on. I was glad about the Katyushas, thinking he'd forget what he had been about to do, what I'd said to him. No chance. Neither the Katyushas nor the electricity had any effect on him. I promised that as soon as I left the shelter I'd find out about the end of the film, but he wasn't listening. He'd locked his mind again. He didn't care how films ended, said, 'I can always guess the end.' He always did make decisions by himself, and when he made up his mind about something, that was it. I said maybe the feathers would change back in a couple of days. He didn't reply. I ran out of things to say then, so I shut up.

He gave me Delilah's leather cord, told me to tie it to a bench in the gym. I did. Then he told me to take off his hat. I took it off and put it on his knees. He grabbed Delilah with both hands, put her in the hat. He wanted me to cut the feathers on her head and body, just like I did when I shaved him. He said, 'I don't care if they all change. I don't care what the book says. She's not like everyone. Out of all the birds, I chose her, and I made her a queen. I won't let her change.' I grabbed the scissors, but my hands were shaking. She's delicate. Strong but delicate. He said so himself. I said, 'This is dangerous. What do you have against her? Leave her be.' He got up then, and pushed her at me, shouting, 'Cut, cut! I don't care.' I said, 'I can't.' He shouted again, 'Cut! Shave her!' I stepped back but he came after me, until he had to stop because of the leather cord tied to the bench. I threw the scissors on the floor; he picked them up. It took him an hour, but finally he managed to stick them on his fingers. At last, he sat on the bench and started to work on her head. His hand was huge, and her head was like an egg. But he couldn't cut, even though he was trying hard, and she stuck her beak into his other hand, the one that doesn't have any feeling, the hand he lets Oshri and Chaim stick pins in while he pretends to be asleep. They can't believe the pins don't bother him.

I stood there, looking at them. I couldn't do a thing, not even something small. It seemed to happen so fast. All I could think of was not standing there, not seeing everything. But I saw it all. How her head wouldn't stay on any more. How could it? No head could stay on that way. In no time at all, it fell into his hat, which was full of her blood, and then Itzik was staring and staring, and starting to cry, quietly, quietly, deep inside, though the tears took their time to rise to his eyes. He wiped them away with his fists, and his fists were still full of her hair, her feathers. All I could think now was: Delilah's dead. Delilah's dead. He killed her. She's dead. I went to the door and I left. I left him there.

Down in the wadi, by the stream, I knew what I was doing, even if it was dark. Delilah was dead.

Delilah was dead and the plan with her. I remembered where I had put the strings of flags but I sat down until I had worked up the strength to take them down. I drank from the stream and made my way to the red tree, slowly, so I wouldn't fall into the the pit. I didn't know how I was going to climb it in the dark, so I just started to jump and grab, grab and jump, until I caught a flag. I pulled it hard, but the next flag caught on a branch and tore, so I jumped again and again until I caught the branch and pulled it down. I pulled the string of the flag-chain and the branch smacked my face, scratching me. I didn't care. I pulled the whole chain until I had it all, with just the one, torn flag. I knew if I pulled it, it would tear in two. My whole body shook, and I felt I should apologise to someone, but there was no one there to hear it. You can't say sorry to a piece of cloth.

In the dark I heard Itzik's voice in my head: 'You can't tell a piece of cloth you're sorry, Dudi, Get it?' I felt angry then, because it felt as though he was pretending he'd come up with that thought, even though I'd thought it before he'd even opened his mouth. At last I thought I'd say sorry to Herzl, so I shouted, 'Sorry, Herzl! Sorry, Herzl!' I lifted my head high and shouted it so he'd hear it on his balcony. I'll make a new one, Herzl. For every flag I tear I'll make ten new ones. I couldn't stop shouting sorry.

Suddenly, the wind picked up, a wind that blew from every direction, driving me mad, but I still climbed up through the wadi. The big rocks were waiting, quiet and black, and I couldn't remember how I climbed them when I hung the flags, because as soon as I got close to one, it seemed much too big, as if it was swollen by the wind or the darkness. It began to tease me, saying, 'Of course we know you. You're Itzik's little brother. Come on, let's see how you do without him to help you climb!' So I looked up at the sky, and the stars seemed to be on my side, and when I looked at the ground, it felt as though they were tied to me by a string.

I looked up then, and I began to climb the rocks, not looking up to the stars because I didn't want them to think I had no faith in them. I walked quickly. I didn't have to listen for Itzik's breathing behind me. I didn't have to stop and wait for him. And I didn't notice that I'd arrived at the carob tree until I'd seen the chain of flags that I'd hung on the highest branches. I was glad to see the moon standing guard over them. I went up to the tree and took hold of its trunk. In fact, I found it easier to climb it in the dark; I could feel the hand-holds myself, the holes and knots. I climbed all the way up to the top and thought I could get all the flags down in one piece, but there were already rips and tears in them, and for every flag that tore I said sorry to someone: Herzl, King David, Abraham, Isaac, Jacob, the four Mothers, and Hagar, who was thrown into the desert to die with Ishmael. I said sorry to the soldiers, too, whether they were in the north, south, east or west, here or there, buried in the ground or up in Heaven, and last of all I said, quietly but strongly, 'Liat, I'm sorry.' But I knew Liat would never forgive me.

I thought then that it was lucky I was here doing this, because the carob tree was on the path home, and if the Katyushas weren't enough, there might be terrorists on their way there. Now that Delilah was dead and couldn't scratch out their eyes, they'd get everyone in one go: Mum, Oshri and Chaim, Etti and Kobi. 'Kobi, Kobi,' I said out loud, now that Itzik wasn't there to get angry and jump on me.

And then I thought about how Mum had given birth to me, a healthy baby, and about Itzik, how I was born to give him spare parts. God wanted my hands to be Itzik's spare hands. And as if it was getting angry, too, the wind picked up again, whistling as though inviting its whole family into the wadi for a party – brothers, sisters, uncles, cousins, coming from all directions. By now I was walking up the path to our building, past the tall trees with the acorns. I didn't hear the wind. I didn't feel any cuts on my body – my hands, my feet and my face were numb.

Suddenly, the town's electricity came back on. From the wadi, in the middle of the mountains, I saw the lights of the town like a television in a darkened room, our building seeming closer, and I could feel my hands and my feet and my face again, and I said out loud, 'Dudi's thought isn't like the wind! No one's going to change it!'

Our building stood between two others, like a bride that has spent all day getting ready for her groom. In the entrance was Mike's painting of snowy mountains and waterfalls, and all the windows were lit up. I could see the chain of flags waving in our window and I didn't have to take them down any more. There was no need. They were just forgotten Independence Day flags, not an invitation to terrorists.

My face was cold and I was dying to go down to the shelter, to collapse onto a mattress. But if I went into the shelter in the middle of the night when everyone was asleep, they'd die of fright or punch my lights out. But I just wanted to promise everyone there that I wouldn't break into houses any more. I'd use the door rather than the window. I nearly swore on Dad's name, then I remembered that Itzik said we shouldn't do that as we didn't have a dad. Now I wanted to argue: Yes, we do! Yes, we do! Yes, we do! We have a dead dad. I think about him all the time. There isn't a day when I don't think of him, feel his hand on my shoulder, as soft and warm as a pillow. I remember how he'd peel the paper off an ice cream for me, slowly so the chocolate wouldn't break, and put it in my hand, the paper like a banana skin so it wouldn't drip. And I remember him at the end. I saw it all. How could Itzik think I'd forget?

How could I forget Dad, how he was the most handsome person there, the others standing around and shouting, moving me, pulling me away from the circle of people so I wouldn't see him, and how I crawled back in and looked. He was still the most handsome, even if they were alive and he was lying on the floor, dead.

That made me think of something else, about his six-year memorial, which they wouldn't do now because of the Katyushas. And without asking anyone, I, Dudi, decided that if no one was going to have a memorial for him because they were afraid of the Katyushas, I'd do it for him! I was outside anyway, and shouldn't have been wandering around. I might as well be at the cemetery if everyone else was in the shelter. As I made my way there, past the football pitch, I decided I'd make my vow there. It would be the place to promise Dad that I was never, ever going to steal again, never climb up the houses of strangers, break in through the windows. I'm only going to use doors from now on. All the way to the cemetery I said, 'Dad', the start of my vow, except I couldn't get any further. Whenever I opened my mouth, only the word 'Dad' came out, 'Dad, Dad'. All I could do was walk and say, 'Dad, Dad'. I don't know what came over me. 'Dad, Dad, Dad, Dad, Dad.' I just couldn't stop.

Dad Dad Dad Dad Dad Dad Dad Dad Dad

KOBI DADON

1   Kobi Dadon. Try writing it: Kobi Dadon.

All the middle letters are holes. My name is full of holes. If only I had an 'l', a long, thin loop, the whole thing would be better. I could write it as high as I liked, to make up for the holes, tying everything together. Done. It's not as if there's a shortage of names with an 'l': Aflalu, Elmakeis, Iluz, Amsalam, Lilo. I'm not after two – just one would make my signature right. My handwriting doesn't help. I can't seem to make my signature any bigger. I measured it with a ruler – it isn't more than an inch and a half. It looks shrivelled, the letters like a row of burnt matches. I've traced over Israel's signature with a black pen: Talmon Israel. It's like a painter's signature. How did he manage it?

Whenever he sends a letter, I immediately get out my ruler. I measure the length first, then the height. His signature is never smaller than three inches long and an inch high.

So, I sit down to write my signature. Sitting as he does, holding the pen as he does. It doesn't work. The letters of my name will never join together properly, and I don't know how to make the whole thing bigger. If I make the capital 'D' bigger, all I get is a bigger hole. If I make all the letters bigger, it looks like the writing of a six-year-old. I try one way, then another. Nothing works. Today the new storeroom papers are supposed to arrive via internal mail: form number 328 is for department orders and form number 412 is for permission to take it from the storeroom. I've worked so hard to organise it all, but my signature will let me down. It'll be seen all over the factory. It could have been something to make people respect me.

If you let someone clever wander around the factory for the day, then asked him to name Talmon's deputy, he might say the department managers, the foremen, the workers. But if he gave ten answers he wouldn't be right. If they asked him who decides what comes in and out of the factory, from the smallest thing – drawing pins for the noticeboard, say – to the biggest – hiring and firing, promotions – there's no chance he'd look at me. And if I told him, he'd laugh. But I'm not worried about it. I walk around with my head high. I've got nothing to hide.

What did they all think of me in those first six months? They didn't even know my name, just called me 'the kid who took poor Rosette's place'. The machine I worked on they called 'the Monster'. When we walked onto the factory floor at ten o'clock at night, the girls would spit on it as they walked past. No one wanted to go near it. They'd take their places, and their spit would drip in front of my face. I wanted to ask them to stop doing it, but I didn't have the guts. The spit aside, it wasn't a good place to be. Not one drop of beauty to the place. I used to dress up every night, as if I was going out somewhere special, just so I'd remember I was going to get out of there one day, to climb the career ladder, not get stuck there for twenty or thirty years. As everyone knows, clothes maketh the man. If you only ever wear dirty clothes that stink of cooking oil, you'll be knocked out in the first round.

I got my bad back because of that night shift. I could hardly stand up straight and I couldn't ask for a chair, either. I was afraid they'd fire me if I did. Everyone said, 'Ah, you're Rosette's replacement' in a way that made me feel guilty, as if it was my fault her head got smashed in.

On my first night at the factory I learned that the machines stop every time there's a hole in the thread. The electricity cuts out, but it doesn't make any difference to the machines if they ruin a human life. Three-thirty in the morning is when you start to go mad. You can't believe you'll get through the next hour. You look at the clock ten times in thirty seconds, then up to the windows in the roof to see if there's any light, then back to the clock. Nothing moves. The clock, the darkness, both stay as they are. You start to think that time really is standing still, that God fell asleep without leaving instructions to move the hours. If someone came to the factory at 2 a.m. and asked us to give a year of our lives just to go to sleep there and then, we'd all sign up to it. People would be queuing up. But after what happened to Rosette, for a while no one went to sleep at three-thirty. Everyone seemed to wake up, to turn and look at me. The factory would buzz at the same time every night. It was a kind of memorial, even though she's still alive. I'd think a thousand thoughts at that time of night. I wanted to stop the noise, to stick an axe into a machine to break it, and, along with everyone else, I'd think about Rosette.

One Thursday, Rosette was standing exactly where I used to, her hand passing the thread into the machine. Everyone says she had the best touch for the job, that she could feel if the thread was a quarter of a millimetre too thick or thin. Maybe she just looked up to the roof windows to see if dawn had begun. Whatever happened, her long hair was suddenly caught in the wheels, pulled through like the thread, until her head smashed against the machine. It can process 30 centimetres of hair or thread in five seconds, it doesn't matter which. Whatever goes into the forest of wheels has to come out the other side. At break-time, the same refrain over and over: Why didn't we jump up and turn off the machine? Then they'd start to get angry. If they didn't make us work back to back like robots, so we can't look at each other, we would have seen her. But over the noise of the machines, how could we have heard anything?

Then they talked about the workers who were facing her but were too far away. Four of them jumped up immediately, but it was no good. Five seconds is nothing. What can you do in five seconds? It's no time at all.

When the whole Rosette business had calmed down, I began to see the factory for real. The laughter at break-time, when the weak electric current of the machines is connected to the kettle, so that when someone tries to make themselves a cup of tea, they get a little shock. The tape cassette of 'The Flower in my Garden' on constant play, turned over a hundred times. The way they aren't as safety-conscious after half an hour on shift, taking off the goggles and the ear protectors – they can't stand wearing them in the heat – but still putting up their hair, of course. From time to time someone still went to visit Rosette, and would come and tell us about her. But the 3.30 a.m. moment was in the past. They forgot all about it. Suddenly, they were fighting over my machine, remembering it was the best machine, clocking in quickly and running to grab it.

I'd get home at six-fifteen on the factory bus. Mum would have been up for some time already. She'd make me tea, and I'd fall into her bed, which was still warm. I'd breathe in her smell, not sour like it was when she was breastfeeding. I'd sleep on her side until the afternoon, then go back into work for the night shift. That was how it was every day for ten months. Then Talmon came to the factory.

Today everyone knows me. There isn't a person who hasn't poured out her heart to Kobi. Ever since I was a boy, people have told me everything. I don't know why. I don't tell them about my life, just listen and remember what they've told me, then keep my mouth shut. I don't gossip. That's what Talmon saw when he took me off the machines and put me in the storeroom. When he called me into his office, three days after he'd arrived as the new manager, everyone thought he was going to fire me. People still think that. Others think we're like cat and mouse. How did they come to that conclusion? Are they blind? Can't they see I'm climbing the ladder?

I might have understood that at the start, when he took me off the factory line, made me carry things, rearrange shelves. I worked until I broke into a sweat. They all thought I'd been screwed. And then he gave me a drinks corner, the best heater, his old desk and chairs when he got new ones. Why can't they see we're as thick as thieves?

My salary is one-and-a-half times theirs. I have my own room. I wear a jacket. My sweating days are long gone. I've become white collar. Little Siso drags the heavy stuff around now. And just because Talmon likes to put on a little show now and again, giving me a dressing-down on the factory floor, pretending he's not happy with an order, or appearing at the door of the cafeteria and demanding something when I'm in the middle of eating, they think he doesn't respect me, that he'll soon fire me. Fire me? *Me*? Once I've finished doing what he wants, I go back to the cafeteria and my plate, counting, one by one, the people who got their jobs because me, and thinking about the ones Talmon and I fired together. Then I'm calm.

What shall I do now? Until the new forms arrive, my time is my own. My storeroom is as closely guarded as a pharmacy now. Since Talmon agreed to a lock on the door, no one is allowed in here alone. If someone needs something, I have to watch them take it off the shelves. They can drink coffee at my table outside, as much as they like. Let them drink, let them pour it out. Kobi's OK with all that. But they can't go into the storeroom alone. Today the forms are coming, and then the whole factory will have to write down what they want and wait for my signature. They'll think twice before asking for something.

It's seven o'clock. I take Talmon's papers from the bottom drawer, the papers from our first meeting. He asked me a thousand questions, and I sat there and told him about my life and my family, what everyone knows and some secrets, too. And with every word that came out, I'd think: Is that really what happened? Is that my life? Until that meeting, I didn't talk to anybody about it, and now all I can think about is how I would tell it differently, and what he would say.

After I'd told him everything, he started talking. 'Look, Kobi,' he said – and I'll never forget this – 'I'm going to put all my cards on the table. I have no choice. I need to let somebody see my hand, and I've chosen you. My biggest problem, my lowest card, is that I'm a new immigrant here, and I can't afford to be new. Look,' he went on, taking a paper out of his briefcase, 'this factory has been going for four-and-a-half years, and it's gone through six managers. Six managers in four-and-a-half years. I'm the seventh. It's simple arithmetic – each manager lasts an average of nine months. That really bothers me. They were all good, all clever, all department managers in the main factory. They were successful, yet they were tossed out of here before they even got their feet under the desk. Afterwards, they were given some dead-end job. I started work here three days ago, and I want to stay here for five years. That's what I want.'

On another piece of paper he wrote the year five years from now and signed it. That was the first time I saw his signature. It was the first time I saw his drawings, too. He'd drawn our factory surrounded by the sea, and six people – the previous managers – holding their briefcases over their heads with both hands, flying, and falling into the sea.

At that point, all I could think of was whether he was going to hire me or fire me. My mind was locked. Hire, fire. Then, when I guessed he wasn't going to kick me out, I didn't want to say a thing because I was afraid he would stop talking and I wouldn't understand what he wanted. I said to myself: Careful, Kobi. This isn't a film. He might be putting on a performance, but this is real life.

'For two days I've been ringing around,' he went on. 'I didn't leave a stone unturned, and this is what I found out: those managers were thrown out because they got on the wrong side of the Council. Everyone knows you've got to be cautious with the authorities, but it's not easy. Not at all. It's stupid to think the ones who were fired were stupid. They were all clever and they all tripped up. So I have to be really clever. And you, Kobi, have to help me be a clever old-timer rather than a stupid newcomer.'

As he talked, he filled the desk with paper. He was either drawing, or writing just one word on a whole piece of paper, then underlining it. When he figured out the average duration of the managers and underlined it, the pen tore the paper. When he said the managers were clever, he wrote 'clever' on their briefcases. He told me the factory workers were like pieces of fruit in a crate. If just one started to rot, you had to take it out before it rotted the fruit next to it. He talked about knowing what was to his right and to his left, saying, 'I have to know what's behind my back and what's right in front of me. A wise man's eyes are in his head. I'm like a blind man and you're helping me cross the street.' Then he drew a picture of it. You wouldn't believe a factory manager could draw so well. Zvika, the previous manager, wasn't a match for Talmon. He was heavy, always nervous and tired. I've never seen Talmon tired. Whenever you see him it's as if he just started work that very minute.

When his desk started overflowing, he threw the paper in the bin and talked about the storeroom. He said, 'You'll have a storeroom with your own desk. It'll be like an office. A falafel shop is too small for you.' Then he told me what I had do in the factory, with the workforce, and what I had to get from the town hall, the Council, the Union, and the people in the market. 'What are people saying in the market?' he always says. 'Don't forget the people in the market.' He must think the whole town does nothing, that everyone just stands around talking at the Thursday morning market.

Afterwards, when he was walking around the factory, I rescued all the paper from his bin, including the last picture he drew. There are two circles. In one the two of us are tied together with a rope, standing on a mountain and laughing; and in the other circle we're both hanging from our rope, dead, with a big X drawn next to us.

I'm dying to sit in his office again like that first time. What wouldn't I give? Back then he didn't have his secretary Leah, who came from his old company a month later. She took Heli's place, after I gave him the OK to fire her. It's a shame really, because Leah made me feel smaller than a fly when I tried to walk past her into his room once. I'm not doing that again. Back then he didn't have those people with him, either, the ones he brings from outside and walks around with. He wasn't confident of his place yet. I look at the drawings to remember our first meeting, when he asked me all those questions about my life, making me feel I was number one. Me and him alone in the room. His cards on the table. To succeed, Israel Talmon needs Kobi. Without Kobi, he's nothing. He does take most of my advice, although not all of it. He fired Zion even though I told him to be careful. He probably thought he was a rotten fruit in the crate, just because he complained about overtime. But he still respects my opinion. He lets me hire people for the crappy jobs, throws me a question here and there, so I always feel we're still tied with the rope he drew, that he can't move without me, the blind man's white stick, to show him the way.

How I wish he would sit with me and lay his cards on the table again. It's eating me up. I wish he'd show Leah who I really am in this place. I wish he'd stand with me at the factory assembly before Rosh Hashana or Passover, when he raises a plastic cup and announces the factory's new and improved production numbers. I wish he'd tell them all who I really am, that without Kobi, he wouldn't have made it through the two years he's been here, wouldn't have expanded the factory from twenty-four workers to seventy-three, from one to two buildings, from fifty orders to two-hundred and twenty, that without Kobi he would have been tossed into the sea, buried in some dead-end job with no prospects. But no, nothing. He makes everyone feel important. He doesn't raise anyone up or bring them down, just finishes every meeting with 'Those who sow in tears will reap with songs of joy' or 'Those who prepare for the Sabbath will eat on the Sabbath'. It's like being back in school. Then he straightens his *yarmulke*, everyone goes back to their places, and he leaves without saying a single word to me. When I think about that, my life seems so black. I can't see any good in it.

Then, when I remember I'm not just his white stick, I feel happier, because I know how to keep quiet, to have patience like no one else. I'm as patient as a stone. Talmon is just one course in my life, and he'll never know what's right under his nose. I have another avenue that gives me the strength to be quiet when he's shitty to me in front of everyone, the strength not to get up and tell everyone what I've done for him.

2   I clean my desk with a rag. There's nothing on it. I won't allow a single piece of paper to be seen on it. Everything is in the drawers.

I wait a few minutes so it's exactly the right time: 7.30 a.m. I take the white plastic folder out of the second drawer, and, one by one, I go through the papers inside. I trace over the lines of the apartment plan with a pen – the walls, the circles that show how the doors open and close, the beds, the sofas, the kitchen, the sinks, the circles of the hob, the square of the fridge, the table in the dining alcove. I trace over everything. If I took a piece of blank paper, I think I could draw it from memory.

I first saw the apartment a year and two months ago, and when I went in, all I wanted to do was run away. We arrived in Rishon LeZion on the mini-bus and dropped the passengers off. I was dying for a shit. Mordi said, 'Let's go in here. I'll pretend I'm interested in buying; you find a toilet.' So we went in. Mordi chatted up the girl there, and I found the bathroom easily. I opened the door, and I thought I'd died and gone to Heaven.

Was it really a bathroom? The toilet seat was covered with green carpet, and on the floor, cut around the base of toilet, was more carpet in the same colour. I didn't know what to do. I took off my shoes so I wouldn't dirty the carpet, then I sat down slowly and put my feet on it really carefully. Then I started to cry. Shitting, crying. Wiping myself, crying. I got up to flush the toilet and I was still crying. I put the carpeted seat back down and sat on it. I didn't have the strength to get up again. I'd aged a hundred years in one minute. I looked around. It was all shiny and new. The big sink was a delicate pink and

133

the mirror was surrounded by small lightbulbs, and you could move it up and down to see yourself from all angles. There were red and violet and pink flowers on the tiles, and the towel was the green of the leaves and the toilet seat carpet.

The soap was new, the bath huge and shiny, and the taps were gold. On the floor next to the bath was a little rug. A rug in the bathroom! Who would have thought it?

The window was ajar, wafting in clean air. There was no noisy black boiler. The floor wasn't black, either. There was no mould on the ceiling, no condensation. Everything was white and new. At last I got up and went to the sink. I stood there, washing my hands and watching myself cry, then wiping my face and crying again, until I turned the mirror to the ceiling so I wouldn't have to look at my tears. I grabbed the towel, pressed it to my face for a few minutes like a bandage. Then I opened my eyes and wiped the sink with the towel until it was shiny again.

I put on my shoes and went back out. Mordi was looking as pleased as if he had won the lottery, but all I could think was that in another minute I was going to faint. I tried to drag him out but he didn't want to come. So I went out by myself, and waited for him outside. After a while he came out, too. 'What's the matter with you?' he said. 'What's the hurry? I'll never understand you. A few more minutes and she'd have made us some coffee.'

We wandered around the construction site for a while. I turned back every minute to see the sign, written in green: 'Model Apartment'. Mordi was talking about the girl there, but I kept turning back to the sign so I wouldn't forget it: Model Apartment. Mordi was talking and talking, laughing as he found a bin and threw away all the brochures she gave him. I'm in agony. I want to put my hand in and take them back out, but I stop myself. I don't want Mordi to know what's on my mind. So I shut up. I take the cigarette he offers me and we wander around the city together.

It was my first time in Rishon, but I didn't see anything of the city. All I saw was my crying face in the bathroom mirror of the Model Apartment. I just walked and thought about my crying face. Then my back pains started, moving up from the backs of my shoes. Little pains at first, then so big they shot up to the middle of my back as they searched for a place to land. Shoot and search, over and over again. The first one was like a test run, like taking a measurement and making a pencil mark on the wall before you drill a hole. Before the drilling started, I swore with all my heart, on Oshri and Chaim, that I would never cry in that mirror again. One day Kobi Dadon will stand in the bathroom of the Model Apartment and laugh into that mirror. I swore so hard that I was sure the person who went to get the drill couldn't find it. That's how I do it: I keep swearing until the pain in my back disappears. But I don't have the strength now. I lost it fighting the pain.

We went back to the bus, ate the food that Fannie and Mordi's mum gave him. 'I tell them both I've got no food, so I get double,' he laughed. 'They push me to each other, from here to there – that's how I make sure they both spoil me.' Then he showed me new photos of his kid. 'We're on the same wavelength,' he told me. 'Lucky I caught you in the draft board in the first call-up. Were you really thinking of going? The ones who joined the army think they're men but they're like boys. They haven't seen anything of life. But somebody who had kids calling him Dad when he was only sixteen is in another league. What do you think of Lior? As soon as he was born, you could see he was a man.' I looked at the photos of his kid and I add to my vow: one day I'm going to laugh in the mirror of the Model Apartment, and take photos of Oshri and Chaim laughing, too.

At last it was four o'clock, and it was time to take home the people we brought to Rishon in the morning. I sat at the back, wanting to sleep, and I heard it like a song: 'What, what, what is a model? The apartment's a model.' For a month I waited to take another day off from the factory. I worked overtime, I worked night shifts. I was still at the machines then; it was before I had the storeroom. I went to Mordi and asked, 'When's your next trip to Rishon?'

Mordi laughed. 'You've got a crush on the city, have you? There's nowhere like Rishon, believe me. Not even Tel Aviv. I go every Thursday.'

I said, 'If you can pick me up at my house, I'll come with you every last Thursday of the month.'

So I'd boxed myself in: my vow to Oshri and Chaim on one side, and Mordi, who wouldn't let me off, on the other.

3 It's eight o'clock. Just as I take the bunch of keys to get out the money notebook, I'm told they're closing the factory. The army's announced a Katyusha alert. We made a mistake last night and shot a couple of shells onto some village. Their radio's reporting that a woman and five children died. Now we're afraid they'll go crazy, and so everyone's being sent home. At 8.15 p.m. the factory's closed. I go outside to wait for the buses with everyone else. Talmon, who'd just arrived, jumps back into his car and starts the engine. You'd have thought the factory was on fire. He drives off like a speeding bullet. People try to talk to him, but he turns the steering wheel and shouts out of the window, 'Tomorrow, it can wait till tomorrow. Where's the fire?'

Everyone's talking about it. This time it's serious. They wouldn't close a whole factory for no reason. The buses are here to take us home. What kind of serious is it? Really serious? I can't work out what they'll achieve from this alert. Not a single person is in the shelter. And it's such a nice day, too. Who'd sit in the shelter on a day like this? The sun is perfect. Somebody up there set the thermostat to a perfect heat.

As soon as work, school and the nursery were let out, all the shops closed, and the street got so full you'd have thought you were in the city. Buses and taxis were getting the schoolteachers, nursery workers and social workers out as fast as they could. A few families grab suitcases, get into a taxi or on a bus, and go to relatives in the south. After half an hour only the locals are left. I go down to the shelter with everyone, and count the minutes. For thirty-five minutes they sit in the shelter, eat all the food they've brought with them – nibbled sunflower seeds, drank coffee – until it is all gone. Then they start going out. First, the men open the door and stand outside to smoke; they obviously can't bear sitting inside with the kids any more. Then everyone starts doing the same. The women go to sit with each other, and send the kids outside to their dads. By ten o'clock no one is sitting in the shelter; they're all wandering the streets like millionaires that don't need to work. Raphi's dad opens up his backgammon set in the middle of town, and starts a game with Shushan. Ten guys come to watch, their kids running around. Reuven, the head of the Union, stands there in his slippers, smoking and looking pleased with himself.

What can you do? No one realises the danger until something happens. Every peaceful minute that passes is a sign that the next minute will be peaceful, too.

By twelve-thirty I'm wandering the streets too, my hands in my pockets. I've got to hide my hands. I don't want anyone to see them. My mouth is fine; everything that leaves my mouth has authorisation, just like the storeroom. My eyes are the same. But I can't control my hands. They do whatever they like, betraying me. When I'm around people I don't know what to do with them. After the trip to Rishon I can't stand wandering around town any more, can't stand talking to the locals. On Independence Day I stood with Mordi and the little kids to watch the fireworks, and Mordi said to me, 'The ones that just go up and up and up drive me mad. You watch them going up and think something's going to happen, and nothing does. They just fall down again without opening.' After Rishon I thought: People here, my dad included, are not even as good as those fireworks.

I make my way to Mordi's house, thinking I'll wait it out there. But I can't. I had to leave the factory while I was in the middle of sorting out my drawers. Every Tuesday, from seven o'clock to eight-fifteen, I work out how much money I can put into my apartment fund that week and I write it into a notebook. I add it all up, work out how much more I have to save, then put it in the drawer and start my day. But today I had to leave before I could write up my notebook. I can't go to Mordi's. I've got to go back and do it so I can start my day right.

I walk back to the factory. It takes me twenty-five minutes. Luckily, I've got the keys, which probably weigh half a kilo. The industrial estate is dead, like it is on a Saturday. I look up at the sky, and feel a little afraid, with one hand trembling I try to open the factory and it doesn't budge. Only when I use both hands can I get in. Last year a Katyusha fell in the industrial estate on Lag b'Omer. If one falls now, who will find me? They'll just say, 'Thank God it didn't fall on the houses.' No one will come. I'll just go in for five minutes, write down the money and then go back up to town.

I go to my room, open the drawer quickly, take out the notebook. I want to write down the date and how much I've saved. It's a good week. A $120 week. Added to the rest, I've now got $7,000. How much more do I need? Just another $7,000 and then I can get out of here. Today I'm halfway. As I write the date, my hand's shaking. It's my birthday today and I'm nineteen. It just so happened that I got to the halfway point on my birthday. I underline the date twice. What a day! I've got half of the deposit for the apartment! I feel as though I've climbed to the top of a mountain and I can see where I'm going. From today, every dollar I earn is pushing me downhill towards my real life. It's lucky I didn't enlist in the army. Where would I be now if I'd wasted time doing that?

I look at the calendar on the wall. I mark the end of every day with an X, tear off the page at the end of every month, put a new calendar up every year. It's the calendar that shows me how time passes, not the clock. The clock is a liar. Every time you look at it, it's as if it has just started ticking, giving no sign that time has passed. It's as if every hour is the first hour of the world. A proper clock should have a hand like a knife, cutting out circles inside, so you can see time working, producing something.

I get up and look at the calendar, to mark the X on today's date before I go. As soon as I do it, I can see that my birthday is today in the Hebrew calendar – 14 Sivan – as well as the standard calendar. How can that be? The two never coincide. Tomorrow is 15 Sivan, Dad's memorial day. Why didn't Mum mention it? She always talks about the memorial two weeks beforehand, so I can get ready. As I think about her, I realise she's not talking at the moment. She hasn't said a word for a week. She's quiet all the time. When I looked at her face this morning as I woke up, I thought maybe I'd said something about the apartment in my sleep, but there's no way I'd do that. I'm like a safe. I keep everything locked away, twenty-four seven. So what's going on? Why didn't she look at me when we went into the shelter this morning? Maybe she's just realised we've missed Itzik's bar mitzvah, that we didn't do anything for him, and didn't know how to talk to me about it. She's probably afraid I'll say no. She knows I'm not Dad. He'd just give her anything she wanted.

I haven't said a word about the bar mitzvah to her or to Itzik. I don't understand why he hasn't mentioned it. Since he left school and brought the bird home, nothing seems to interest him. That bird is his life now. Because of her, he went back to sleep in the old apartment, and in the kitchen, no less. Just because it has a sink. He doesn't look after himself. It's as if he's thinks he's already dead. A cage with two animals in it wouldn't stink as much as that kitchen. If I give her money to throw away on a bar mitzvah, even half of what she spent on mine, I'll fall behind on the Model Apartment schedule. The notebook will be back to where it was four months ago. I had a bar mitzvah fit for a king. No one had ever seen anything like it. You couldn't have asked for more. But just when you feel life is smiling down on you, your dad goes and fucks everything up.

Two days after my bar mitzvah I was told, 'Your dad died at the falafel shop.' At the bar mitzvah everyone said, 'Now you're a man. Do you feel you've turned into a man?' They slapped me on the back so hard I almost fell over, and I laughed like an idiot.

I was treated like a king at my bar mitzvah. No one could avoid hearing about it. Everyone was talking about me and my family. We all looked great, with our new clothes and haircuts, and the whole house was full of flowers and presents.

Two days later I was wandering around the town centre wearing my bar mitzvah jacket, shiny shoes and new watch, and everyone was still saying '*mazel tov*' wherever I went. The town centre started to fill up; everyone had come to hear Rabbi Kahane. I looked at the people with him, figured out who was the real boss, and started to help them set up their things. I didn't talk much, just gestured to two strong kids to carry the platform the rabbi would stand on, grabbed Abutbul's eldest son and told him he'd get five shekels to beat up anyone who heckled, with half up front so he knew I was serious. I called Albert Biton to help them with the electricity. After ten minutes they were mine. They couldn't manage without Kobi. They didn't know my name, yet they ran to me with a question every two minutes. When

I saw they were nearly finished, I whistled to Dudi, who was playing with his friends near the phone booth, sent him to get a few bottles of juice from the falafel shop. I didn't think he'd have a problem. Just a few bottles. But Dad never understood how to choose sides. That was why he died.

So I got the drinks myself, opened them and handed them round. We sat down and drank together, started to chat. One way or another, I got to hear all sorts of things about the rabbi. Things no one knows. I pretended not to be interested, as if I heard stories about important people every day. But I was fizzing inside. They thought I worked for the Council, didn't realise how young I was. Maybe because I was already shaving, they thought I was four or five years older. They said, 'They don't help us like this everywhere. *Shkoyakh*! *Shkoyakh*!' I didn't know what they meant, but I didn't let on. Inside I was laughing, as cool as a cucumber.

After the rabbi finished his speech and the dancing had stopped, they introduced me. He blessed me, calling me 'Yakov'. People started to drift away, and the rabbi and his people finished loading their van. I looked at the van until it disappeared. At the bend in the road one of them waved goodbye to me. I was full of it. He might have been going away but he wouldn't forget me. Maybe he'd talk about me. Then, suddenly, they were shouting: 'Kobi, come quick, your dad's collapsed at the falafel shop.'

What do you mean? Collapsed? How? I ran there and saw everything: Dad lying on the floor in the falafel oil, the pot upside down on the floor, the big knife in his hand, full of bits of parsley, his eyes half-open, the left one swollen. Later Albert Biton found the bee that stung him in the oil. The centre of town had been empty, but in less than a minute it was crammed with people again. I stood there with everyone else, watching them pull my dad out like he would pull a sack of chickpeas, lying him on the floor. His shirt was pulled out of his trousers and you could see his whole belly. I thought I would die. I don't know why. I wanted to cover him up but I couldn't move. I wanted them all to shut up, to stand still, not to keep moving. He looked to me like Yehiel the Bible teacher who used to gaze at us with hooded eyes, waiting for us to be quiet before he opened his mouth. I wanted to say, 'Don't you see he's waiting for you to be quiet?' But Dad just lay still, his hair glued to the floor with oil, and people shouted.

Chico started CPR. All the time everyone kept saying, 'Isn't this bad for the kids? They shouldn't see him like this. Take them away.' But no one did take us away. Why would they when they had such a good view? Every other minute somebody shouted, 'When will the ambulance be here?' But everyone knew he was dead before the ambulance arrived. In the end they took us home. Itzik was with us, too. Me and Dudi and Itzik. I can still hear Mum's screeches as she tried to run to the centre, the women in our building stopping her. They grabbed her, brought her into the house, laid her down on the sofa in the living room, poured water on her.

I don't remember the funeral. It has just flown out of my head. But I do remember coming home afterwards. Every door was open as we climbed the stairs. The whole building was like one big house, and everything was turned over. I didn't know where to put my feet. I was turfed out of all the usual places and I couldn't go outside. In the end they sat me on a mattress on the floor. People started coming into the house. Stand, sit. More came in. I looked up at a thousand faces. They were using all the air. I couldn't breathe. I went to the bathroom. There was a queue, but they let me go first. I did everything quickly – washed my face, wet my hair, fixed my bar mitzvah *yarmulke* with a pin. To make myself cry I said into the mirror, 'Dad's dead. Dad's dead.' But I couldn't cry. Nothing. Not a single tear. I tried out different expressions, decided on one for the day so I could be sure how they'd see me. Someone knocked on the door. I grabbed the shirt they tore. It was a new shirt, what good did it do to tear it? Another knock. I opened the door and went back to my mattress. Now there were serious faces instead of the handshakes and laughs of the bar mitzvah, but they shook my hand once more, repeating what they'd said at my bar mitzvah: 'Now you're the man of the family. You have to be a man now.'

Mum's brothers from Ashdod were there for the day. They were afraid for her, afraid to leave her alone. They told me the same thing. What could I say? I nodded, keeping my head down, putting my hand over my face, waiting until they went to talk to someone else – Mum, Dad's brothers, Grandma, anyone just so long as they left me alone. When I stood with Dad's brothers to say Kaddish for him, I felt I wasn't alone. But I didn't know what was going to happen. I didn't know that one year later I'd discover their true faces when they left me alone to be the man of the house.

After about a month and a half or two months, Mum came home from the clinic crying, and went into her room. Ricki Amar, who works with her at the nursery, followed her. After a while she came out of the room alone, went into the kitchen to boil water for tea. We followed her. She said, 'Come in here, I have something to tell you. Your mum is pregnant. You've got to take care of her, make sure she doesn't work too hard.' At first I didn't understand. What did she mean? Pregnant? How could she get pregnant now? I didn't get it. I don't know why. I was angry. And disgusted, too. There are guys who run onto the football pitch after a game and kick a ball into the goal. It's their chance to been seen on the pitch. They like to score a goal, without a goalkeeper or other players, just for the hell of it. I can't stand that. It makes me sick.

4   I close the notebook and lock it in the drawer. I want to run away from the factory. Without the noise of the machines, it's worse than a graveyard. The last time it was so quiet was my first day. It was six o'clock on a Sunday morning and I was sixteen and two months. The workers went onto the factory floor with the foreman. In the dark all the machines were like rocks. Why not? I thought. We'll stand next to each other, talk, laugh, and, chic-choc, the day's over. Suddenly they turned on all the machines, all of them at once, the women's and the men's. I thought my ears would explode. The machines started moving like animals that had slept all Saturday. I wanted to escape, to find the schoolbag I had thrown away, to go back to school. Every day for a month I wanted to go back to school. Then I got my salary and I felt like a man who knows how to earn some cash. After the fifteenth of the month, when I went to the bank, I didn't want to go back to school any more. It's like being in first grade and walking past the nursery. You look over the fence at your old teacher sitting outside with the children, and see there's no reason to go back there. And when my first draft board letter came, I saw the army wasn't the right thing for me, either. It's lucky I met Mordi. He taught me what to do, and so did Talmon. I don't know who he talked to, but they say his brother is a high-ranking officer in the army. A week later, the exemption letter arrived in the post.

I get up and walk down the corridor, past Jamil's room. Talmon will never know the truth. Jamil is the factory book-keeper, and he cottoned on to our game right from the start. He worked it out at the job interview. A day later he caught me on my way to the storeroom and quietly said, 'Thanks.' My face started to burn. I was rooted to the spot, and he went to his room. Just 'thanks'. How he got wind of us, I don't know. How could he have worked out that I can put in a word with Talmon? How did he realise I helped him get the job? Maybe he knew there was a Jew who wanted the job, too. When I was at nursery, we'd play a game when we all had to copy one person, and another has to guess who it is. Motti Ipergan would be sent out of the room, then come back in, look for a second and quietly say the right name, then sit down in his chair. The teacher would go mad. She did everything she could to confuse him, but he never got confused. He now works in Army Intelligence – what else? Jamil's the same. His brain is fast and accurate. Immediately he gets what no one else does, and says only what he needs to. He has diplomas in accountancy and tax, and all his diplomas say he qualified with distinction.

I walked into Talmon's room in the middle of his interview,

pretended I was filing, and looked up at the ceiling. That was our signal. Looking up at the ceiling meant 'he's the one to hire'. The week before interviews, Talmon gives me the list of candidates, and I do my work: I ask questions, listen to the answers, get into places – the Union, the head of the Council and his secretary – to know who's pulling one way and who's pulling the other. I know which candidate has been sent to trip him up, and which one they don't want hired, although they don't want to look prejudiced, as well as the person they recommend for friendship's sake, who's screwed up every job he ever had. If I don't have the time to slip him the paper on the sly, he calls me into the interview and I give him my signal. He never talks about it. Sometimes it's as easy as pie, like the brother-in-law of the head of the Council, or a member of some family that everyone knows you can't touch. I don't understand how he can't see it. It's as if he's blind and deaf. Sometimes I feel I'm sweating bullets to help him, pleading with Mordi to talk to the right person when he drives them, maybe crack a few jokes with the poker-faced secretary to the head of the Council when they're arranging transportation. I do everything so I can write two words to Talmon on a piece of paper, or go into his room to give him our signal before going back to the store-room. He doesn't want anything more from me.

The truth is, Jamil was hired because my cousin Gabi wanted the job, too. He'd finished studying and had come back to the *moshav*. He sat and talked to Talmon like the job was already his. He knew that the only other candidate was an Arab from the village. If Mordi knew I gave a Jew's job to an Arab he'd kill me. He's always saying, 'You can't even trust an Arab that's been dead forty years.' But what do I care if he's an Arab or a Jew? He could be a Bedouin for all I care. I'll scratch the back of whoever scratches mine. I just opened the door during Gabi's interview, stuck my head in, and left. I didn't even say hello, just looked at the floor so Talmon wouldn't make a mistake. No way are any of Dad's family getting a foot in this factory. After what they did to us when Dad died, the whole business with the falafel shop, I've got no time for them. I wouldn't lift my little finger to help any of them.

Two weeks after he started work at the factory, Jamil came to me with his proposal: 'For every worker of mine that you bring in, you get ten per cent of his first salary.' I said, 'Twenty per cent.' We settled on fifteen. I don't know his percentage. I don't ask. Then I went away and, a minute later, came back with the Model Apartment brochure. I sat there, shaking. I put the brochure down and I couldn't open my mouth. I was going mad dreaming about it. Jamil took the folder, pulled out everything with his long fingers, opened it all on the table. I didn't say a word. He asked questions about money, took an adding machine and some blank paper, sat for a few minutes, wrote some numbers on the paper and, there and then, made me a plan to bring the Model Apartment out of my dreams and into my life. I almost kissed his hand.

When he brought me money the first time, I walked around with it in my pocket all day. I didn't know where to put it. There was nowhere safe at home. In any case, there's always somebody around when I get in. If I put it in the bank, into savings, the cashiers there could hint to Mum or the Housing Office that I have means of paying. People here don't know how to keep their mouths shut. Only yesterday Itzik's teacher grabbed me in the town centre, in front of everyone, and started talking about how he hadn't been to school for two months, that she'd send a truant officer or the new street youthworker. She shouted at me right in front of the supermarket, when everyone could hear.

That first night I slept with the money on me. In the morning I went back to the factory and asked Jamil what to do. He said, 'I'll keep it all for you in dollars, until you have fourteen thousand for the deposit.' I thought: What do I have to lose? I'm in his hands, and he's in mine. We're bound with the same rope.

From that day, on the fifteenth of every month, I withdraw my whole salary from the bank in cash. I give half to him, and he changes it into dollars, then keeps it in the village. When someone from his village gets a job, he writes down how many dollars he's putting away for me, and that's it. I've never seen my dollars, but I'm not worried. Jamil is completely straight. His word is his bond. And having it in dollars means I can't spend it. I'm dying to see my dollars one day, to hold them in my hand, to count them, to walk around with them in my pocket, to feel them on my body, but I gave him my word I wouldn't go to his village, and my word is my bond, too. And no one in the factory would guess we've got something going. I never sit next to him in the cafeteria, and he doesn't drink coffee with me like everyone else. I've promised I won't go to the village, and Jamil has promised that, even if I beg, he won't give me a single dollar before the time comes to buy.

We agreed that soon after, when Mum was putting pressure on me to let Itzik have private lessons in the city. She said, 'If he doesn't have private lessons, what will become of him? He spends all day with that bird. What kind of a life is that?' I said, 'There's no money.' She looked me straight in the eye, but I didn't blink. Anyway, I wasn't really lying. It's not money – it's walls, a sink, an oven, a bathroom, carpet. As soon as I started thinking that way about the money, it got easy for me to say no to them. I think the same when I feel like buying a new jacket. So we're all living on half my salary and the child allowance and the pennies she earns at the nursery. Everyone understands there's no money. Even Dudi, who's dying to have a few pounds in his pocket, doesn't ask. But I allow one trip to the cinema every two weeks. What can I do? You can't live without films here. You'd die. And they've stopped wanting a television, an electric heater, or clothes. They know they don't have a good reason to ask me. I also stopped paying Council tax and water rates. The Council cut it off once, and I went to talk to them. They settled for half the debt and turned it back on. And the Housing Office hasn't seen a penny from me for a year. They've started to threaten, so I'll make a settlement with them, too.

I don't buy anything for the house. It's not a *home*. I've seen what a *home* looks like. This is a pigsty. I'm just working to get myself and her and the twins out of this place. Itzik and Dudi and Etti will have to manage by themselves. I was working at Etti's age. I don't spend money for the sake of it. Don't get me wrong, I'd love to buy Mum a nice necklace, a new bracelet or a watch. I'm dying to buy her things, to see her face when she opens the box. But I'm not like Dad, who wanted her to be happy every day, throwing his money around like a kid. I know how to keep quiet, to keep everything locked inside.

When I make up my mind not to talk, I don't say a word. In the end I'll bring her the most precious jewel in the world: the keys to the apartment.

I haven't said a word to her about the Model Apartment. When she holds the keys, that's the first she'll hear about it. She'll stand there in Rishon with me and Chaim and Oshri. I won't bring a thing from the house. Not a single rag is going to move to Rishon with us. Everything there will be clean, waiting for her. I picture her unlocking the door, the keys falling out of her hand. She'll need to sit down, she'll ask for a chair. A chair? I'll take her to the armchair in the living room, bring her a glass of cold water from the kitchen. Then the colour will come back to her face and she can start her life again. New sheets, new towels, new pots. Everything will be new. Every day, when she falls into bed beside me, I hear her saying she aches all over. There's less than half a metre between us. I'm dying to say, 'Leave the nursery. We have money; you don't have to work.' But I don't let myself. I close my eyes and imagine her lying in the big bed in Rishon, the same wood colour as the wardrobe. There's nothing more stylish.

Every month I walk the streets in Rishon for an hour and a half, looking in people's windows to see what's in their houses, what they do, what they buy. How they talk to each other, how they are with their kids, when they come back from nursery and school. I keep it all in my head ready for the day I move. As I walk the streets, I picture her getting off the bus on Herzl Street after a good night's sleep, washed in the new bathroom, well dressed. Her face has returned to how it was in my bar mitzvah photo. She has a nice handbag, not the white bar mitzvah one but a new handbag with a purse full of money inside. She walks into shops, buys what she feels like. I've also picked out her hairdresser. In Rishon I'm sure she'll throw away that scarf and all the mourning clothes. I already know the clothes shops she'll like. I can see her life in Rishon. It's a nice life, a life fit for humans.

I go there every four weeks. No one at home knows. I get to the construction site at ten-thirty. The first thing I do is walk around to see how they've progressed. I don't want them to finish quickly. I need time to get the money together. I look at all the buildings, but I know where my apartment is. The only one I want is the Model Apartment itself, none of the others. I want it exactly as it is, fully fitted and furnished. I sit down outside it, take off my shoes and pour out all the sand that has crept in. There isn't any soil. The ground, the air, the sun are all different there. Nothing's the same. I put my shoes back on, tie the laces, and walk into my house. Every time I check what has happened to it that month, room by room. The bedroom, Mum's room, the twins' room, the bathroom. I check every corner, afraid things will get ruined. It's a pity I can't lock it, so my stuff won't get worn out. It's the carpet, dirtied by all the shoes, that annoys me the most.

One day I said to Yafit, 'Can't we cover the rug with some plastic?'

She laughed and said, 'You and your jokes.'

I said, 'Come on, let's take the toilet paper out of the bathroom so people will use the small toilet instead.'

She laughed again.

Every month I wet a rag and polish all the taps. The house is clean, the floor and the windows gleaming. Yafit goes mad. 'If I wasn't dying of boredom, I wouldn't talk to you,' she says. At first she thought I was mad, but at the end of the morning she always does what I want. At twenty-five past one she locks the door of the Model Apartment, leaves the keys on the small balcony for me. I come at one-thirty on the dot, take the keys, put them in my pocket, and pretend I'm walking into my own house with my own keys. I lock the door from the inside, throw the keys on the dining table in the alcove, drink some water. Yafit is usually sleeping on her stomach, legs crossed, in the master bedroom. She doesn't even take off her shoes. But I don't allow her to put them on the bedspread. So she crosses her legs in the air, her jeans as tight as can be. If Mordi was here he wouldn't be able to control himself. But I don't fancy her. She's like a substitute teacher, going from one man to another, filling in where she's needed.

She tells me everything. Kobi's the only ear she's got. Every time I get the name of someone new. I don't need a girl who sleeps around. She likes to pretend she's my wife, but if I didn't come home one day then she'd be off with someone else. Everything she does is an act. But she gets nothing out of me. She doesn't even know where I live. Once she asked me what my dad did for a living. I told him he owned a restaurant, just to see how it felt. I've heard that's what people say in Rishon. She hasn't a clue he's dead. Sometimes she asks when I'm going to bring the deposit, says the main office is putting pressure on her. I say, 'My dad's swamped with work. In another month, two months at the most, when he has time, he'll settle up. Don't worry about it.' I'm not worried, after all. She told me the Model Apartment would be the last one sold because they need it until the end.

I don't look at her for long. I go into the room to wake her, and she gets up, pecks me on the cheek. We go into the kitchen and she says,

153

'Do you want a coffee? How was work?' I always bring her something for the house, either flowers or fruit. Happily, she takes out the plastic ones from the bowl or the vase, puts in the ones I brought her. Before we leave, I go into the bathroom, check my face carefully. I don't lie to myself – the mirror still doesn't show me the face I swore I would have. When we leave the apartment together, she lets me lock the door. Just holding the keys in my hand drives me mad. One day, as I was wandering, I bought the nicest keyring in the city. It's made out of plastic, although it looks like glass, with real dried flowers inside. It took me hours to find the right one. Yafit says, '*Yalla*, Kobi, it's late. Don't forget I have to be back at four.' I know I have to leave the keys in her hands, and I can't. It gets harder every time. The keyring has become like holding a child's hand, then having to let it go. Yafit knows how hard it is for me and tries to help. The last time she said, 'Kobi, you have to talk to the neighbours about making a mess in the entrance hall, and you should go to the next tenants' committee meeting. I never want to see Markovitz on the third floor after what happened on Saturday.' I said, 'Don't worry, I'll talk to them.' Then I put the keys in her hand and she left.

I always stand there for about fifteen minutes after she's gone. I can't move. I'm dying to ask what the tenants' committee is, what their meetings are like and what they talk about. It's not as if it's a factory. It's only a building. What is there to talk about at building meetings? But I don't ask. In Rishon I don't ask questions. I just take it all in and find out afterwards. I don't let anyone get a sense of where I'm from. I dress like someone from Rishon. You'd think I was one of them.

I've already learned everything I need. Just from hanging around, from talking with Yafit. I know how to show people around the Model Apartment, too. One day an older couple came to view it while she was resting. She often goes out to late-night parties and comes into work tired. I send her to the bedroom, so she can lie down, and I watch the place for her. When the couple arrived, I knocked softly on her door, so she could get herself together, and I began to walk around with them myself. When she came out she went mad. But there's no question I can't answer. I know everything she knows, even how sometimes to focus on the wife and sometimes on the husband.

Yafit said to me, 'If one of them wants it and the other doesn't, I don't make the gulf between them any bigger. I take a thread and I start to repair it. I help them find common ground, what they both want. Did you know how to darn clothes? You go from one side of the hole to the other. You have to have a lot of patience, stitching in the strong cloth that won't fall apart, and you go from side to side and up and down, until the hole has gone.'

'Of course,' I said. 'My mum does it that way, too.'

She said, 'Mum-mum, Mum-mum. You're a baby, Kobi. Don't tell me you sit at home with her every night.'

I took that on the chin. I see how she keeps her cool every time people leave without wanting to buy, pretending she doesn't care. She says to me, like she's talking about somebody she's never met, 'Let them go. Who needs them? After you've seen a hundred people view the apartment, you know who's serious and who isn't. I'm on to them straight away. What's the point of arguing with the ones who are looking for everything that's wrong with the apartment? Let them go

155

and do up their old house. Good for them. Compared to the price of a new apartment, doing up a house is chicken feed.'

I like it most when she says to me, 'You're the only person I didn't have to show the apartment. You told me you wanted to buy without ever putting a foot in the place. You're quite a guy. But I don't understand: can you see through walls or something? How did you fall in love with the apartment? Through the door? Through the windows?'

When Mordi and I went to Rishon the second time, and I wanted to go to the Model Apartment, Mordi was sure it was because of the girl. I thought he wouldn't notice while the people on the mini-bus were getting off, so I asked him to take me to the new housing estate. He stopped at the side of the road for a heart to heart.

'If it's because of the girl there, what's her name, Yafit? If it's for that Yafit, I'm not taking you. You're my friend, and I won't let you get into my kind of nonsense. Don't forget I was just a boy. I was playing with Fannie. I didn't think I was playing with my life. What can you do? It was my fault and I paid for it. I'll be paying for the rest of my life. I'm not saying . . . Fannie's a good woman . . . It's just my life, a life you wouldn't think twice about. It's the life of someone who walks into a nice shop – the one over there, see?' He reversed a few metres and stopped in front of the shop. 'I went in there, a fifteen-year-old boy with some money, a gift you might get once in your life. I picked up the first thing that caught my eye. I wasn't thinking, didn't even look around properly. The thing slipped out of my hand. What could I do? I had to pay up and go home with what I broke. Don't look at me like that. People think I'm a joker, always laughing. They have no idea that Mordi is burning up inside every day, that he's dying for a chance to go back to the shop just once more.'

What could I tell him? What was there to tell him? If I said it wasn't to see Yafit, then I'd have to say it was to see the Model Apartment. But I'm not saying a word about the apartment. Only Jamil knows about it.

Mordi's problem is that he doesn't like silence, so he just carried on talking. 'You're not a kid, Kobi. Also, in your situation, you can't mess around. If you've any sense, you'll get a foreign wife. Look at Eliko. What a life he's got, eh? What girl would say no to him? There's not a girl in the town who wouldn't have married him like a shot if he so much as looked at her, but did he take the easy option? No! He took his time, got out of the army, went to Tel Aviv for a year, where he realised he was a no one – couldn't get a classy girlfriend – and went to Norway instead. When you get off the plane there you don't get, "You look Moroccan to me", "Where in Israel are you from?" or "Who's your dad?" There, you are what you are. You're taken at face value – judged on your body and your strength and your looks. It's an international language. If you work as a fisherman like Eliko, you'll make a packet in half a year. You learn the language, wander around, get a pretty girlfriend, but not too pretty, with money, but not too much money, so she won't think it all comes from her.'

He started the bus again. I thought he'd finished so I switched on the radio. He reached out and switched it off, interrupting a jingle mid-tune: 'Nothing beats the heat like ice-cold Crystal.'

'He's got brains,' he continued. 'He picked a wife like he was picking a flower, then put her in a vase of water. To her he's everything: father, mother, brother, friend. And most important, she knows his mother is queen bee. What more could he want? He spoils her rotten, too. She's his princess. So everyone knows their place.' I'm sitting in the car, thinking about how I can get to the apartment. I don't know how I'm going to get away. 'And best of all, his mother and his wife can't talk to each other. They don't speak each other's language. They need him to translate the tiniest thing. Eliko's a genius, I tell you, a genius. He's got a girl who speaks Norwegian and a little English, and a mother who speaks Moroccan, French and Hebrew. Five languages between them and they can't talk to each other. Eliko's their only bridge. And he knows how to use it to get some peace and quiet.'

I said nothing, but still he carried on talking. When we were in the same class at school, he wouldn't say a word. I tried to remember how he was then, but it's as if he's not the same person. Now he can hardly keep his mouth shut. He's always laughing, smoking, eating, spitting, talking, singing, drinking, telling jokes, whistling. He even opens letters with his teeth. I think it's a habit from driving the bus. All day every day his hands are on the steering wheel, his eyes on the road, his feet on the accelerator, brake and clutch. He's like a para-plegic; the only thing he can move is his mouth.

As we drove back to town, I wondered if he'd put a foreign girl in the Model Apartment for me. As I dozed off, I heard Mordi's words in my sleep: 'When you're abroad, you've got to make her understand that your mum and the twins are part of the package. She's got no choice in that.' I pictured the Model Apartment, the living room there, the big brown corduroy sofa, the shiny table and its fruit bowl decorated with camels in the desert, the large sandy-coloured ashtray. I saw in my mind's eye the black vase with flowers on the little side table, the rug with its pattern of circles, the floor-to-ceiling curtains the colour of milky coffee, the giant flower pot with its plant the size of a tree. I moved on to the television cabinet, looked at the pictures on the wall behind the sofa. One picture is of a river with flowers floating on it. Sometimes they look like flowers, sometimes like little green boats, carrying girls in white and yellow dresses. It's pretty either way. I don't have to decide. Every time I go, I sit in a chair and look at it for about half an hour. It's a picture that is always moving but it calms me, too. When I've finished looking at it, I close my eyes and when I open them again, the picture is all around me.

I thought about the picture as I listened to Mordi: 'Once I went to Eliko's and the wife was sitting in the living room, like a china doll, feeding the baby with a bottle. His mother was bringing her tea and cookies, and Eliko was just sitting quietly, happy with his lot.'

I transferred the foreign wife onto the sofa in the Model Apartment. She was drinking coffee, watching television, her hair the same shiny dark-blonde as the ashtray. Her clothes were patterned with circles, like the rug, but smaller. She breathed quietly and I breathed in time with her, until I fell asleep, floating on water like the flowers in the picture. I opened my eyes just as we were coming back into town. It was evening.

5   I walk home from the factory, thinking about Rishon and the apartment all the way. When I get to the centre of town, it's dead, like the industrial estate. No one's there. It's two-thirty, so everyone's probably having lunch. I'm thirsty and dying to get home. I glance towards the street that leads to the clinic and I see Mum. It's definitely her, even though she has her back to me. The headscarf, the dress, the shoes. It's her. I can't believe it, though. It's as if another woman has dressed in her clothes. Where is she going in the middle of an alert? Everything's closed. I can't whistle to my mother in the street. What goes on at home is our business, but even if there's no one in the street, someone might be looking out of a window. I want to shout to her, but I don't know what to shout. I haven't called her 'Mum' since I turned into the twins' dad. What would Oshri and Chaim think if I called her 'Mum', too? I'm trapped: I can't call her Mum and I can't call her Simona. If I call her Simona, people will think I'm not respecting my mother. What should I say? Simi, like Dad used to?

At first, I used to think about it at school, that I'd call her Simi in front of Oshri and Chaim when she got home. What would she do? So every day I'd wait for her to come home, and I would try to say Simi but I couldn't. It stuck in my throat and I couldn't get it out. It's like lighting a fire on the Sabbath. You think about it a hundred times, but you can't go through with it. Even if you don't wear a *yarmulke*, or if you go to the beach instead of the synagogue on Saturday, your hand refuses to strike the match.

She doesn't have the same problem. She always calls me 'Kobi'. But when she's talking to Oshri and Chaim she says, 'Tell Dad' or 'Go to Dad' or 'Be quiet when Dad's asleep'. I look at her walking down the street, and I know I just need her name to leave my mouth once, and then it will be easy. I just can't do it in the street. Lately, I've been thinking that I could start doing it in Rishon. No one knows us there.

As soon we arrive in Rishon, I'll let the house keys fall into her hand and I'll say, 'Congratulations, Simi, enjoy yourself.' What will happen? Will Dad pop out of the ground and give me a slap? What could possibly happen? She'll be so happy about the new house that she won't realise what I've said.

She walks to the end of the street. I don't stop her. She's carrying the bar mitzvah handbag, which she hasn't used since Dad died. The shoulder strap is made of two white cords, attached to the bag with big gold rings. The gold clasp shines in the sunlight. She never goes out with that handbag. She goes to work with a plastic bag, and in the market she throws her purse into a basket. Why is she carrying it now? I watch her cross the street, then she disappears from view. I don't know where she's going. Where could she be going? Sylvie's house is nearby – maybe she's visiting her. I can't think why, though. She never visits people.

I turn around and head for home. I'm hungry. I walk up the stairs and go into the apartment. Oshri and Chaim and Etti are in their rooms having afternoon naps. I go into the kitchen, heat up the couscous, spoon it onto a plate with a big piece of pumpkin. I take a mouthful, but I can't swallow. All I can see is her walking down the street, the handbag swinging from side to side and hitting her in the back. I can't eat. I need the bathroom. I've got to stop this. I take off my jacket and shoes, go into the bathroom, and put the mop handle against the door so no one can open it from outside while I'm having a shower. I take off all my clothes, put them on the sink, draw the shower curtain, turn on the water and sit on the floor. The floor is cold and the water is boiling as it pummels my head. I lower my head, so the water hits me on the back instead. That feels good. I don't touch myself. I can't touch myself and think about Mum in the street at the same time. I look down. I feel like a wild animal in danger. I can't help it. I'm in trouble. I close my eyes and focus on the foreign wife. I manage to bring her into the shower, but she's like air. There's nothing underneath her clothes. I try to think about Yafit then, but that doesn't work, either. She screws up her face, tells me I'm mad, laughs at me. She'd never set foot in a house like this. Instead I picture her on the sofa at the Model Apartment, then on the bed in the bedroom, her back to me. She doesn't take off her clothes, but throws her high heels on the floor, and rubs her bare legs together. I hold myself, moving slowly up and down, up and down, slowly, slowly. My hand is slow but my blood is rushing now and I'm breathing fast and I don't want it ever to stop and it's driving me crazy and I want it to stop and my hand's still moving slow and my legs and my arms and my head are like a spring and my lips are dry and my heart is beating till I have to do it fast now and I do it fast and hard and faster and faster and I give a small shout as it shoots out of me.

I sit there, not moving, until the hot water is finished and the cold water starts to fall. I lift my hand and turn off the shower. I get up, mop the water that has crept as far as the door, dry myself, quickly dress, and walk out. I don't look in the mirror. I'm cold. The shirt I put on the sink has a circle of wet from the dripping tap, and the bottoms of my trousers are wet from the water on the floor. I go to the bedroom, change my clothes, then get into bed in the middle of the day, covering myself from head to toe.

Please let her not come now. That would be all I need. What a shitty day. I don't understand what the army gains from the alert. What difference does it make to them to ruin the day for thousands of people, turning everything upside-down and sending everyone home. An empty day to wander the streets or wait until the sky falls in. It'd be better not to tell us anything. If we're alive, then we're alive, and if we're dead, then we'll have died living a normal day. At work, at school, doing whatever we normally do. I'm angry with the army. The bed's too hot. It smells clean. I check the sheet. Did she change it again? I don't know what's got into her. A week ago, she started changing it every day. How does she have the strength to take it off the bed, wash it and put a new one on every day?

I close my eyes, remember how we were when Oshri and Chaim were babies. For a year and a half, in this bed, we fenced them in. Two baby lambs between us, she'd say. We were neither properly asleep nor properly awake. Once I thought she was looking at me, so I said something and she replied in her sleep. Another time she was feeding both of them at the same time, and I thought she'd fallen asleep, when suddenly she started talking: 'In Morocco, my Aunt Tamu had a snake in the house. When she breastfed the baby on one side, the snake would feed from the other side.' I don't know if I believed those stories about the female snake, a pet in her aunt's house where Mum grew up. The snake lived in a basket and ate *sehina* with them on the Sabbath. And the house was made of mud and straw. 'One day,' she told me, 'we came home and we couldn't get in because the snake had wrapped itself around the doorknob. We found out afterwards that there was a viper inside. She'd saved us.' She had a thousand stories about snakes in Morocco, a place where there was a market of snakes.

But she'd only ever tell the stories in bed. I don't know why. Maybe she was dreaming about the snakes.

I wouldn't dream. I was always the first to know when one of them was going to wake up – I'd place my hand on him, put the dummy in – and I'd always remember who'd fed last and who'd filled his nappy. She couldn't remember a thing. It was like she was drunk. I'd pick them up, wake her, arrange two pillows behind her – one at the bottom and one behind her stiff neck – give her the babies, take them from her, change them and bathe them in the dark. Oshri was always quiet when he was eating or bathing. Before bedtime I'd fill the baby bath with water and put it on a chair, then, when he cried, I'd add boiling water from the kettle and wash him with soap, so he'd feel nice and clean. I'd undress him and wrap a towel around him so he wouldn't get cold. My heart would beat faster when he cried. I'd imagine he was shouting at me, telling me to stop being nasty to him. When I held him in the towel, my shadow rose up the wall almost to the ceiling. There wasn't much light, just one in the bathroom, as Dudi couldn't sleep if it wasn't pitch-black. At bedtime we'd turn off all the lights, then, once he was asleep, we'd turn on the bathroom light and open the door a crack. I'd take Oshri out of the towel and he'd scream, but as soon as his body touched the water he'd be quiet. I washed him the way she taught me. First I'd take a little water in my hand and pour it over his face three times: Abraham, Isaac, Jacob. The blessing made my heart quiet, too. Then I'd pour water onto his belly, swishing him back and forth, then turning him over and holding him by the chest, so his head wouldn't go under the water, and pouring water on his back and bottom, then onto his back again, letting him push his feet against the edge of the bath. It was like a merry-go-round. When the water had cooled, I'd take him out and give him to her so she could dress him.

The whole room was filled with their smell. What a smell. There's nothing in the world like it. If the dummy hadn't managed to calm them, I'd cuddle them and they'd start nosing around my shirt, searching for milk. Her shirt would be open all the time. She never closed it. I'd give them to her and watch how they opened their mouths wide to feed. It was like a game – her red circles swallowed up by theirs. I'd watch how she pushed with two fingers to take out the nipple when she thought her milk had finished, and I'd listen to the sound of their gulping. I loved looking at her face when they got into a good rhythm, because it made her feel good. I'd lie on my side and let them hold my finger with their whole hand as they were feeding, and stroke their hair with my other hand. It was beautiful hair. When you touched it, it was as if the hair rose up to stroke you instead.

Not once did she mention Dad. I was waiting for her to say his name. But even when there was a memorial for him, she didn't talk about him, just about what we had to do and who would babysit the twins while we were at the cemetery. She didn't shed any tears for him. She cried for her mum, who died in Morocco. When I thought about him, I'd wait for Mum to leave the room. Then I'd lie down on the left-hand side of the bed, his side. I'd fold the pillow in two, just as he did, put my head on it, and stretch my feet downwards, waiting for the day I could touch the end of the bed. Every time I did it, I'd see that I would soon be as tall as he was, that I'd soon cover the place where he slept. Dad was tall, taller than his brothers and the rest of his family. I'm 1.68m, and when I lie on the bed, I imagine his foot sticking out underneath mine.

Sometimes she'd close her eyes and talk to me. She'd say, 'Kobi, precious, go and wake Etti so she can help me. You get some sleep. You have school. Go on, it'd be a shame to miss all your studies.' So I'd go and see Etti, then come back and tell her Etti was dead to the world, that I couldn't wake her.

Before she finished feeding the twins, I knew she had to replace what she had given them. How else would she feed them again when they woke up? I'd stand in the kitchen, my face against the little coffee pot, close my eyes, feeling the milk boil. My skin would be as soft as a baby's again. When I heard the milk rise, I'd open my eyes, turn off the stove, put in two sugars and half a teaspoon of instant coffee, and take it into the bedroom. I'd also bring in three or four almonds from the bag I'd hidden at the top of the cabinet, because Rikki said I should only give them to her for her milk so it would be white and strong, not watery. We'd sit in bed and drink coffee and look at the twins together. Even when they went to sleep, we couldn't close our eyes. We just felt like looking at them all the time. I loved the quietness. Before the twins arrived, she shouted all the time. She'd raise her voice and never lower it. But when she came back from hospital with the twins, she talked quietly so they wouldn't wake up. After they'd fed, she'd wind them, patting them on the back: ha-ha-ha-hi, ha-ha-ha-hi.

Once I had a dream that she was holding a baby against her shoulder and the baby was me. The dream's coming back to me now. That's how it is with dreams: when you try to remember them, nothing;

when you turn your back, they ambush you. I dreamed I was a baby, making little throaty noises. She was holding me and patting me on the back to wind me. Again and again on my back and my bottom, again and again, quite hard, lifting me up to see if I've filled my nappy, and hitting me on the back, ha-ha-ha-hi, and on the bottom and pushing against me with her whole hand. I come on her, and she says, 'To your good health.' Why did I let her do that? And why couldn't I feel it?

Suddenly, the back pain. The screw is hammered into me with one mighty blow – no pencil, no drill, just shoved straight in.

But I don't double up. I just pull the sheet straight, put on my jacket, and walk down the hallway, holding on to the walls. Oshri and Chaim call me from the bedroom. I don't reply. They follow me. I sit down to put on my shoes, but my back won't allow me to do it. I don't have to say a word. Each twin takes a shoe and puts it on, tying the laces the way I taught them. It takes them ages. As I sit there, watching them, the pain melts away. They're beautiful when they're trying to be nice. Their heads are bent over the laces, and they hold the knot tightly so it won't slip. I glance at the picture of Dad on the wall. Why did I sit opposite it right now? So I'll look at Dad and remember I must not think of them as my children? When he died, it was as if his face was copied twice, like a key, and tossed back into the world. What can I do? I can't stand his picture being there. I wish I could take it down. I try to tell myself he can't see me, but his eyes land on me as soon as I set foot in the house.

They finish tying the laces, kiss me on both cheeks. I can tell who's who just from the kiss. Oshri's side is wet.

I get up and wrench open the door. I don't know what to say to them. I walk down the hallway of the old apartment and they're following me. I hold onto the terrorists' cupboard, and I say, 'This is the terrorists' cupboard. When you hear a big boom, you know terrorists are here, but you don't need to be afraid. Kobi's built somewhere for you to go. You climb up on a chair, take the key from the top of the cupboard, open it and go inside. There was a girl who stood behind the door of a cupboard and the terrorists didn't find her. They won't find you in here, either. Inside is a bottle of oil. You pour the oil on the floor, so the terrorists will slip on it and die, and then you close the door and sit quietly until I come to get you.' That's what I tell them, even though I know I won't be the one to come and get them. I'm dying to say: One day I'll take you away from all of this, not just the cupboard, or the house or the town, not just away from the Katyushas and the terrorists, but from everything. In Rishon they have no idea what we're going through here. They hear it on the radio, but they don't understand.

The twins can't wait to get into the cupboard. They're jumping around, going off to get a chair and drag it over, climbing on to it. It makes me feel like crying. I don't know why. It's just that when I see them happy, I feel like crying. It's not just with my own children, either. I always feel like crying when I see happy little kids.

I want to go, but they won't let me. They want me to stay with them all the time. I'm their dad. I take off my bar mitzvah watch. They can't believe I'm giving it to them. They look at it, feel its weight, put it to their ears. They both want to wear it. I haven't got the time. I don't want Mum to come back. Luckily Etti's fast asleep.

I tell them to check how long it takes them to run from their bed to the terrorists' cupboard, and make them take turns so they won't fight over who's the runner and who's the timekeeper.

Now I know what to do. I'm going to see Jamil. I go down the stairs, holding on to both sides. There's only one thing that'll get me out. I'm going to take all the money now. I've waited long enough and I can't wait any more. How long can a man wait? There's nothing here for me. I'm going abroad with my dollars. I'll fly to Norway, get married there. I don't need to learn Norwegian. Mordi says my looks will speak for themselves. I'll go and make a load of money, then I'll come back with my wife. I'll go to Rishon straight from the airport, suitcases and all, sign on the dotted line for the Model Apartment, give them the deposit there and then. I'll find a girl who's got the rest of the money for the apartment. I have to do it now. I've run out of time. I can't spend one more day in this hole.

I leave the building, walk to Mordi's house, and whistle. He sticks his head out of the window, shouts that he'll be down. I go and stand next to his car, and he follows me there, opening the door for me before getting in the driver's side. 'Go,' is all I say. 'Let's get out of here.' Mordi sees the mood I'm in and keeps quiet. He releases the handbrake, puts the car into gear. Two minutes later we're driving out of the town. I give him directions with nods – right, then left. He glances at me, drives silently. We drive for ten minutes. When we get to Jamil's village I tell him to stop. He puts a hand on my shoulder and says, 'Why, what's the matter?' I don't look at him. I can't. He says nothing more, removes his hand so I can get out. He doesn't drive away. I wave, telling him to go, and start walking. He drives after me, his window down, saying, 'I'm not leaving you here alone with the Arabs.' I tell him I'm going to see someone from the factory, smile to reassure him, so he won't worry about me, remind him about the alert, that it's not good to leave Fannie and the kid on their own. Finally, when he realises I'm serious, he drives away. I walk into the village. I don't know where to go. How am I supposed to know? The village is dead. There's not a single person walking around.

Why did I let Mordi drive away? I thought it was my own business, that I could manage. I didn't think it through. Now I wish he'd stayed. Why didn't I bring him into the village to get the money and then escape, fast? Why didn't I tell him about the Model Apartment? As I walk, all I can think is, 'Why, why, why?' What was I thinking to let him drive away? I'm not walking straight. The pain in my back is holding me in its grip, deciding what it'll do with my body, hammering that screw in with another mighty blow. If I do something to annoy the pain, it shoots a surge of electricity from my head to my legs. I have no answer; the little screw in my back controls everything I do.

I look around. Not one house is finished here. Everything is moving, growing, half-built, wherever you look. In one house there are stairs on the roof, but nothing above them; in another, stone cladding is finished on one wall and begun on the next. On some houses you can see where they've filled in with two or three rows of cinder bricks. There's sand, gravel and boarding everywhere. Nothing is completed. I walk around until I almost forget where I am. Suddenly it's starting to get dark. I don't want to believe it.

I don't know where to go, whether to head right or left. It seems as though the only colour left is black, as if they stole the colours while my back was turned, dragged them away from the houses, the closed shops, the clothes on the washing lines, the rubbish bins.

I wish I could lie down but there isn't a single pavement in the whole place. I'm dying to straighten out my back, to push it the other way. It's the only thing that helps with the pain. In the factory I close my door and lie on the floor until it passes. But as I sit down on the road, thinking about taking off my jacket so it won't get dirty, I hear the sound of children. I get up, wanting to run, but my back mocks me, making me walk like an old woman.

The children see me cross the street, and come over. I ask for the Khouri family. One of them speaks Hebrew and says, 'Which Khouris? There are lots of Khouris.'

I say, 'Jamil Khouri.'

'There are lots of those, too.'

I say, 'He's got blue eyes.'

He laughs, tells the rest of them in Arabic, and they laugh as well. 'All the Khouris have got blue eyes.'

In the end I say, 'The factory book-keeper.'

Then they take me to him, all of them. First they run ahead, but when they see I can hardly move, they walk next to me slowly, chattering all the time in Arabic. What are they talking about? Why are they laughing?

I catch a word here and there, but I can't understand the whole. It's not the Moroccan of my parents. Why did I let Mordi leave? What was I thinking? Why didn't I take him to Jamil's with me? Why-why, why-why. My head is pounding, as though the hammer is pounding in nails, twice for good measure – why-why, why-why – then, with its claw, taking them out again. The answer is: I don't know. I just don't know.

Seven or eight kids are standing behind me. '*Shoukran*,' I shout. I want them to go, but they don't move. I want to go back to the factory, take my clocking-in card, erase the last hour and start the whole day again. How can I go into his house now, with all these children looking at me? How can I break my word, the promise I made that he'd never see my face in his village so no one would suspect our deal. I can't forget how he looked at me with those blue eyes when I said, 'Either you trust me or you don't. There's no half-way house.'

The children knock on the door, and who opens it but Amin, who organises the factory transportation for people who live out in villages. The children call him Abu-Jamil. They say, '*Fi wahad yahdi bishal 'an Jamil.*' He shows me in, shakes my hand, goes and calls Jamil. I never realised that was his dad. I look at him in a different light, thinking maybe I was only seeing half the picture. Maybe he's in on the deal. Maybe everyone in the house knows. Maybe they're all spending my money.

I look around. The house is clean and neat. In the middle of one wall is a sink with soap and a towel. No bathroom, just a sink in the hallway. Jamil comes and takes me to a side room. A woman is sitting on the floor, chopping meat with a small knife. The room is tiny, and she's fat, taking up half the space. Her big blue dress, the same blue as her eyes, circles her like a pool of water. She's obviously Jamil's mother and it's also obvious that, on the plastic sheet in front of her, she's dicing a dead sheep. She throws the cubes of meat into a deep tray, takes out the liver and laughs. 'Want some? It's good for you, gives you strength. You eat it raw.' She cuts a few bloody slices and eats a slice raw, just like that.

Jamil is the Jamil I know from work. His white shirt is ironed and buttoned up to the neck. He doesn't laugh or cry or move. He's blank, like his mum. I can't understand how an educated, elegantly dressed guy has a mother like that, sitting barefoot on the floor in an old dress. We go past her and through another door into an inner room. I sit on the sofa. He takes a chair. He looks out of the window, doesn't look me in the eye. 'I'm not giving you the money,' he says. 'You can stay here for a while, having something to eat and drink, and my brother will take you back. Tomorrow, when you get up and go to work, you'll have forgotten. It'd be a shame to lose everything you've saved. Just a little more patience, and you can go and buy your apartment.' Now he's looking at me with those blue eyes, and I don't know what to do. He has all my money. It's as if it's locked away, with his promise as the password, and I don't know how to get to it. I don't have the password. He promised me, and his word is his bond. What can I do? I want to go mad, to start shouting, but I can't take it out on him. He sits there quietly, so I am powerless. If he shouted, 'Why did you come into my village?' I'd stand up to him, make no mistake. I'd take everything. In five minutes I'd be out of there.

But we sit in silence instead. My back's killing me. The sofa's missing a support, and sags in the middle. My back can't cope with it and I start to fidget. Jamil thinks we're finished. He gets up to go, but I don't move, grabbing the sofa arm instead.

Suddenly I see Mordi laughing at me. 'You're letting him make plans for you? Who does he think he is? Did you really think he wouldn't steal from you? You'll believe anyone, even an Arab. I can't believe you, Kobi. You gave all your money to an Arab? An Arab? How many times have I told you about not trusting an Arab, even one that's been dead forty years? How many times? You gave him seven thousand dollars? You've just thrown it away!'

I picture Mum, the white handbag banging against her, the brown stains I made on the mattress, the keys to the Model Apartment slipping away from me. I hear Yafit laughing at me, giving the keys to someone else. All of a sudden I'm going mad, jumping up and shouting, 'Give me the money. Where did you put my money?' Part of the sofa's wooden armrest has come off in my hand. I'm standing right in front of him. 'Kobi, what are you doing?' he says, and I hit him on the head with the armrest. He dodges to one side. I fall on to the chair. My back is shot to pieces.

I fall to the floor and curl up. I hear the door close. My head is exploding. I think I've twisted my foot. I can't feel my back – it's as though it has taken off, is flying somewhere. When it returns the screw has gone. The pain has moved down to my legs. I put my hands into my armpits. My jacket is torn on one side and my shirt has come undone, my belly sticking out. I want to get up, but my foot can't take my weight, and I fall back to the floor.

Someone opens the door. I turn my head. Jamil's mother is standing there, the knife in her hand. I close my eyes. She'll rip out my liver with one twist, and eat it raw, taking my strength.

6   The mother leaves. Jamil comes back in, helps me into a chair as if nothing happened, puts a package in my hand. He doesn't say a thing. There's a little scratch next to his eye from the armrest. His face is still blank. You wouldn't think I nearly took his eye out. I don't know where he's put his anger, how his blood isn't boiling, how he's looking at me with his blue eyes as if nothing happened. I open the plastic package and take out a brown envelope with 'Kobi' written on it, as well as some Arabic figures. I start to count the dollars. When I reach a thousand, I know the whole seven thousand is there. I can't look Jamil in the eye. I put the dollars back in the brown envelope and the envelope into the plastic bag, then I let the package fall to the floor. I start to cry and, like a kid, I can't stop.

I just sit there, holding my head and crying. Where are all the tears coming from? I can't see a thing. All I can feel is the water pouring out of my eyes. I don't know how to stop it. I'll have to wait for it to stop by itself. Crazy thoughts creep into my mind: maybe if I don't pay the water bill, they'll cut me off; all my blood is turning into water and coming out of my eyes. I can't do anything about it. What can I do? I'll just sit in Jamil's chair and wait until I have no more blood to shed.

Jamil takes off my shoe and my sock, then goes away and brings in another of his brothers, Zoheir, a nurse at the hospital. Jamil's scrawny but he's the opposite. He looks as though he could smash me into a pulp with one finger. My foot hurts. A dark-blue ball has swollen up. I'm suffering the pain in silence. I don't want to be a nuisance. He wraps a bandage around my foot. I don't want him to stop wrapping. His hands feel so good I want to kiss them. As smooth and fat as a baby's. It's as if the world is topsy-turvy and the babies are looking after the grown-ups. I wish he could wrap me in a bandage from my head to my feet.

His mother comes in with a cup of tea and a painkiller. They talk in Arabic. I don't want to understand them, don't even try to listen for words I know. I don't look for the package. I don't want to see it. What do I want? Just for them to take me somewhere, feed me, put me to sleep, talk in their language about what to do with me. I want them to tuck me in, wake me in the morning, send me to work, take my salary and guard it for me. I want them to bring me a woman to marry, to tell me what I have to do every minute of the day.

Jamil's brother puts a sock over the bandage. They take me to eat with them. I put one hand on Jamil's shoulder and the other on his brother's shoulder. At the table they sit me in a chair. From elsewhere in the house, other people come. Where were they hiding? I just sit there. Everyone comes to me, so I won't have to stand up. I shake hands with his dad, his brothers. They all sit down and start to eat. Two minutes later, we hear two loud booms, one after the other.

I don't know how I could have forgotten about the alert. I get up when I hear the first boom, wanting to go to the shelter, and they say, 'What shelter? We don't have shelters like you. Sit down and eat. This is the best room – the wall is almost a metre thick.' So we eat the meat, the rice, the salads, hear the second boom, and carry on eating. I never imagined that Katyushas might land here. I don't know why. I just didn't think Katyushas would fall in an Arab village. A few minutes later, a short, thin guy comes in, talking quickly. Jamil translates into Hebrew for me: 'Two Katyushas fell in the town. The electricity's out. The second one landed in the town centre, no doubt about it. He's the uncle, the headteacher of the school. He saw everything from his roof – the ambulances and fire engines, too.'

They sit me back down, put more food on my plate. The headteacher says in Hebrew, 'I'm begging the Katyusha to come and fall on the school, but it didn't happen.' Everyone at the table laughs with him, and he looks at me because I'm not laughing. 'The school is empty and each Katyusha means millions of government money. With two I could build a gym so good that all the villages in the area would use it.'

I think that if I've got any human decency, I should be worrying about my family. I have to run and help them. Our apartment is fifty metres from the centre of town. I look at Jamil. But he hasn't realised what he's said. He doesn't know where I live. I don't tell him. I don't want to think about what might have happened. I don't want to decide who will live and who will die. I don't want to decide about money. I don't want to decide where they should live and what they should do. Instead I pretend I'm someone from the village, someone who eats lamb prepared by his mother every day. Take another pitta. Don't think about shelters.

Zoheir hands me another pitta. 'Eat, eat. Don't be shy.' I scoop the food from the little bowls with the pitta like everyone else. I start to taste the food, to feel my hunger, to love their house. I sit and I eat just like everyone else.

Jamil's little brother catches my eye, laughter racing all over his face, coming and going quickly so the grown-ups don't see. I'm the only one who sees him laughing, the only one who knows he's playing with a ball under the table. When his dad picks him up to give him a nice piece of meat, he catches my eye again and rolls the ball over to me so I can keep it for him. When he sits down, I roll it back with my good foot. He's the little one in the family. Someone's always watching out for him, or thinking about what's good for him. We eat, the two of us, not looking at each other, but rolling the ball back and forth underneath the table. I glance at him, catch the laughter as it runs from his eye to the side of his mouth. Suddenly I feel his laughter setting me alight, and I'm laughing, too, though no one can see. When he sees that, he passes the ball to one side so I have to move quickly to catch it. Then I bring the ball back to the middle, keep it under my chair, wait, drink, eat, until I see it's driving him mad, and then I roll it back to him. He gets up again, sitting with his uncle this time. The ball's under my chair. After he's gone I ask Jamil, 'How old is the kid?' Jamil doesn't understand who I mean. It's only when the kid sits back down that he catches on. 'Who, Amir?' he says. 'He's the little one of the house. He'll be thirteen this month.'

ETTI DADON

1

My mind went blank when it fell. It was a horrible one. The electricity went out. Then another fell straight away, a million times stronger and even more horrible. I couldn't think of a thing, couldn't remember a thing, and everyone else was the same: grown-ups, old people, children, babies. We all forgot everything. We just screamed.

The scream seemed to spread out in the darkness of the stairwell where we were, making us into a single mass, a monster with many feet, trembling hands and open mouths. Then, afterwards, memory began to resurface. Children started to yell 'Mama' and 'Papa', parents called out their children's names, someone shouted, 'Why is the shelter closed?'

With its dozens of mouths – asking, accusing, imploring – the monster repeated, 'Why is the shelter closed?'

A voice thundered, 'Where's the key? Someone should bring the key.'

The monster echoed, 'The key.'

Hands met in the darkness. 'Is that you, Eliko? Is that you?'

'Meital, where's Meital? I can't see Meital?'

'I'm here, Mum,' chirped a voice.

The monster began to move, sorting itself into families. Its limbs tore themselves apart and melted into six storeys of darkness, calling the names of absent children, begging for them. The echoes of the names went up and down the stairwell like an out-of-control lift, hitting the monster on the head.

'Where's the key?' the monster screamed again. 'Quick, somebody, bring the key before another one falls on us!' The scream changed to a wail, and one head climbed the stairs to look for the key.

Before he came back, the monster swelled again, its limbs complete once more, the missing ones sobbing, complaining, accusing.

'How can you stay in the house when you hear Katyushas?'

'I almost got killed trying to find you!'

'Don't shout at him. Look how white he is!'

'How can you see he's white when I can't see a thing?'

'Let him pass!'

'Let him . . .'

'He's got the key. Let him pass. He's got the key.'

The monster pleaded with itself, but instead of thinning out, it becomes even more solid, pushing against the shelter door. Then a calm, assured voice managed to soften the monster's body, to slip inside.

Then the shelter was open.

Inside everything was bare. The light of torches and candles was the opposite of the midday sun, which now seemed more beautiful than any holiday or Sabbath. It was a Cinderella light, weak and yellow, a light of tattered rags, waiting for the fairy godmother to arrive.

Small children clinging to their parents suddenly pulled back. Something in the hug suddenly seemed strange, and they wanted to reassure themselves it really was Mama or Papa. Everyone moved as though they were in the belly of a whale. I was trembling. I couldn't breathe. My stomach felt like a bag of sharp stones, felling me to the floor in one swoop. My hands flew up to my frozen cheeks, to support my forehead, which felt as cold and as heavy as iron.

In the silence I watched people moving their lips. Marcelle said something and passed her baby to me, along with the bottle and the muslin. I held Asher tightly – he was kicking and his face was red, his eyes swollen. I put the bottle near his little open mouth and he attached himself to it straight away, sucking on the teat. Then he stopped fighting me and closed his eyes.

The heavy buzz of voices began to disperse. Marcelle touched my hand. 'Hold the bottle high,' she said. 'Then he won't gulp air. What can I do? Yehuda's never here when I need him.' Asher sucked in a steady rhythm. 'I have to go to Yasmin,' she said. 'Take it easy; you're shaking.' The stones in my belly became soft, and round like pebbles.

The bottle wasn't empty, but Asher was asleep. Now and then, his eyes closed, he took another sip. I felt my bra pinching me. I didn't know if I was supposed to take the bottle out of his mouth, but I didn't dare move to ask. I didn't want him to wake up, and I didn't want to look at anyone. It felt good, sitting with him, as if we were the only two people in the shelter.

But we weren't. Yasmin was screaming and Marcelle was trying to calm her down. 'Sweetheart, the vents just let the air in,' she said. 'Katyushas can't get in. They aren't windows, just tubes that bring us air. Don't look at them, darling. Come and put your head down here. Look at Eliko sitting quietly – what a sweetie.'

But Yasmin kept crying, breathing in the smell of fear created by the parts of the monster now scattered around the shelter.

Asher's hair was damp with sweat and stuck to his head. I saw a louse crawling between the hairs, and for the first time noticed the parts of its body: the head, the legs, the transparent parts, the brown back. Lice disgust me. As my arm fell asleep under his head, the louse began to look like Little Red Riding Hood walking through the forest, not knowing when the wolf would pop out. I suddenly wanted to scratch my head, just as I do when other people scratch themselves or talk about lice, but I didn't have a spare hand to scratch with.

Yasmin burst into a long wail and started running towards the shelter door. Everyone told Marcelle she should give her daughter a slap, that it was the only way she'd snap out of her hysterics.

Suddenly, other voices piped up, loud ones. People were fighting: over mattresses, over blankets, over who was taking the most room. Others untied the chains attaching the iron bed frames to the walls, opening them out, and immediately climbing up and lying down, sticking Sabbath candles to the iron frame with candle wax. Faces flickered from the beds, just like the picture we saw in school on Holocaust Day. I can't forget it. I close my eyes and whisper, 'Everyone knows there's no comparison. It's not the same thing at all.' But other pictures came into my head then, a chain of them: the double-decker bus where skeletons lay in striped pyjamas, the wagons heaped with white corpses, the barbed wire . . . my thin, trembling hand stretched through a hole in the wire to grasp a crust of bread someone was passing to me.

Then I hear shouts. Five or six people were attacking Shmuel Cohen, who had locked the shelter at midday and gone to sleep with the key.

'He was fast asleep. It was the Katyushas that woke him. He was by himself, Ziona and the children have gone to her sister's in Beersheba,' Marcelle said. 'He was shaking in his bed in the dark. He couldn't move until Yehuda went to get the key and found him gripping it in his hand. I don't understand what he could have been thinking, Etti. Did he think the key would save him?'

Shmuel looked at the floor, his chin sunk into his collar. 'I locked it because of the children,' he said. 'They were going wild playing in here. *Your* children' – he raised his head a little – 'not mine.'

'We almost died because of you, Shmuel, *died*,' they moaned, then rebuked themselves for not kicking up a fuss at the water company, so they'd finally come to fix the drains, for not cleaning up a little, for not bringing some blankets and women's magazines.

'*Halas,* stop moaning,' someone said. 'How would you have kept it all safe? It would have been stolen or wrecked.'

Everyone quietened down then, turning their backs on each other, drawing imaginary lines around themselves and settling down on their mattresses. I leaned against the wall, watching the children being tucked in, four to a mattress, head to toe. 'Put your head down, sweetheart,' soothed their parents, and sleep began to open little doors here and there, sneaking the children inside, one after another, until they were all gathered up inside. Then it was night-time.

It was just seven or eight o'clock, but night had fallen upon us in a moment, a private, local night, like rain falling from a single cloud. There were no hours, no minutes. It was as if our time was separated from normal time, racing ahead until it had to stop and rest, to wait for normal time to catch up. Only then will we become part of the daily news programme, maybe even the main headline.

I heard everything that happened, saw it and smelled it, but I remember nothing. I felt like a part of the baby and the bottle, my hand attached to the bottle, the hand of a girl with a mother and siblings. But they're not here.

Not one of them was here. In the darkness, I went into a different building by mistake, number 122. I ran here – my legs remember – right after the first Katyusha, like a little girl who sees someone who looks like her papa from behind and grabs his sleeve by mistake.

2   Yehuda, Marcelle's husband, came in. He works in the maintenance department at the Council. He's the one that opened the shelter for us then disappeared. All the men got up the minute he came, and the women stood, too. I looked at him through a tunnel of people, and saw his mouth open to speak like a red cave inside his moustache and beard.

'It's Big Amsalam,' said the mouth. 'We took him to hospital. They don't know if he'll be OK. You know Big Amsalam – his wife was six months pregnant when she lost the baby last year.'

She used to work at Mama's nursery, but not everyone knew who he meant. The ones who didn't know got an explanation from those who did, leading them on a twisting path to remembering that man, whose face they would have recognised in the street and only now attach to his name.

'Big Amsalam, Itzik Amsalam. Suddenly no one knows who that is?'

'Amsalam from the hardware shop?'

'No, not him.'

'You mean Meir from Housing. With a wife called Susie?'

'Susie? *Shequn huway abuah*?'

'*Bint Elyahu "Amar"*?'

'*Aywa*!'

'Why didn't you just say it was Eliyahu's daughter?'

'That's what I said. Not her sister Mazal, the one with the limp?'

'Nu, who's her husband?'

'Who's her husband? Hasiba's son?'

'The guy who almost won a million in the pools?'

'Not him – his older brother, Amsalam, who works in the defence industry.'

Over and over, without tiring of it, they traced their own paths to Big Amsalam, before someone lost their way and had to start again.

In minutes, names and stories were flying around the shelter, each summed up in one sentence: 'the one who once went out with Simcha from the building where the mad woman lives'; 'the one whose sister-in-law's daughter once went out with an Arab, an educated one, actually, who went to Romania to become a dentist – he's back now';

'the one whose brother works on a new Volvo truck that has ten gears'; 'the one whose baby was born handicapped on Maimouna night and they left it in the hospital – didn't you hear about that?'

All this new information rustled in the cramped space, and the confused faces looked squashed and tense and as if they were about to split, like tangerines with a thin peel. I knew my face looked exactly the same.

Now everyone was talking softly, passing water bottles back and forth, offering clean nappies, toilet paper, rubbish bags, headache pills, blankets, even mattresses: 'Go on, have it. Don't be shy. We have two already, and they could sleep together, warm each other up.'

They started to replay the explosions, to compare them with others. 'There's no question, this time was the worst,' someone would throw out, and immediately a reply would bounce back: 'What about the Katyushas that fell last Lag b'Omer?' Then another would say, 'What about the ones that fell on the industrial estate? We all heard those and everyone ran to see where they had landed.' People joined in on one side or another, like teams in a game. 'He's right!' 'What do you mean?' 'It's true. There's no comparison.' But then everyone started putting their own cards on the table – they looked just like card sharps – and comparing anyway. I thought about how old I was when the terrorists came that first time and then what happened the second time, and then where I was and what I was doing in all the bombings and raids and alerts that came after. As I looked around I realised we'd got a new card, a valuable new card that we could use later.

'*Dir balqum*, be careful of the candles,' Yehuda said. 'I brought some torches with me. Everyone keep an eye on their candles so that nothing catches fire.' People asked him more questions about the wounded man and about the damage outside, but instead he announced that bread would be given out by the Council first thing tomorrow morning, that everyone needed to be patient, that the chief of staff himself was on his way here, and that the electricity company were working as fast as they could to restore power, and that there was a good chance they'd fix it in three or four hours.

I could see everyone was listening to Yehuda. They were almost relaxed, wanting him to start again, to make something up. Who cared? Let him stand there and tell us anything – dreams, lies, whatever.

We'll believe you, I vowed with all my heart. No one will stop you. No one will argue with you. We almost died but we didn't, and here we're stripped of everything: responsibilities, work, homework, quarrels and troubles. We have all the time in the world, time is sitting here with us on a mattress in a shelter.

Time wasn't skipping ahead of us for once. We could rest and imagine we were the lead actors in a film about life and death.

The silence Yehuda created was broad and deep, like the Red Sea before Moses split it in two. He stroked his beard, opened his red cave of a mouth, silence flooding it. He coughed a little, maybe skipping over what he didn't want to tell us, and anyway, none of us wanted to hear where we were and what we did when the second Katyusha fell, or where Yehuda was and what he was doing. A brave man among cowards. I wondered if he would tell other people in other shelters about us, how we shoved against the locked shelter door, how we screamed, and how he was the only one to act like a man and go to find the key. I knew, too, that by tomorrow morning, everyone in town would know that our shelter was locked, and that, when Shmuel Cohen's family came back from Beersheba, they'd lock themselves in their apartment, as if they were in a shelter, to avoid people's stares. From today they'd be known as 'the one whose husband was sleeping with the key to the shelter during the bombing' or 'the daughter of Cohen, who locked the shelter of one-twenty-two during the bombing' or even 'the one who nearly killed us all during the bombing'.

But Yehuda skipped over that part, taking us instead out of the shelter and into the town centre. We followed him in our minds, as if we too had the courage to wander about outside on such a night. 'There's broken glass everywhere,' he said. 'The supermarket windows exploded in the blast. The second Katyusha fell a hundred metres from here – eighty metres perhaps. We're the closest building,' he added, and the together-monster was happy to hear that, because now it was safe so it wanted death to be as close as possible so it could feel how lucky it was to have been saved by a miracle.

'It won't be easy to get the centre back to how it was,' Yehuda said. 'It'll take months and months.' The army was all over the place at the moment, he told us, but there would be a guard there by early tomorrow morning to stop looting. As soon as the mêlée was over, they'd start rebuilding. 'The phone booth was hit, too,' he continued. 'You wouldn't think shrapnel could go so far. It's lucky, really lucky, that the supermarket was closed because of the alert. Just think what could have happened if the second Katyusha had fallen on a normal day when the supermarket was busy! You don't want to think about it happening on a Thursday night when it's full of people.' He paused, leaving us just enough time to picture every detail, before going on to talk about the mayor, who had reached the area first. He had no idea how he got to places so quickly. 'He pops up every time something happens, wherever it is,' he said, his voice seeming torn between admiration for the mayor and disappointment that he was never caught out.

Then he turned our minds to Big Amsalam (now everyone knew who he was), who was hit by shrapnel from the first Katyusha, which fell on the pavement of the north side of town – and he was lucky it was only shrapnel. 'If he'd crossed the street half a minute earlier, he'd be dead now,' Yehuda said, looking at the mass of people opposite him, the many hands, feet and ears of the together-monster, which looked disappointed, its thirst for his stories still not slaked. He coughed a little and brought death even closer. 'Did I say half a minute? It wasn't even a quarter of a minute. He was at most ten seconds away from a direct hit.' The monster growled in thanks, and edged closer to hear how Amsalam lay in his blood.

'They tried to treat him on the spot, but it was too dark to see anything. So I got into the car, put my foot to the floor, turned the car around and parked with two wheels on the pavement, shining the headlights on him.' The picture in the monster's mind was sharp and clear. We all knew Big Amsalam now, his broad shoulders and neck which looked as though they could carry the whole planet rather than just his head, and we all knew the maintenance department's pickup truck, too, which Yehuda drives with the door half open, ready to jump out, like a horse that knows the right moment to stop.

'What can I tell you? I'm looking at him and I can't see where he was hit because of all the blood. It's all over his face and legs, too, and his hands, but maybe that was because he touched the blood and spread it around. He was conscious, awake, but in shock. We couldn't get a word out of him. It was twenty-five minutes before the ambulance arrived. Avi Suissa went with him, his sister Esti's husband. They didn't tell his wife because of her condition – she had a miscarriage last time, poor thing. They'll tell her when they know more.'

In the darkness of the shelter, the together-monster heard the ambulance siren fading into the distance, saw the pickup's headlights on the yawning crater left by the Katyusha and the scraps of shrapnel scattered everywhere. The electricity pylon was twisted, which was why the town's electricity had been cut off, the tree next to it sliced in two, and chickens lay dead on the ground. 'I couldn't believe my eyes,' said Yehuda, shutting both of them for some reason, both witnesses, and putting his hand on his heart, 'but Ziva and Shimi's chickens had all been slaughtered.' That word finished his story, like a seamstress fitting a new dress on a client and then tearing off the collar at the end. That one word, thrown into the hollow of the shelter, exploded people's restraint, and everyone started screaming at once: 'We won't keep quiet this time!' 'We'll show them what we're made of!' 'Who do they think they are?' They wanted a quick and bloody revenge, because what else could they do with their shame? Shame about the way they behaved when the Katyusha fell, the way they screamed and trembled and trampled, the way they only looked out for themselves, the way they became a part of the together-monster.

Yehuda came up to me, leaning over to take the sleeping Asher from me. My arms were revealed – painful, red and damp. He turned back, seeming to remember something. 'Don't worry,' he said. 'I'll get to your shelter in a while and I'll tell them you're OK.' My arms, used to Oshri and Chaim – one twin on the right, the other on the left – were empty.

3 I tried with all my might. I really tried, but I couldn't remember a thing. I was still trapped within the monster, breathing, thinking, being with everyone else.

The first thing that came to me was that I had to go to the toilet. I took a prayer candle with me. As usual, the floor was covered with water. I tried to tiptoe but my feet still got wet. I closed the iron door behind me and bolted it. I managed to pee without sitting on the seat, which looked disgusting even by candle-light, having practised this at school, where the toilet is also filthy. I just put my legs either side of the toilet and moved my hips forward, like a belly dancer.

Afterwards I left the candle on the floor and walked out. Three women were queuing in front of the puddle, their gazes trained to the floor. I lowered my head, too. This wasn't the time to be sociable. Back in the shelter it was as if I had been gone for hours. A great drowsiness had fallen upon everyone, but then I saw people gathering in little hands that had fallen off mattresses here and there, fixing their hair, hugging their knees, rubbing a cracked heel. Marcelle waved at me from the other end of the shelter. Yasmin and Asher were lying sideways on the mattress, and she'd made a space for me, too.

It was only when I sat down, leaning my back against the wall and closing my eyes – pretending to be asleep so no one would talk to me – that I remembered everything: the sixth anniversary of my father's death tomorrow, and the memorial that might be cancelled because of the raid; Dudi and Itzik and their kestrel; Mama and Kobi; Oshri and Chaim, who had disappeared and I didn't know where. And finally – finally, like an unneeded tail that can't be discarded – I remembered our family's lie, which has itself become a family member, a lie born after Chaim and Oshri, a lie which changed all of our lives.

The shelter was quiet. Almost everyone was asleep or pretending to be asleep. Husband and wife lay, not touching, one or two children sleeping between them. Coughs were heard here and there. Maybe a speck of dust was happy about the slurry of people that had come its way, and was jumping merrily from one person to the next, bursting out of one mouth and then another, before flying and landing somewhere else, enjoying the chorus of coughs it was causing. Marcelle and her children lay mingled together. She looked like a little girl, too, one who had fallen asleep crying. On her fingers were Asher's dummy, Yasmin's hair band, and Yehuda's wedding ring, as if she had married all three and could hold the whole family in one hand.

The most important thing was to find Oshri and Chaim.

Yesterday we came back from nursery as we do every day – Oshri on my right hand and Chaim on my left. Their soft little hands make me forget everything, the awful mornings, the school – Etti who counts the hours, hoping people will ignore her, will just let her listen and not ask her questions or notice that she finds it hard to read, not ask her to talk, to be their friend, to touch them. All she wants is her radio, and every time someone gets too close, her hand reaches into her bag for it. All this is wiped away when my brothers stick their little hands in mine and ask, 'Etti, come and play "who's my twin".'

I took out Mama's headscarf, which I also kept in my bag, right at the bottom. She won't wear it because it's not widowish enough. It's been in my bag for six years, along with everything else: notebooks, books, food, handouts, tests, pencils, rubbers, plasters, cotton wool all come and go, but Mama's colourful headscarf and my radio stay put. I tied the scarf around my eyes, and they made sure I couldn't see. Then they let me feel their hand or foot, or an ear or some hair. When I touched it, I knew immediately but I felt it for a minute before saying 'Chaim' or 'Oshri'. I was always right. They couldn't understand how I did it, because everyone in town, with their eyes wide open, gets them mixed up. Even the nursery teacher writes their names on a cardboard label and pins it to their shirts.

Then we played the candle game. I close my eyes and put my fist out, the thumb sticking up like a candle. One of them blows on it to put out the candle, and I have to guess which one it is by the breath that tickles my thumb.

I made three wrong guesses, but the fourth time I noticed that when Oshri blows, tiny droplets as light as air touch my skin, like a distant sprinkler blown by the wind.

Then they climbed the fence behind me for the next game. One jumps onto my back, hugging my neck. I turn him round quickly and lower him on to the pavement. Oshri and Chaim weigh exactly the same. When they were weighed at the baby clinic, the nurse was always amazed. 'The same weight to the gram,' she'd say to Mama. 'Are you sure I haven't weighed the same one twice?'

I can't tell which one is which by weight. But Chaim, who is more anxious, almost chokes me when I turn quickly, so I can identify him that way.

4 There in the shelter, I examined our lie. Face to face. No one made it up; it was just born by and from itself. It's the kind of lie that doesn't hide inside a secret. It came home, stood up straight, and said, 'I'm the lie. I believe you invited me?' Then it got so excited and confused it almost fell down the stairs, so we ushered it into the apartment, closed the door, and stood around it in a circle. 'Stop making so much noise,' we said to it. 'We know you're not the truth. You don't have to shout. We all know who you are and why you're here.'

Then it became a little lie, a small thing, easy to swallow. A one-word lie, that was all. It was like an aspirin, which leaves a bitter taste in your mouth if you insist on chewing it. But no one insists. Why would they? You swallow it and then forget it.

It started when Chaim and Oshri were almost a year old and saying 'ba-ba-ba' and then 'ba-ba pa-pa'. I said, 'Why are they saying "papa" when they don't have a papa?'

Babies that don't have a father should say 'ma-ma' first.

196

But for some reason it took them a long time before they managed to say 'mama'. They'd purse their lips and say 'ti-ti', which is what they called me.

So they said 'ba-ba-ba-ba', and when Kobi came home, they'd reach up their hands to be picked up. That's how it was. He'd come home from school, pick the two of them up together and spin them around and throw them in the air. They were scared but laughing, so he'd do it again, and they'd say 'pa-pa, pa-pa' and that was it. From then on he was Papa. Papa's home.

But Chaim and Oshri grew, and so did the lie. I could see it was getting bigger and bigger, spreading into every corner of the apartment without asking permission, and I started to worry it would try to get into my head, too. I decided to fight it, but I didn't know how, so I waited and I waited. I saw how the lie was making Mama and Kobi sleep together in the big bed, as if they were bride and groom, how Kobi wasn't going out with girls like his friends, how he made decisions instead of Mama and how she let him get angry with us, as though he wasn't just our brother. And she didn't even organise a bar mitzvah for Itzik. How could she if she gives Kobi all her salary from the nursery?

I spent every day in despair because of the lie. I didn't know what to do about it. Then in school we learned the story of Jacob, who became tangled in his own lies and those of other people, becoming the first-born because of a lie, and then marrying a first-born daughter because of lie. So I decided to invent a new story for the twins, one that would be strong enough to fight against the lie.

I kept thinking: Why don't Oshri and Chaim see the lie? Why

haven't they worked it out? They could if they wanted to. It isn't difficult to see that someone of Kobi's age couldn't be my father, or Itzik and Dudi's. It's not hard to notice that we don't call him 'Papa'. Kobi's bar mitzvah photo is evidence enough. But when I look at Papa in the photo, I remember he didn't know about the twins before he died. He felt no excitement or expectation. He never even began to be their father.

I got up from the mattress. I straightened my knees but they hurt. I wanted to walk. My whole body was crying out to move, especially my legs, but there wasn't room to take a single step. The shelter seemed fuller, suddenly, as if everyone had swollen up mid-sleep, like baking rolls in an oven. I rolled my neck to loosen my neck muscles, then felt dizzy and had to lean against a wall. My shirt was wrinkled, and a button had fallen off – the top one, of course. I held onto it to stop it opening. Marcelle, who had woken up, saw me doing this, and, whispering to Ahuva, got a safety-pin from her bag. 'So there won't be any trouble,' Marcelle said, and carefully pinned my shirt together.

I took the rubber band off my plait and spread out my hair. Then I ploughed it with my fingers until it was divided into three long snakes – one in one hand, and two in the other – which I passed from hand to hand, until they were twisted and plaited. I smoothed the plait to the end, to check whether any strands of hair had twisted out, and then I wrapped the band around it. My head felt alive then, and there was a pleasant feeling in the nape of my neck, where my hair was gathered.

I undid it and spread it out again. I made a parting at the back with my fingers and made it into two equal parts. Then I started making two plaits, strand after strand, tightening and tightening again. I borrowed Yasmin's hair band from Marcelle for the second plait. She smiled a sleepy smile, and I felt a smile rise in my cheeks and eyes, too. Half asleep, Marcelle drank in my smile, like a baby drinking *kiddush* wine from his father's fingers. I remembered how Papa used to dip his little finger in the silver cup and put the end of it to Dudi's mouth for him to suck.

It was very hot yesterday, and Chaim and Oshri had fallen asleep. Itzik was in his room with the bird, and I listened outside the door. He was talking to it the way men in films talk to their lovers. 'Delilah, Delilah,' he repeated. He and Dudi gave it a girl's name, not knowing it was a male. The plumage of a male kestrel looks female when it's young. By chance I heard Azaria Allon talking about it on my radio, and I turned it off immediately. I didn't want to hear about kestrels.

I've never got close to the bird, not even when Oshri begged me, tugging my hand and pulling me towards the old kitchen. I don't get close to Itzik, either. Maybe it's because of his hands, because he makes a show of them, so that people will see how twisted they are. His eyes are like shovels, always turning things over, and I was afraid they'd make him think I was repelled by him rather than his hands.

I took out the rubbish and hid the bucket in the bushes. Then I made my way to the nursery, to Mama. My feet started running almost by themselves, as if they too wanted to talk. Then I wondered if I was really running away, trying to get to the nursery before I was caught by 'You'll Be Sorry' and 'You'll Be Ashamed', who follow me everywhere. They certainly had discovered that I'd left the house without them, because they immediately started shouting after me, 'You'll-Be-Ashamed-and-You'll-Be-Sorry', so loud the whole street could hear. But I didn't listen.

It was afternoon nap-time, I thought. The children are asleep and I can talk to her. I'll just tell her, in simple terms, that it's impossible to carry on like this, that she has to tell the twins the truth before someone says something horrible in the street or in school. They'll be at school in a few months and then it'll be too late. Mama never went to school here and she doesn't know how cruel the playground can be. What does she know about school? Just what she hears at parents' meetings. I stood up to my pursuers and said exactly what my brothers will hear in a few months at break-time:

'My brother Zion swears to me on the Torah that your dad is dead!'

'Everyone knows Kobi is just your brother!'

'You don't have a dad!'

'Tell me, who doesn't know who their dad is?'

And, as if that won't be enough:

'Who doesn't know your mum is fucking your brother Kobi?'

5   'A woman can do without it, but, for a man, one week is like eternity!'

It was the voice of Ricki, the cook. I stopped on my way up the path, hugged the wall and walked quietly, so they couldn't see me. They only had the screen door closed. Every day at the same time they sit near the entrance on low children's chairs around the little table. I could hear laughter, but didn't recognise Mama's laugh, which always sounds as though she's trying to cough it up. I couldn't hear Aliza's melodious laugh, either.

'There isn't a man alive who'll get my body before the wedding,' Sylvie declared.

Levana replied in Moroccan and they laughed again.

'*Yalla*, girls,' Ricki prodded them, 'are you glued to the chairs? No cleaning elves are coming to help us today.'

I heard them moving the table back to its usual place, and reminded myself why I was here. But, for a moment, all I could think about was the man of their conversation. I pictured him as a letter, as I did when I was a girl, with the broad shoulders of the letter 'm' in 'man'. One leg kicking forward, with a little head and protruding eyes. He looked a little like Itzik's kestrel. His hands were jammed into his pockets, hugging his body – it was hard for him to do without. Then I saw a woman in the letter 'w'. She was belly-dancing, as if she were alone in the world, her hands raised and her legs spread, her long hair covering her bottom.

Suddenly the screen door opened and dirty mopping water splashed onto me. Levana, mop in hand, said, 'My goodness, you gave me a fright! Come in, come in. Are you here to see your mama? Wait for me to put a dry cloth down so you don't bring in any water.'

I went to the toddler room where Mama and Aliza worked. The kids were asleep on little iron beds. The air was full of sleepy breathing. One bed was empty, its sagging green canvas inviting me to climb in and go to sleep in the sweet-smelling cloud of pee and vegetable soup.

I found Mama and Aliza in the children's toilet. They were taking white cloth nappies out of the children's bags, all clean and dry, and, one by one, dipping them in the toilet where they had rinsed the dirty nappies. They didn't notice me, and when they did, Mama was worried until I swore everything was fine at home. Then she went back to what she had been doing, wetting dry, clean nappies in the toilet.

'Etti, my precious,' said Aliza, 'just guard the door so no mothers come in. Then we can finish these, *chic-choc.*'

And Mama said, 'You never get a word of thanks from them, never. Not even for a good job sewing doll's clothes. Where do they look first? In the bag of shit, counting the nappies. What do they think they're going to find? A diamond?' She dips another nappy in the toilet. 'If there aren't four dirty nappies in the bag, they jump on you: "Why didn't you change his nappy?" She starts yelling, then, saying her kid was running around in pee half the day. If their bottoms are red, it's the nursery's fault. God forbid you should say it's because they forgot to change their kid at night.'

She stood up, then, her hand on her hip. She said she was dying for a cup of instant coffee with milk, that it was the only thing which would help her back.

Aliza gestured to me to take Mama's place. I looked at them for a minute. I wanted to say something but I didn't. Instead I took a dry nappy from Mama. As I leaned over the toilet, I saw my face reflected there, as if I'd fallen into the water in Mama's wake.

'Aliza's dipped the nappies in the toilet,' Aliza said in a bitter yet sugary tone. 'She's done one each for Rosette and Shula, two for Yaffa, another one for Annette, but there's none left for Sima! So she went and looked, she looked everywhere, and lo and behold, she found one for Sima.' I kept looking at my face in the toilet. Every time Aliza wrung out a nappy, the image was distorted. I've already started thinking like them: 'Moshiko's got two dirty ones, so we'll wet him another, and then, when he gets up, we'll change him again. That way he'll have four dirty ones and his mum will be happy.'

Aliza passed me the soap. She washed her hands, dried them, and looked at herself in the mirror. Her face seemed cleaned of anger and resentment. From the pocket of her smock she took out a pair of tweezers and expertly plucked the hairs that had grown outside the narrow line of her eyebrows. 'Wash your hands properly and then come and sit with us,' she said to me, still looking in the mirror. 'Whoever works deserves to rest.'

I realised that if I tried to talk to Mama, to say that the time had come to tell the truth, I'd sound like a baby who wouldn't let go of a broken doll. 'Oh, Etti, where are you, and where is life!' she'd say.

I went back home and decided to tell them myself.

I tried to picture my family in the shelter. Kobi would be standing near the door, waiting to go out, as if he was saying to himself, 'I'm just here for a while – this isn't really me', like a mannequin in a shop window telling herself she's not part of the noisy, dirty street. Oshri and Chaim would hardly take up half a mattress. They sometimes curl up in the washing tub, saying, 'Look, Etti, look! This is how we were in Mama's tummy!' Dudi would be wandering around, looking to make people laugh, to make friends. Itzik would be calling Dudi to come and help with the kestrel, which would be annoying everyone in the shelter. Mama would be trying to make everyone sit quietly, so that people wouldn't talk about us after it was all over, not even about Itzik and his bird. And if Oshri and Chaim aren't in the shelter, she'd be praying that Yehuda would come in and tell her he found the little ones in a different shelter, just like he found me.

Where are they, though? I can't remember where I left them, where I was before the Katyushas fell.

I made my way home from the nursery with a new lie, then I did my Bible study homework. It was a normal evening, and then night fell. I went to sleep with Oshri and Chaim. A few hours later I woke up, got out of their bed, and drew the covers up to their necks. It was late. I saw Dudi was sleeping, and I went into the hallway and stood outside Mama and Kobi's door. I pressed my ear to the door but I didn't hear anything. I thought about opening it, but I didn't dare.

I went to my own bed, but I couldn't sleep. I went out onto the balcony and looked at the washing that Mama had pegged out that evening. The washing lines look like the lines of a poem. 'Mama's dress' or 'Itzik's trousers' sit on them like words, the pegs like commas. Mama's dress, comma, Itzik's elasticated trousers, comma, Dudi and Itzik's shirts, comma, Kobi's white shirt, comma, Oshri and Chaim's socks, comma, my school skirt, comma, Mama and Kobi's sheet, full stop. In simple, clear language, our clothes told the outside world we were a family, but inside it was a different story. In truth, there wasn't a single day when everyone's clothes – Papa, Mama and six children – hung together on one line.

6   Quietly I went back into the twins' room and covered them up again. I was wide awake. I took my bag and went to the terrorists' cupboard. I had never opened it. Every time I passed it, I was reminded that it was Kobi's cupboard, not mine.

The year Papa died, Kobi took all the shelves out of the cupboard and began to practise going in and coming out. He'd go in, sit down, then come out, over and over again, until the cupboard was wobbly. Even then he didn't stop. With his new bar mitzvah watch, he'd measure how long it took to get to the cupboard from anywhere in the house, how long it took to get in and close the doors from the inside. He'd jump out of the bathroom, or even run off in the middle of a meal, shoving aside whoever was in his way, timing himself, and announcing the result when he got back. Once he jumped inside and one of the cupboard's feet broke, so he stopped training and put a rock in its place, pestering Mama to have it fixed. Mama rang Uncle Avram – that was before the big bust-up, when Papa's brothers were still talking to her – and he lay the cupboard down on its side, re-attaching the foot with a few nails. Kobi was pleased. No one said a thing about it, or about the fact we didn't need a hiding place when Papa was alive. Anyway, there wasn't enough room in it until he cleared his clothes out of it (all Mama's colourful clothes had been thrown out first).

I crawled into the cupboard barefoot. Once inside, I folded my legs and closed one door, leaving the other ajar for light. There was room for two adults, or three small children. I lifted my head to see how high it was, and caught sight of a pair of boy's underpants pinned to the ceiling of the cupboard, with a bottle of oil inside them. Something was written on the bottle in blue pen. As I stood up to read it, my head bumped the bottle. There were six words in Kobi's neat handwriting: 'Don't forget: pour oil on floor.' As I read, I thought of Hanukkah that year. Papa's year.

Mama went to work in the nursery that day, and before she left she fried us some *sfinj*. Oshri and Chaim hadn't yet been born, and neither had the lie. Back then the youngest in the family was Papa's death. It was just half a year old, a baby death with a fresh smell. At that point you don't know how it will grow up. Death changes fast. In the first month it just lies on its back, crying and not moving. Then it starts to turn over and around, to crawl and knock things over. You have to be with it all the time, to follow it so it won't destroy everything that was there before it was born. But it's faster than we are, finds breakables within its reach. Everything that Papa held dear, we didn't know how to protect. Death would touch, feel, eat, examine, throw, break, destroy and tear. And you couldn't leave it alone, not for a minute.

And when we left the house we'd take death with us. It came to school in the sandwich Mama had made for us; got into our dreams at night, waking us in tears. In the morning it would get up before us, standing next to our beds before we even opened our eyes, so we couldn't get up without remembering it was there, couldn't see the sun without looking first into its baby eyes with their false innocence: 'What have I done?'

That afternoon, Kobi took the deep frying pan with the cooled oil from the *sfinj*. He went into the hallway with it and poured the oil onto the floor. Then he slid on it, the way we used to slide in the corridors at school. I stood in the bathroom doorway, laughing. I hadn't laughed like that for six months. Dudi and Itzik waited their turn to slide. Just then, Mama came home.

She already had a big belly by then, the biggest I had ever seen. It was a week before the twins were born. When she saw us laughing and Kobi lying on the floor in a puddle of oil, she cried out, 'Oh my God!' Then she put her hand to her mouth and began to cry. In that moment we saw ourselves through her eyes. Like baby chicks; we crowded into her eye sockets, and saw what we hadn't seen until then: her children, her orphans, making fun of how their father had died.

'It's for the terrorists,' Kobi told her. 'To prepare for when they come. I wanted to see how much oil you'd need.' Then he went and changed his trousers, leaving us to clean up. It was an impossible job. The oil never completely washed away, and neither did that moment, that image.

I sat in the cupboard, my legs crossed, the bottle of oil swinging above my head. I opened my bag and took the radio out of its plastic bag, as well as the batteries, which I keep in a sock so they won't get used too often. I didn't know whether it was worth using them now. I tasted them with the tip of my tongue and put them into the radio. It was Papa's little transistor. All the knobs were missing. I rescued it from the rubbish bucket behind the falafel shop. Using my teeth, I managed to twist what was left of the tuning dial to hear the radio-woman talking.

That's what I called her when I first heard her voice. Later I found out that her name was Reuma. I liked saying it: Reuma, Re-u-ma. In Hebrew it can mean 'look'. I played around with her name, wondering who had come up with it, and whether she was called Reuma from birth or whether it came afterwards when she started to say: '*Look* what happened' or '*Look* how good that is'.

A month after Papa died, on the way back from a school trip to Jerusalem, the guide pointed at two tall antennae that looked to me like a pair of Eiffel Towers. 'That is where the news is broadcast from,' he said. I was drawn to those towers more than all the important places we had visited, and was sorry we didn't go inside. But ever since that day, every time I pressed the radio to my ear, I'd tell myself that the radio-woman was patiently waiting for me to finish school, that I'd learn how to speak Hebrew just like her, with beautiful words that sound as though they come from distant lands. Without shame, I kept saying them until I understood them. And before I went to sleep, I'd imagine how I'd climb the steps of her tower, more pointed the higher it goes, and under a tiny roof beneath the sky I'd find a place for just one chair. Reuma would be sitting there, waiting for me to come and to say, 'You can come down now, Reuma. I'll take over.'

Then I'll talk to her, pronouncing '*heit*' just as she does. I've practised this using the daily Bible quotation. To do it properly you have to think about the ice cream scoop on Shimon's stand, where he also sells sunflower seeds and salted nuts. You have to imagine it curving inside your mouth, slipping into the hollow of your palate. I'll also see what she thinks of my '*ayin*', a sound like a round coin rising gently from the throat. Every word that comes out of my mouth will be like a glossy ripe grape. I picture Reuma getting off her chair, sitting me down in her place, showing me the microphone and the other equipment. When she leaves, I stay, and I know I'm going to stay at the top of the tower for ever.

I hear the news programme's theme tune, my voice talking into the microphone for the first time: 'This is Etti, speaking to you from Jerusalem. First, the old stuff.' The news doesn't interest me, just the things they don't bother reporting, or lie about if they do.

After the news, I got out of the cupboard and went for a nap. In the morning, because of the alert, they sent everyone home from school at eight-thirty. Mama came home from the nursery and we went down to the shelter with the neighbours. Then, because nothing happened, we went home again, and I fell asleep with Chaim and Oshri at midday. When they woke me, the whole apartment was empty. It was just the three of us. Mama had disappeared, too, without saying a thing. I stayed with Chaim and Oshri. I didn't know how to begin telling them about Papa. I thought maybe we'd start with a story they already knew.

So we sat on my bed, and I took the pillowcase off and put my hand in, pretending to stir the stories – they like me doing this – and then . . . oh! I caught a story.

7   I took out my fist and peered into it to see what I had caught. I opened my fingers a little, pushing the twins away so they wouldn't peek, and said, 'You won't believe what I've got – the story about the woman who turned into an octopus.'

And Oshri said, 'Etti, promise you'll make it have a happy ending.'

They jumped on the bed until the springs creaked, then fell on it together like two burst balloons.

Chaim said, 'Promise, Etti! Otherwise I won't listen!' And he covered his ears, screaming, 'I can't hear a thing, can't hear a thing!'

'I can't hear anything, either!' Oshri crowed. 'I'll shout so I can't hear myself.' He opened his mouth wide and shouted, 'Aaaaaahhhhhh . . .' until he ran out of puff, and Chaim took over.

'That's enough!' I said. 'You'd better stop shouting now, or there won't be a story.' Then they were quiet.

'Today I'll go beyond the end of the story,' I told them. 'I'll go on until we have a happy ending, I promise. Put your hands on your knees, just like you do in your pre-school assembly.' Their expressions were suddenly obedient, and I panicked about my hasty promise. Gentle afternoon light streamed in through the window behind them, and when I looked at them again, they had relaxed, their hands slipping from their knees to the mattress.

'The name of the story,' I said, 'is "The Woman Who Turned into an Octopus".'

And then I began.

'Once upon a time, a long time ago, there was a woman, a completely normal woman. She had two arms, two legs, a tummy and a back. She had a face with two eyes, one nose and two ears. Everything about her was totally normal. She was just like any other woman.'

'You didn't say what she was wearing. Tell us about her clothes!'

'Thanks for reminding me,' I said, and they looked pleased, concentrating even harder to make sure I didn't forget anything. 'The woman had long, smooth, brown hair, and everyone wanted to touch it. And her clothes were all sorts of colours. She had a dress in every colour you can think of: red and blue—'

'And yellow!'

'And green!'

'Yes,' I said, 'and turquoise and purple and violet. And they were covered with every type of pattern: flowers and hearts and circles and triangles.'

'And stars, Etti. You didn't say stars!'

'And stars. Every pattern there is. And this woman also had children and a husband. But one day, something bad happened. A witch came into the woman's house. She had one wobbly tooth – just one – and a long, twisted nose with a disgusting wart on the end. She flew around looking into people's windows, and what do you think she saw in this woman's house? She saw this woman had everything she wanted, and she got really cross. Why is that woman so happy when I'm not? she thought. Why does she have such pretty clothes when I have horrible clothes with holes? Why does she have pretty long hair when my hair is horrible and green? Why does she have a husband and sweet children when I have—'

'Why can't she get married, too?'

'All the womans that are married have got children, don't they, Etti?'

'She wanted to get married, she really did, but no one wanted to marry her.'

'Because she was horrible!'

'And because she was bad!'

'Yes, because she was bad and horrible. So the witch decided to put a spell on the woman's husband, so he'd die. In less than a minute.'

In the stairwell we could hear heavy steps. Perhaps the Dahans' grandmother had come to visit.

Oshri stood up on the bed. 'He fell down. Boom, dead. Like that, Etti? Look how I do it.' He walked to the end of the bed and let his little body fall forward.

'Ow! You fell on my foot!' Chaim said. 'That's not how people die! It's not, is it, Etti? I'll show you. You don't jump when you die because you haven't got any strength, so you just slide down onto the floor.' Chaim got off the bed to demonstrate. He ran two steps, then slipped and let his body fall backwards. 'Did you see how my head bumped? That's how people die! And your tongue comes out, doesn't it?' He tried to talk and stick his tongue out at the same time, mangling the words.

'That's enough,' I said. 'If you don't sit on the bed with your hands on your knees, I won't tell you the rest.' They sat down on the bed again, clasping their knees and waiting for me to continue. I hoped my voice wouldn't shake.

'No one saw how the man died. He was alone when it happened. Only the witch was watching, laughing her evil laugh. She laughed and laughed until she almost died: hee-hee-hee, ha-ha-ha . . .' As always, they were clinging to each other by this point in the story.

'OK, that bit's finished,' I said. 'You can take your hands off your ears.'

They each took off one hand, only removing the other when they were sure the witch's laugh had stopped.

'The witch flew up into the sky on her broom: buzz, buzz, buzz, buzz, buzzzzzz . . .'

'Buzzzzzz,' they joined in. 'Buzzzzzz.'

'After the woman's husband had died, the woman threw away all her pretty, colourful clothes and would only wear black and blue. That's what you do when someone dies – you don't wear colours any more. But the witch lifted the top of the rubbish bin and put her hand in—'

'Disgusting!'

'Stinky!'

'— and she took all the woman's pretty clothes out of the bin – her dresses, her blouses, her skirts. But they didn't fit her. She didn't look pretty wearing them.'

'Because she was all twisted!'

'Because of her twisted legs!'

'Yes, it was because the clothes weren't her size. The woman had lots and lots of work now. From early in the morning until late at night she had to cook and clean and do the laundry all by herself, as well as go to work. She had to do everything by herself.'

I stopped for a moment, and they waited quietly for the next bit.

'When the children got sick,' I continued, 'she took them to the doctor, and she went to the bank and the supermarket, and to the market every Thursday, and she did it all by herself.'

'Because her husband was dead.'

'He fell down – boom, dead!'

'And one winter's day, when it was freezing cold, they didn't have enough money to buy oil for the heater. The woman's strength had gone. She was tired. Her whole body ached. That night, when every-one was sleeping, she sat and cried and cried and cried. Her tears soaked her dress and dripped onto the floor, washing the floor and then slipping under the door—'

'And down the stairs—'

'And into the street, Etti?'

'And then the witch saw the woman's tears flowing down the street, and she laughed—'

'You're not going to make her laugh again, are you, Etti?'

'We're scared of her laugh, Etti—'

'She flew on her broom: buzzzzzz, buzzzzzz—'

'Buzzzzzz! Buzzzzzz!'

'I'm waiting . . .'

'Buzzzzzzzzzzzzzz . . .'

'Buzzzzzzzzzzzzzz . . .'

I looked at them enjoying the sound, their little teeth bared, and waited until they'd tired of it. I wanted them to listen to me, really listen to the truth, not just the story.

Then I remembered I'd promised them a happy ending; they'd insisted on it. They settled down at last – I didn't have to ask – and fixed their eyes on me again, as if they'd just noticed something.

'The witch', I went on, 'disguised herself as an old woman in a headscarf, a very pretty scarf, actually. She came to the woman and asked, "What's the matter? Why are you crying?" The woman said, "I'm fine. Just something in my eye." Then she invited the witch to sit down, gave her tea with sage, and peanut and jam cookies. The witch ate everything – she didn't leave a single cookie – and as she drank her tea she said, "To your good health." She spoke so nicely that the woman thought she was a good person. Then the witch asked again: "What's the matter? You can tell me anything. I'm an old woman and I've heard lots and lots of stories in my life. I can keep a secret." So the woman told her everything. It did her good to tell someone, because that's what you do when something happens to you. You even tell me what happens to you in pre-school, don't you?'

'Yes,' they said together.

'The woman didn't have anyone to talk to about what was hurting her. Since her husband died she was all alone. There was no one except her children. The witch listened to her from start to finish, wiped her tears and calmed her down. Then she said, "I'll help you because it's my job. I'm a fairy—"'

'Liar! Liar! Don't listen to her!'

'She's lying. She's not a fairy. She's bad!'

'The woman didn't know she was a witch. How was she to know? You can't always tell people are bad just by looking at them. And she spoke in such a sweet voice, like sugar or honey. She said, "I'll help you. I know a magic charm that will give you two more arms to help you do your work – to cook, wash the dishes, sweep, clean the wall panelling, hang out the washing, everything!"'

I paused. They were tense, ready to jump in with the answer to whatever question I asked. I could see Oshri was about to interrupt – he never gets the timing quite right – and went on, '"After I attach two more hands to you you'll have—"'

'Four hands!'

'I wanted to say it!'

'Go on, say it now,' I said to Oshri. 'Pretend he didn't say it.'

'But he did say it! I wanted to be the first!'

'So you can be first at the end. That's important, too. Some people always want to be last, to say the last word, because then everyone will remember what they said.'

'You're just saying that! You always take his side!'

Oshri lay on his stomach and pummelled the mattress, as he always does, and for a moment I forgot today wasn't an ordinary day. When he started hitting Chaim, too, I separated them and put them either side of me, hugging Oshri close but he wouldn't calm down.

'OK, I'm not telling the rest until you're quiet,' I said, turning my hand in front of my mouth as if I was turning a key.

'My mouth is locked!' said Chaim.

'My mouth is stuck together with glue!' said Oshri. 'Now I'm first at the end!'

I went on. 'The woman was pleased by the idea of having two more hands. But, suddenly, the witch, still in her nice voice, said something that was not very nice at all. She said, "There is a condition. You have to give me a part of yourself before I give you more hands." The woman thought and thought and thought, until she realised what she could give to the witch.'

'Her hair!' they chorused, looking pleased with themselves.

'Yes. The woman thought: My hair will grow. I can give it away and it'll come back as long and as pretty as before. Anyway, I don't have time to comb it every day with all the work I have. But the witch didn't give her a nice hairstyle, like they would at the hairdressers. She took all her pretty hair and the roots, too, so it wouldn't grow any more. She was left with little bristles, like the witch. Then the witch put the woman's beautiful hair on her own head like a wig, and flew out of the window.'

'She flew on her broom. Buzzzzzzzzzzzzzz—'

'Buzzzzzzzzzzzzzz—'

'Yes. Now the woman managed to do lots of things that she couldn't do before. With four hands she could hang out the washing in a flash, put two pots on the stove at the same time, and four chairs on the table, so she could mop. She could wash two children at a time — two soaps in each pair of hands — and dry them in two towels. She even went to the market on Thursday before work with four baskets: one for vegetables, one for—'

'Fruit!'

'One for fish and the last one for—'

'For Makhlouf's odds and ends!'

'Yes, that's right. But one day — a day just like this, even the weather was the same — she felt two kicks in her tummy, and that's how she knew there were two babies inside.'

'Twins?'

'Like us?'

'Yes, just like you. Two boys. She was pregnant and started to get fat. Every day she grew fatter and fatter, until she could hardly move. Luckily she had four hands to do all the work. Without them she would never have coped. After nine months the woman went to the hospital and the twins were born. She took them home, and even though they were lovely, she was—'

'Sad again!'

'She had no strength!'

'That's right. She didn't have a single drop of strength. Even her four hands weren't enough to manage all the work she had with the twins. She sat down to cry again. She cried and cried and cried, until her tears—'

'Went down to the street.'

'Yes, her tears flowed all the way down to the street.'

'And the witch came again, didn't she, Etti? Don't do the laugh, Etti.'

'I don't care. I'll put my hands over my ears and I won't hear a thing!'

'I promise I won't do the laugh if you promise you won't do the broom.'

'We won't.'

'The witch disguised herself as a nice person again, and this time she didn't have to say much. As soon as the woman saw her she thought: What wouldn't I give for two more hands? I'll have to give her something. She thought and thought and thought, and decided to give her the middle of her body – including her tummy and her back. I'm not going to have any more children, thought the woman, so why should I care if she takes my belly? And I can't sleep at night, so what use is my back? I can give the babies milk in a bottle like everyone else. And I don't need the middle of my body, either. So the woman—'

'I'll say how many hands this time!'

'Go on then, say it—'

'Now she had five hands!'

'Not five! Not five!'

'Six. Six. It's all your fault! I was afraid you'd say it first.'

'Yes. Now she got six hands.'

'She *had* six hands, not *got*. But she didn't have a belly or a back, although she did still have her heart. The woman didn't cry any more. She held on to each baby with two hands, gave them milk in bottles and changed their nappies at the same time. And she still had two hands to fold the washing and mend the torn clothes of the older children—'

'Like us, when our trousers got torn—'

'On the slide!'

'And when the twins went to sleep,' I said, looking at their innocent, unsuspecting, trusting faces, 'and the big children went to sleep, too, she could wash the floor in ten minutes with three mops and three rags. It was easy. But she wasn't happy—'

'Sad again!'

'Crying and crying and crying!'

'That's right. She was crying and wiping the tears away with her hands, but even six hands weren't enough, because this was the day that the woman looked at herself in the mirror for the first time. And what did she see?'

'A scary animal with lots of arms!'

'Yes. In the mirror was a scary animal with a head and six arms and two legs. She sat on her bed that night and cried and cried and cried—'

'The street!'

'And the witch came again—'

'Yes, the witch came again. Now she wasn't even pretending to be nice. She didn't care if the woman was crying, and she wouldn't agree to give the woman back what she had taken from her. Instead she said, "If you don't want to be a scary animal, something no one's ever seen before, then give me your legs and I'll give you two more arms. Then you'll be an octopus, and everyone knows what that is." The woman said, "Octopus? What's an octopus?"'

'Not like that! Make her scared: "What's an octopus? Why an octopus?"'

'Yes. Now the woman didn't know what an octopus was. She was scared of the word she didn't know, so the witch explained what it was, showing her a picture of one, and calming her down.'

'Just like the picture you brought us.'

'I put it in my pocket. Here's an octopus! Eight arms.'

'He tore it!'

'I didn't tear it! It was like that before, wasn't it, Etti? Tell him it was torn when you gave it to me.'

'It's my turn to keep the octopus, isn't it, Etti?'

'I'll give it to you when the story's finished.'

'No way. You'll tear it even more, won't he, Etti?'

I promised I'd glue the picture afterwards, and they both settled down to listen again.

'The woman looked at the picture of the octopus. In the blue sea it looked beautiful, not at all like a strange and ugly monster. The woman agreed. She didn't think twice. So she let the witch take away her legs and give her two more arms, and now she had—'

'Eight!'

'Eight arms, that's right. Just like an octopus. And that's how she was turned into an octopus. She had a head and eight arms, and that's what she saw in the mirror. And then the witch, who now had her hair and her face and her whole body, looked exactly as the woman used to, as identical as a drop of water. The woman looked at herself in the mirror again, and she was frightened. That's it, she thought, I'll never go back to the way I was. So she said to the witch, "You know what, take my heart, too. Why would I need it? It just causes me pain. Take it, take it. Why would I need it?" And she gave away her heart.

'Now what was left of the woman? Just a head and eight arms. All she could think was: What do I have to do now? What do I have to do now? That's the only thing left to think about because I don't have a body any more. I have no legs with which to dance, no tummy with which to enjoy a delicious cake or an ice cream cone or some chocolate, no mouth to laugh at a joke, no heart to want to hug my children with all eight of my arms, or to tell them stories they loved. Now her arms just did what her head thought they should do – work and work from morning until night.'

I was so caught up in the description that I didn't notice their faces falling. In a small, disappointed voice, Oshri said, 'And the witch was laughing, wasn't she, Etti?'

But Chaim sat up. 'You said it would be a happy ending, Etti,' he insisted. 'This isn't a happy ending at all!'

'It's a bad end!'

'It's scary and horrible!'

'Wait, I haven't finished,' I said, although I'd forgotten my promise and had no idea how to carry on. 'I'll go on until we have a happy ending,' I said confidently. 'Just sit quietly.'

'I'm always quiet. He started it.'

'Not true. Liar!'

'Etti, he said I'm a liar!'

'That's enough. Now you should both be quiet and listen, because this is the most important part of the story. Something happened which you've forgotten: the witch took the heart for herself, didn't she? The woman gave it to her, and she took it, OK? So what do you think happened next?'

'The woman died because she didn't have a heart!'

'You can't live without a heart! Boom-boom, you're dead!'

'The woman didn't die,' I told them, although I still didn't have an ending and knew I somehow had to make a u-turn so the story would finish differently this time. 'The witch made it so that the woman could live without a heart.'

'She turned her into a fish,' said Oshri helpfully.

Chaim said, 'In the supermarket, we saw fish that still jump about after they're dead.'

'And an octopus doesn't have a heart, does it, Etti?'

'What do they need a heart for?'

'They got no nose, neither.'

'No, because they never catch a cold!'

They were both laughing now, so I went on. 'I'll tell you what happened,' I said. 'The witch now had the heart of a good woman.'

They looked at me with huge, surprised eyes.

'She stopped being a witch?'

'She turned into a good woman!'

'I said it first, didn't I, Etti?'

'So the witch tried to laugh her evil laugh, but she couldn't do it. Instead, a nice laugh came out. She tried to fly on her broom, but she couldn't do that, either. She got on, and the broomstick fell down and broke. Her heart was already soft, like . . . like . . .'

'Like butter!'

'Like a banana!'

'Her heart was as soft as a really ripe banana, and all she wanted to do was help everyone. It was all she could think about. The woman didn't believe it at first. She thought the witch was pretending again. But then she saw it was true, that the witch really had become a good woman. So she asked for her body back, because she missed it terribly and was sorry she had given it away. She didn't need to ask twice: the witch agreed immediately. And because she was really good, she returned everything: her hair, her body, her legs. Finally, the woman said to the witch, "Would you mind giving me back my heart?"'

I stopped, waiting for them to say something, but they clung to me more tightly than before. Maybe they thought a frightening bit was coming up, something they hadn't heard before that would spoil everything.

'And the witch', I said, 'was so good now that she gave the woman her heart and died on the spot.'

'Boom, dead!'

'She deserved it!'

'For what she did to the woman!'

'Is that the happy end, Etti? No more witches are going to come for her?'

'Of course not! And that one's in her grave.'

'You can't come out of your grave, can you, Etti?'

As I hugged them I sensed something about the new end was still worrying them.

'But who'll do the woman's work now, Etti?'

'Yes, who will do it?'

'The woman's children will help her,' I replied. 'Even her twins can help with the housework. They're both very good boys, and they're big enough.'

'Like us? Like when we helped you bring in the rubbish bin?'

'What do you mean "like us"? You're talking nonsense. We didn't get a visit from a witch, did we, Etti?'

'And no one's died, have they, Etti? It's only in the story that he died, her husband.'

'Why are you crying, Etti?'

'I'm scared when you cry, Etti. You said it was a happy end, so why are you crying?'

'Don't cry, Etti. The witch is dead. The minute you took out her heart. Boom, she died.'

'Look – I'm the witch dying. Look, Etti, you're not looking.'

'Look at me, too, Etti. Move over – you don't know how to die. I'm a better dead person!'

'Now you're laughing.'

What happened next? We drank tea with *shiba*, and they dunked their cookies the way they like to. I can still see the pieces of cookie tangled in the *shiba* leaves, then sinking to the bottom, and the bright sesame seeds floating on the top. It was already getting dark outside, and Oshri dragged a chair over and stood on it to turn on the light, and then all I remember is the boom and running alone in the dark, running in the street as I've never run before, thinking I'd found my building, pushing with everyone else on the locked door of the shelter when the second Katyusha fell and I was in the middle of the big scream, just a throat and nothing else.

I can't seem to remember why I went down to the street and where the twins were. Every day when I was their age, I ran straight from school to the falafel shop, saying 'Papa-Papa' all the way. It didn't hurt to say it then.

I was his helper from the age of seven. When I went into the shop, I'd see him standing behind the low wall that hid the stove. I could only see his hair, but I knew that, in a minute, I'd see all of him. I liked the anticipation.

I never went around the wall. Instead I'd take off my schoolbag and throw it onto the floor. I'd drag over a wooden vegetable crate, lifting it onto one side and putting it down over my schoolbag like a cage, pushing in the bag's straps. Then I'd pull over another crate, lift it onto the first one, and make it secure. On tip-toe, I'd push the little pillow into place. Papa would hear me, and, before turning around, he'd say his seven words: 'Watch out for the metal, Etti *binti*!' He was worried I'd get cut on the sharp, rusty crates. I'd go back out of the door, climb up onto an empty pickle can and from there climb to the window. I'd go in through the window, turn and come down, bottom first, onto the flowered pillow, ready for work. When I turned my head, I'd see all of Papa, and he could see me. His forehead was ironed free of wrinkles, and he looked full of happiness, like orange juice being poured into a cup, the orange line getting higher and higher. That's the face I used to see when he discovered me on my crates every afternoon.

I'd open the till, jiggling it to the right and left, because it always got stuck. The drawer was divided into squares. I'd open the little bags with the coins and pour them into the compartments, and I'd straighten and arrange the notes. The bills were quiet and serious like the faces painted on them, and the coins were like mischievous children, rolling around and making noise.

The other children would come a little later. Everyone who passed our falafel shop had to stop themselves from buying something. The smell drove everyone crazy because Papa started frying before there were customers. He didn't care if he had to throw some out. He knew the smell would do its work for him, that the smell of falafel is stronger than all the smells in the centre of town. It attracts people. That was his first trade secret. For that alone he deserved to be the king. All day long he flooded the town centre with the smell of falafel. It made everyone hungry, and he never sold old or cold balls.

The year he died, I'd learned everything, even how to make the portions. I was eleven. I wanted to explain it all to my uncles, Papa's brothers from the *moshav* – Morris and Avram and Pinchas and Shimi and Eli – but they didn't ask me. They'd agreed with Mama that they'd manage the falafel shop and give us some of the profits every month.

They took over the shop the day after the shiva and they all agreed it was impossible to continue running that place in the same way, that there was an urgent need for renovation, that everyone would put in some money, and that they would do all the work themselves. They changed the floor and painted the walls and made a plaster ceiling with white stalactites hanging down. They bought a new deep-fryer, shining stainless steel and a big fridge, ordered a neon sign, 'Falafel of the North – Always First', hung a huge mirror on the entrance wall, brought in an aquarium with goldfish and plastic plants to stand in the corner, made the entrance wider so people could help themselves to salads from the bar, and added three new lights. And people passed by and said, 'Very beautiful!' and 'You've done a great job!' But they didn't buy falafel.

Their whole approach was wrong. The five brothers thought it would be enough if each of them worked a day in the falafel shop. On Fridays they decided not to open, because it was a short day. They didn't know that Friday at noon was as busy as the rest of the week put together, and that if you feel like falafel on Friday but see the door closed, you'll get used to buying somewhere else.

After Papa died, my legs still ran to the falafel shop after school. I couldn't stop them. The sign, 'Falafel of the North – Always First', used to stick in my throat, and I'd turn away and run and cry in the bushes with the yellow flowers that were near the town centre. I'd sit in the middle of the bushes, put my head on my schoolbag, and cry quietly until I fell asleep. Once I managed not to run away, and got so close I could see the crack in the sign. It had only been there a month. And as I got closer still, I could see there was only one fish left in the aquarium. It was Uncle Avram's day on the stand, and it was obvious he didn't know a thing. After that, I came back again, day after day. I stood there and I could see none of them knew what they were doing. My uncles thought a portion of falafel meant throwing a few balls into a pitta, and then letting people add what they wanted. How could I explain to them that Papa would make portions individual? He'd say, 'This one likes a thick pitta', and we'd sift around to find an especially thick one. Or he'd say, 'This woman doesn't like it to drip', and he'd cushion the bottom of the pitta with the piece he'd cut from the top, and wrap it in two napkins. And there were people who would snack on a ball while they were waiting for their portion, and he'd add an extra one on the top. One person wanted the whole thing to taste of tahini, even if it tore, another liked the falafel a little burned, someone else liked them very light, almost raw. And the cheapskates who ordered half a portion when they were hungry got a big half from Papa which was really two-thirds, and he'd throw away the leftovers. People didn't realise how well he knew them. He didn't talk much, but if he managed to surprise them, he'd look at me and his chin would dance a little, like a small victory celebration.

And then there were the ones who put on airs and graces and threw instructions at him from a distance: 'Make my portion for me.' They felt like only children, the only ones to get a special portion, and yet he would only ever make them an ordinary portion. And we had six or seven taxi drivers who would give a little toot from the high-way. By the time they arrived, Papa would have prepared a really spicy portion, wrapped in a bag, with a drink, and I would go and give it to them through the taxi window.

9   I was eleven when he died. I was sitting next to the till on a high chair, with my new hairstyle from Kobi's bar mitzvah. I didn't like it or my dress. I wanted to forget the whole party: the people who pinched my cheeks as if I was still a little girl, the others who, in contrast, saw I was developing and weren't shy about staring, and especially the false smiles flashing in the mirrors around us.

That day masses of people squeezed into the falafel shop and competed with each other to shower praise on Papa for the bar mitzvah – there had never been one like it in the town. I didn't move away from the till for a long time. I took money and added it up and gave people change until Dudi came in with his friend. He opened the fridge and said that Kobi had sent him to fetch some drinks for Rabbi Kahane's people. Papa heard him and said, 'They're not free. Why would they be free?' Then Kobi came. I was cleaning at the back of the shop, to keep the cats away, and I heard Kobi say, 'Why can't you give them away? They're important people!' Papa answered, 'In my place, nothing's free. If Begin himself came, he'd have to pay.' And Kobi said to him, 'You know what, you'll end up in the falafel shop all your life!'

When I went back into the room, Kobi had already taken at least ten bottles out of the fridge. He gave me some, and I didn't know what to do. I looked at Papa, but he turned to face the wall and carried on frying. He didn't say a word. Kobi went out, shouting for me to follow him. Suddenly he seemed grown-up. When we got to the square, he opened the bottles for Kahane's men, and sat down to talk. I stood next to him, listening to them quoting and praising their rabbi. 'He's like a father,' they said, 'one with mercy in his heart who thinks of all Jews as his children.'

They told us that on their journey here the car had a flat tyre. So they all got out and found themselves looking at a wonderful view of Jericho. 'You see,' the rabbi said to them, 'right here is the place where Elijah the Prophet went to Heaven. It's a scandal that there are no Jewish settlements here.' He went on to say that when they came back he'd do everything he could to encourage building of a *yeshiva* there. Everyone else was worried about the flat tyre but not the rabbi. Oh no. For him, everything is an opportunity to show his love for the Jewish people. He never thinks of himself, just the Jews.

Soon afterwards they left Kobi to mingle in the crowd, chanting 'Long Live the Jewish People', raising clenched fists to Heaven. There was a fist on their yellow shirts, too, yellow in a black puddle. No one was taking them seriously. I left the square and walked back to the falafel shop in the shade, next to the shops, with a finger in each of the empty bottles. I had almost reached the falafel shop when the loudspeaker started. I turned and went back. The rabbi spoke strange Hebrew, American Hebrew, and he was stuttering. With his black beard and *yarmulke*, he just looked like an ordinary person. He began quietly, with a verse in every sentence, so only Siso the sailor and his friends stood and listened to him. Everyone else in the centre carried on with what they were doing, until, suddenly, Kahane called out in a loud, imploring, chastising voice: 'Jews! Daughters of Israel are defiling themselves with Arabs! They're taking away our livelihood, our daughters, our State . . .' People began to come out of the shops, and those already in the square stood still with their baskets, bags or strollers, as he raised a hand to Heaven. 'I'm saying what you're all thinking,' he said into the loudspeaker. 'And everyone else is a hypocrite and a coward. Fellow Jews, we have to clean the State of our enemies!' Clapping was heard here and there, and the crowd waited for him to continue. Kahane was quiet for a minute, then threw the name of the neighbouring village into the air, repeating it twice. 'Is that an Arab village?' he asked, stroking his beard. 'It's not an Arab village! It's a Jewish village where Arabs live temporarily.' The crowd laughed and lots more people clapped. The empty bottles clinked against each other, but I didn't care if they broke my fingers. More and more people were streaming into the square now, filling it. They squeezed together, looking up at him, and some started chanting, 'Kahane! Kahane!'

Mama was at home. She was sitting in the living room, her hair up, wearing blusher and mascara, as if she was still at the bar mitzvah. She was surrounded by admirers and didn't hear me come in. I went to the room where we all slept then – Itzik, Dudi, Kobi and I. I got into bed, pulled the covers up to my neck, still listening to Rabbi Kahane and wondering what he meant when he spoke about daughters of Israel defiling themselves.

The screaming woke me. I got up and rushed into the living room in time to see Mama bursting out of the door. I heard her bump into the empty bottles I had left by the door, then shout, 'Mas'ud,

Mas'ud.' She ran down the stairs and into the street, still shouting, and I ran after her, barefoot.

Papa had stayed in the falafel shop when the square began to fill with people and when it emptied again, and when he collapsed there, the whole town was left with a riddle to solve: how did he die? For a year everyone tried to understand what had killed him, what had happened first: The oil or the bee?

The knife or the fall?

The heart or the burn?

The blood or the sting? Like the Passover song 'Chad Gadya', with its mixed-up verses, there was no way of knowing how the angel of death came to my father as he was working. All the clues were on the floor of the falafel shop for people to build or mix up as they wished. Mama said it was the evil eye that killed him. Kobi said angrily that it was the oil. Dudi and Itzik, who were six and seven, saw the knife in his hand, the wound and the bee-sting.

The doctor said that apparently his heart stopped. I was a girl then, and I imagined that Papa's heart stopped just so it would not be drawn to the square, to the hearts that merged into the one common heart of the together-monster. The heart stopped and left my father lying dead on the floor of the falafel stand.

I left the shelter and walked in the pitch-darkness to our building. I climbed the stairs. I didn't want to go back into the shelter. The Cohens' door was wide open, and so were all the other doors. It was dark and the open doors were like the yawning mouths of caves, each with its own smell. Our door was open, too.

I went straight to the kitchen. I groped around on the counter, found matches and lit the stove. I took a Sabbath candle out of the drawer and lit that, too, putting it on a little plate. Papa's picture, cropped across his chest and imprisoned in a carved, gilt frame, still hung in the hall, along with the photo of us all at Kobi's bar mitzvah. 'I wish someone would take down that picture,' Mama begged. 'I can't stand looking at that stupid, laughing woman. She has no idea what's going to happen to her in two days, how her world will fall apart.' I took the picture off the wall. On the table, dishes were heaped with the Tuesday couscous. I tasted them all: too spicy, too salty, lukewarm, cold, repulsive. I shielded the candle with my hand, looking into the flame, at the orange surrounding it. Let it burn, I thought. Let everything burn. I got up from the chair suddenly — it fell with a bang, and then I heard something else. By the light of the candle I walked down the hallway to the old apartment, towards the terrorists' cupboard, then I slipped. Oil.

The candle flickered and almost went out.

Everything happened at once. The door of the cupboard opened, the electricity came back on, and I was standing, swaying, in front of Oshri and Chaim's little faces inside the cupboard. 'Who should we be afraid of now, Etti?' they asked together.

I put out the candle and took a step forward. I slipped off my sandals and got into the cupboard with them. I closed both doors from inside, leaving a crack of light, feeling as though I might burst into tears. But instead of tears, something else burst out: a story.

What hadn't they brought with them? Inside were two pillows, their water gun, a loaf of bread with the middle hollowed out and only the crust left. The three of us mingled together in the womb of the cupboard, and they showered me with all that had happened in the last few hours: how there was a huge boom and it got dark and they ran straight to the cupboard like Kobi had told them to do, and how they heard the second boom and shouts in the building because people didn't know they were supposed to go into the cupboard.

I didn't understand why they weren't scared. I would have died of fright. I didn't know when Kobi had managed to explain about the cupboard and the oil, and I didn't ask. I just kissed them and said, 'You know, I have a new story to tell you, a true story about our family.' But I didn't want to start with Papa dying or the bar mitzvah, where Mama usually began, as if the party in the hall was the top of the mountain and Papa's death a deep valley, and that only by climbing to the mountain's peak could you feel the force of the fall.

I pulled their heads close and stroked their foreheads with a finger, exactly how they like it, until their eyes shut. But they didn't fall asleep. They were listening, I knew they were. 'This story', I said quietly, 'is a special story, which you've never heard before. You tell this story backwards, from the end to the beginning. That's the only way to tell it, and both of you are the end of the story – so, you see, it's a happy ending.'

To find out more about our books, to meet our
authors, to discover new writing, to get inspiration
for your book group, to read exclusive on-line
interviews, blogs and comment, and to sign up for
our newsletter, visit **www.portobellobooks.com**

encouraging voices,
supporting writers,
challenging readers

Portobello
BOOKS